I0689198

Jazzy Kitty Publications Presents
THE LAST CRY THE CONTINUATON
THE UNWANTED DON
YOU CAN'T KILL
WHAT'S MEANT
TORRY FLOWERS
AKA Ravenion Nalls

The Last Cry The Continuation The Unwanted Don

By: Torrey Flowers aka Ravenion Nalls

Cover Designed By: Jazzy Kitty Publications

Cover images: Torrey Flowers and www.photobucket.com

Logo Designs By: Andre M. Saunders

Editor(s): Anelda L. Attaway and Torrey Flowers

Revised: May 2018

© 2014 Torrey Flowers

ISBN 978-0-9892656-9-0

Library of Congress Control Number: 2014935096

ACKNOWLEDGMENTS

To Eric Jones Jr. and Anthony Cook thanks for letting me keep my homey alive.

Angela Hawkins thanks for the love and support; my best friend for life.

Gerald Basden "Pee Wee" and Lois thanks for letting me use your address.

GA Justice Project, my best friends, lawyer, and supporters.

Thanks D. Ammar, J. Smith, and S. Dershimer.

Thanks to my family for your support.

Jamie Foxx, "What's up Cuz?"

Antonio Hightower, Ronaldo Maxwell, Kuli Jackson, Bread, Harvey Jackson, Kenyetta Smith, Billie Miff, Yayo, Eric Yarbrough, Anthony Clark, K. King, Mrs. L. Burke, Easy, John Hart, K. Duncan, DeMarcus Kirkland, Skyler Kilgore, Trinette Kilgore, Tammie Peppers, Debbie Peppers, Anthony Peppers, AJ, LeLe, Bam Bam, Jade, Hose, Lilneil, Miny, Quashay, Diggy, Val, Hanson, Geanva, Audrey, Kwula, John McCoy, N. Hagwood, Vince Lupoe, Famous P, Diana Mincey, KO, Teairra, Wanda, Audrey Sharpe, Quinicea Hawkins, Mr. Johnson, Ms. Thompson, L. Hagan, Kisha G, J. Thornton, Sunshine Norwood, Bishop Harvey Johnson, Angie Boyd, Tyrell Campbell, J. Farmer, James Gray, Nurse Byrd, TesFaye aka Scarface, Abdullah Williamson aka Dual, Travis Barber, Willie Frank Raven, D. Carter, Reginal Warner, Eron Dennis Martin, Leotha Foster Kemp, Ms. K. Ross, S. Avery, Val Holiday, Peaches, (D. Harvey the P.A.) Ms. Carty, June Baker, Kevin Barnes, LeRoy Barnes, P. Ligon, Ms. Chambliss, Ms. Lee, Ms. Francis, Ms. Steven, Blowfish, and Ms. Boo.

Marissa Alexander keep your fight up "Baby girl."

Nene "Hold your head up Cuzin, it will be over soon."

Synia (Teairra's daughter), Mr. Stubbs, Nehemah Hagwood Jr., Marchelle Robinson, The Jenkins Family, R.I.P. Tiffany Rucker.

To my publisher Mrs. Anelda Attaway, we live and breathe together.

Madrika Gray, Chaplain Jordan thanks for the tuff love.

Last but not least, to all my homies in the jail cell missing their block. Read this novel and feel this: You're still there thuggin in your own way.

DEDICATIONS

I dedicate The Last Cry The Continuation The Unwanted Don to all of you. It was written to give hope; hope for a better tomorrow.

And to everyone that's doing life in prison, hold your head up. You're just one day away from tomorrow.

Thank you, Lord, for blessing me with a beautiful family.

Love Y'all!

MY SPECIAL DEDICATIONS

To Trinette My Daughter's Mother:

Trinette, thank you for your love and support.

Most importantly, giving me a beautiful daughter.

To Skyler My Daughter:

Skyler you are my world and I live my life through you.

Trinette and Skyler just hold on, we'll breathe as one!

TABLE OF CONTENTS

INTRODUCTION

The Last Cry The Continuation The Unwanted Don is Part II of my first book The Last Cry published on August 29, 2011.

This book is the continuation of the main characters in the Last Cry: Juan Ellis, Natasha Middle, Sonya, Smokey, Leo, and Nikko to name a few.

The Last Cry was based on a local street dealer that finds himself in a robbery, in which he kills one of the robbers. After being captured by the police the next day, he finds his faith in the hands of a 18-year-old Natasha Middles. Natasha holds a possessive love for him and goes to her grandfather Honorable Judge Harold Middle for help in hope that Ellis would finally notice her and give her the relationship she dreamed of.

Please go to Amazon at http://www.amazon.com/The-Last-Cry-Torrey-Flowers/dp/0983054894 to order my first book and read more. This is the anticipated continuation of The Last Cry (revised on May 30, 2018) and it's available at https://www.amazon.com/Last-Cry-Continuation-Unwanted-Don/dp/0989265692. My books are available now worldwide on all online bookstores. Thank you in advance for your support.

CHAPTER 1

Ravenion Thinking About His Life

Ravenion laid in the bed thinking about his life; the road he had chosen and the people he had hurt. Why he didn't die from the gunshot wound to his neck? Is a question he'll forever ask God. All he knew was that his neck was hurting and he couldn't turn his head to the right. He opened his eyes to visualize the room; trying to become familiar with his surroundings.

He looked to his left and saw a wooden door, there were no windows. He eased his head up and a dim lamp on a brown wooden stand. Still lying on his back, he looked up at the ceiling fan and watched it turn, still remembering that night. All he could remember was shooting his way to the barn, crossing the yard, and falling on his face. He took in a deep breath and said to himself, *"Well, I've gotten myself into some deep shit this time, I guess I gotta face the shit head-on."*

He heard a female voice outside the door saying, "No visitors are allowed."

And a male voice replied, "Step back!"

He knew then that he'd been arrested. Then the door came open and in came a little Cuban lady with red scrubs on. She had a tray in her hands walking towards him. He strained to turn to his left side and see what was on the tray as she set it on the nightstand.

"Why hello!" she said.

"I see you've finally woken up out of that coma. You've been out for twelve days. Ever since you got here the girls have been worried sick. I've got to call Nikko and let him know you've woken up."

"I'm in Cuba?" he asked.

"Yes, they brought you here right after your surgery. I know you have two feuding girls trying to take care of you at the same time. They come in and out of the room fussing at one another about who was first and which one loves you the most. Just let me give you this shot and I'll take that IV out of your arm."

He hadn't even noticed the IV sticking out of his right arm or the tube up his nose. He started dozing again as the woman began removing the IV. Before she could get to his nose, he was already asleep. That meant the pain medicine she had shot him up with had kicked in. She cleaned his gunshot wound and bandaged it and quietly left the room.

In the hallway she watched the male guard lock the door. She heard fussing in the small house, so that meant the girls were at it again.

It was a three-bedroom house in the city. Nikko wanted him well hidden in case the Feds came looking for him. The city would be the last place they would look, knowing his worth.

As she walked down the hallway, she passed two rooms on the right. The hallway led to the living room where Sonya stood wearing a black Fendi dress with black stockings and no shoes. She was in the middle of the living room with her back to the door. Gloria was on the brown leather sofa with a white Prada dress on, listening to Sonya's demands about Ravenion. She demands she was there before Gloria and that she should learn her position when he got well. Gloria just laid there listening and thinking to herself, "*Yeah Bitch, as soon as that baby is born I'm gonna kill you.*"

Gloria tried to tell her that they're always gonna be subject to a threesome, but Sonya didn't want to accept that. She wanted to kill Gloria but not there because she knew the Cubans would kill her. So, she had to use force by putting her foot down while she was pregnant. She no one would touch her or tempt her. The nurse just watched the two with a smile. It was funny how they argued all day but slept in the same room. Neither one of them was allowed in his room anymore because they almost got into a fight four days ago when Gloria kissed him first. The nurse called Nikko and told him how they had nearly knocked down his IV pole and that they almost snatched it out. Nikko came and brought a guard with him. He posted the guard at the door with instructions that neither of them was allowed in the room without him.

Now, they sat in the living room fussing at each other. The nurse enjoyed it because it brought life into the house. She wanted to tell them he had woken up but kept it to herself because she knew they'd stop arguing and probably beat the guard to get in and see him. Deep down everybody knew Ravenion would never let anybody hurt those girls. They knew it too, they were only respecting the guard because they didn't want him to wake up to them fighting. So, she walked to her room. Hers was the middle room, between the living room and his room.

The floor creaked so she would hear if anyone tried to persuade the guard, she would hear them coming. She opened her door and walked into her room, she was a very private person. No grandkids because her two sons died trying to get to the U.S. by boat 12 years ago. She had only one TV in her house and it was in the living room. Her entire bedroom suit was new, Queen size bed with ornate headboard, nightstand with lamps, and big dresser drawers that sat on the base wall, now with money to spend she was very happy. Only 59-years-old, she thought about dating, about playing bingo, something she always wanted to do but could never afford. One thing she did know was she was gonna enjoy herself with this money. Nikko had set her straight, 30 grand was a lot of money, in Cuba or America. Nikko described what kind of person Ravenion was and she knew that she'd be getting company once he was feeling better. She sat on the bed facing the wall and picked up the receiver to call Nikko.

"This is Vanquella, he woke up for a few minutes. I spoke with him briefly and gave him a shot of morphine, and he was back asleep before I could remove the IV tube. I changed his bandage and cleaned his wound. I'm gonna wake him up so I can feed and bathe him. He hasn't been bathed in four days because I don't have any help to move him. Hopefully he can move a little on his own. Can I move him to the bathroom?" she asked.

"Yes, tell the guard to carry him to the bathroom and to keep them girls away! I'll be there in a few minutes, I got to keep everything secretive. I don't want anybody to know he's there because he might have to stay there awhile. How are the girls doing?"

"They're alright," she replied.

"The Americans want all the control, Gloria is just going with the flow. I think Gloria understands why she is like that. She keeps throwing the baby in Gloria's face. So, Gloria won't put up much of a fight."

"Tell Gloria to stay calm because she will win in the end," he said while laughing and hung up the phone.

She noticed that the house had become quiet, so she jumped up and ran to the living room. Sonya was sitting on the sofa watching some TV show.

"Where is Gloria?" asked Vanquella.

"She went to the store to get me some pickles, chips, Kool-Aid, and ice cream," replied Sonya.

"You plan on eating all of that yourself?" asked Vanquella incredulous.

"Well of course, I'm not worried about her trying to harm me. Not while I got this baby. She'll be alright." They both looked at each other, smiled and went back to what they were doing.

When Gloria came back with Sonya's order, Sonya told her to take a bite out of the pickle and the ice cream.

Gloria laughed and said, "So you don't trust me? If I'm going to get to eat your pussy, why would I risk hurting myself? I'm not like you anyway, I love him, and I don't care to harm you."

So, she took a bite out of the pickle and a spoon of the ice cream. Deep down inside Sonya knew Gloria wouldn't hurt her while she carried the baby. She wanted to make peace for now. Ravenion needed both of them to get his strength back, so she made the first move. She hugged her and kissed real hard, catching Gloria off guard. They looked at each other in amazement. They turned toward the room, the room was the same as the rest of the rooms. Sonya closed the door and locked it, they slid their dresses off and looked at each other. Gloria being a beginner, she didn't know what to do. So, Sonya took off Gloria's black bra and helped her out of her black panties. She laid Gloria on the bed and kissed her. Running her hands through her hair. Gloria just laid there looking at the ceiling, smiling. She couldn't believe this shit was really happening. It wasn't long before Sonya was kissing and tonguing her pussy. The feeling of Sonya's tongue licking her clit, her teeth nipping her, her finger rubbing hard against her G-spot, was the best feeling she had ever felt. She found herself throwing it back to Sonya as she cradled her with both of her hands. As Sonya stuck one of her fingers up her ass, Gloria moaned out for Sonya to give her more. Sonya ate Gloria for an hour giving Gloria complete peace between the two. When it was Gloria's turn she wanted to be better than Sonya, so she went at her with Ravenion on her mind, licking her stomach all the way to her ass. Sonya shook as Gloria went from her ass to her pussy.

Sonya locked her legs around Gloria's neck, moaning in ecstasy, "Yes! Yes! Yes!" She pleased her more than herself was pleased.

She stuck her fingers in every hole of Sonya's, giving her a much better nut than hers. She knew she had to get used to doing this, because there was no way she was going to let her and Ravenion go at it by themselves. She looked up at Sonya, she had her eyes closed.

So, she laughed and said, "I'm glad we're getting along."

Gloria slid on top of her kissing her and grinding her deep down, both of them enjoyed it. They made love over and over again, until Gloria got up and put her robe on and went to get Sonya's potato chips. They fed each other, laughing at how, earlier, they were fighting, now they were in bed together. Sonya told her she was hungry. Sonya put her matching white robe and they went into the kitchen together to fix pancakes, bacon, and eggs. When they looked at the clock it was 7:30 a.m. The old lady was coming out of Ravenion's room.

When she saw them she just laughed and said, "I see you two have made up. Well, I guess I'll tell y'all, while you were making out Ravenion was up and talking. I bathed him and he asked how y'all was doing. I told him you were fighting all the time."

"Why did you tell him that?" Sonya asked.

"You knew we were making out."

With a sigh Vanquella answered, "If you let me finish, I told him you were fighting in the beginning and that now y'all had come as one. Now he's up watching TV some movie called, "Reddick."

"Can we go in?" Gloria asked.

"Yes! If you'll promise not to fight!"

"We promise," they both said at the same time.

She told the guard to let them into the room, they ran to the door like two little girls running to their poppa. When they entered Gloria ran to the left side of him. They both kissed his cheeks at the same time. They sat on both sides of him, watching the movie, each one holding a hand. He didn't say anything at all, he just took his hand and patted each one on the thigh. He didn't want to talk about what happened, because deep down inside he knew what had to be done. What had been done was that they had given themselves up to prove their loyalty. So, he had to show his and get them out somehow, some way. That's where his mind was trying to make the great escape.

Sonya knew he was troubled about what, she didn't know. She wanted to ask him what was on his mind, because she could see it in his face. Her sparkling hazel eyes were glued to his. As he blinked tears rolled down his face.

She looked over at Gloria who was glued to the movie, she had no idea how to give attention to her man; and to learn to see the signs of his needs. If this was ever to happen again she wouldn't know how to comfort him. So, Sonya got up and turned the TV off. Gloria looked at him and then at her, still wanting to snap she took in a deep breath.

"Rav, what's wrong? I don't want to hear nothing because I've watched tears fall from your eyes for 30 minutes. Gloria you should learn to watch your man. That movie isn't important. What's important is finding out his problem and helping him solve it."

He closed his eyes and said to them, "Before I die, I got to get Smoky and Leo out of prison."

He closed his eyes to think things out, he wanted to learn how to meditate and clear the world from his mind. He asked Gloria to go find him some Zen meditation books or some Buddhist books. Not to be a Buddhist but to learn to live at peace with his mind. He didn't care about life or death, he cared about people. His mind still pondered about the baby in the microwave and the boy in the oven. He knew deep down inside that kids were just as dangerous as him if they had the right influence. He often wondered who he had looked up to. Who influenced him to be a drug dealer and a murderer. His mind was never focused enough to answer this question, just like then, it's the same way now. So, he understood he needed help, because its times like these when he had to fight his own mind. The child that was in him just never had time to grow. That same child cries out in him every day and it hurts to tell him not today. We can't play today. As he thought, he thought about Blue, *"Was he in love with her sister?"* Not wanting to answer that question because he feared the answer.

He opened his eyes to see Sonya standing there with tears in her eyes. He noticed Gloria was gone, she had left. He motioned his left hand towards his cock and with his right hand pulled the covers back. He was naked and had a bedpan under him. The nurse had just bathed him and cleaned the pan. Sonya sat the pan on the floor, removed her robe, and climbed in bed with him. She kissed him but he pushed her back with his right hand, seeing her naked body aroused him. She knew he wanted to tour her lips and tongue. So, she gave him a grand tour, a slow tour with a lot of sucking and pulling. Then easing off of him to make love to him. She made hard love to him. She wanted to finish before Gloria got back, so she settled for a quickie. After they were finished she covered him and told him to rest.

She walked out smiling because she knew she was number one and Gloria was number two. Gloria returned with a book called, *"There Ain't Nothing Wrong with You"* by Cheri Hubbard. Sonya was in the shower, so she went in the room and locked the door and laid beside him. He told her to remove the pan, because he was able to move around now. She took the pan and sat it on the floor under the bed. She played with the left side of his face, rubbing it with her hand. She explained how she had been trying to bring peace between her and Sonya and how they slept together.

She looked him in the eyes and said, "I love you, that's why I did it. I don't like it, I swear I don't. Her day will come. You don't need her I'm young. I can have a child and take care of it. I'm in training to protect you from her as soon as that baby is born."

She kissed him and started reading the book to him. He closed his eyes, listening to her voice. He had to use the bathroom. He remembered the pan wasn't there, so he got up showing his naked body. Trying to balance himself, he threw out both of his arms, once his balance was straight, he took Frankenstein steps all the way from the right side of the bed, around the bottom, staying close in case he fell. When he made it, he was sweating real bad and he was weak. He called Gloria in to hold him up and as she grabbed him she grabbed his dick and held it while he pissed. He was breathing hard and deep, sweating so bad that he pointed at the tub and told her to run some water. She sat him on the toilet, he put his elbows on his lap and his head on his hands. She sat on the side of the tub looking at him. She was mad with herself because she was supposed to have taken that bullet, not him. She was afraid for him and she knew she needed to get him back in shape. One of the things she could see that was still perfect on him was his waves. Vanquella had been brushing his hair. She cut the water off and helped him in the tub. He relaxed and when he opened his eyes, she was gone. She went and got his pain pills from the nightstand and a glass of water.

She tried to give him the pills, but he spoke very soft to her, "I don't want these pills no more they are what's got me like this now, so just pour them all down the toilet. You know that they have three missing scientists over here, these pills might be mind control pills. I don't feel right. I've been taught the mind heals the body and right now I can't even think straight. My thoughts are racing and jumping all over the place like I've been snorting coke or something."

As she got up and gathered all of the pills to flush, she heard Sonya beating on the door saying, "Rav, Baby are you alright? Come open the door."

She shook the door and asked the guard was anybody in there with him. He didn't answer her, he wasn't about to turn on his own kind.

Sonya just looked at him, reading his mind, she understood. So, she called Vanquella, but Vanquella didn't want to get involved in the girls quarrel so she didn't answer back. Vanquella knew Gloria was in there, just as she knew Sonya had just left out. She knew one of them would try to kill the other, it was just a matter of days.

Gloria returned to the bathroom and closed the door and flushed the pills. He was as comfortable as he could get in the water, so she undressed and stepped in the water.

He opened his arms up to her as she laid back against his chest. He told her she had to help him get better, she answered him saying she would. They laid there thinking, she was thinking how they never really got a chance to spend time together, and he was thinking of getting his boy's out of jail.

She started singing a song she wrote titled, *"Love Take this Pain."*

"Love Take this Pain," she sang, *"Love Take this Pain from Me, Cause I Don't Wanna Cry, Love Take this Pain from Me, Look in My Soul and Watch the Pain Grow. Deep in My Soul I'm Learning to Let Go, Love Take this Pain from Me."*

When she finished he said, "Gloria, with your voice, I'm gonna make you a star. You shouldn't have to be forced into this lifestyle if you don't want to be in it. Do you want to sing?" he asked.

"Yes!" she answered.

"But Nikko won't let me, I'm only supposed to train for combat and go on a mission."

"Well, I'm gonna change all that and send you out to see the world. Maybe marry a fellow that's nice and good to you."

"Oh No! You're all the man I need. I'll sing for you, because all my songs are to you anyway."

She kissed him with a smile on her face. But deep down inside he knew she'd be another Natasha Middle, a young girl with a bright future and a tragic ending. He couldn't mess that up for her so he was gonna let her sing.

She bathed him, wanting badly to make love to him. Unlike Sonya, she could wait. Her momma always told her that good things come to those who wait.

He laid there in the water watching her bathe. It was something about her. She didn't arouse him. But watching her just made him joyful. It gave him a peace he didn't even feel with Tasha. He missed her and his son. He is human and he had a heart. Often, he thought about his life, he was given to this life he didn't choose it. But he was gonna live his life to the fullest. He was happy that Sonya was having a little one. But looking at Gloria, he wanted his seed in her also. Everything about her was unique. If he didn't save anybody, he was gonna save her, even if that meant going against Nikko.

She turned to face him, leaned forward, kissed him and rubbed her nipples across his mouth and said, "This will be waiting on you when you get better. So, you better heal yourself."

She stepped out of the tub and put the towel on off the towel rack next to the door. She grabbed the other one and extended her hand out to him. He eased up and grabbed her with both hands leaning against her and stepped out. She put the towel on him and they made their way to the bed, face to face. She laid him on the bed. He told her to get him some underwear. She got him some black nylon boxers and a black nylon T-shirt from the dresser that the TV sat on. He was drying his under arms when she turned around. She got the Speed Stick Deodorant from beside the TV and gave it to him. He rubbed it under his left arm and then the right, put his underclothes on and laid back down.

The door came open. All she could see was some black suede shoes and silky black pants and Sonya's red leg behind them. She turned around and saw both of them looking at her.

"Nice shirt, Nikko," she said. It was a silk black shirt and Sonya had on her blue cotton gown and some blue slippers.

"How are you doing, Rav?" Nikko asked.

"I'm making it. I need some therapy, I can barely stand up. I need you to send me to the best therapist in this country."

"Ahh Rav, you don't need no therapist. What you need is rest. You're trying to get back to these girls to fast. They ain't going nowhere. Remember what I told you, dick control. With that you will heal fast. I'm gonna come get you tomorrow and take you to the training field. We'll exercise, you, me, and the girls. Pushups, pullups, sit-ups, jogging, we're gonna get it the old-fashioned way. Lift a few weights. The people here want to see you get better. They ask about you every day."

"How can we help Mr. Nalls? Where is he Nikko? I've even heard some say Mr. Nalls should be over Cuba, not Nikko or Castro. I just laugh! Girls, I need y'all to leave. One of y'all bring me a chair to sit in so we can talk."

They left and Nikko stood by the door. Gloria handed him a chair. He sat it in front of him, closed the door and sat down. He looked Rav eye to eye, and then dropped his head.

"Rav, what I'm about to tell you might scare you. No not scare you but catch you off guard. I'm a billionaire. I've got money all over the world and my money has kept me well protected. I'm the last of my families' men besides my brother, but he can't show his face. Just like you, he's dead. With all the money I have, it can't protect me from death. Are you familiar with the word "Shaman?" Rav shook his head.

"Today we call them witch doctors, but back in Africa they called them

Shaman. They come and foretell your future. Well, about four days ago I had this dream and, in this dream, I was in a cornfield chopping stalks. When I got to the middle of the cornfield, every stalk I chopped down came back up against me and started covering me. Rav, I couldn't run or anything. For the first time in my life I found myself powerless. Then I saw my mother descend from the sky with a baby boy. Rav, sometimes our seed isn't born through us, it's given to us. She gave me the baby boy. Once I held it to my heart we both started bleeding; my blood was his and his was mine. The boy grew in my hand and commanded the stalk to bow down. As we continued to chop down more stalks in the east and the west, more stalks rose and went against the boy. I woke up and went for a Shaman. I asked her what was up and she said for me to prepare for death. The people of Cuba are going to rise up against me and the baby boy was you. I was to give you all knowledge of both worlds. The blood is the cutting of the wrist and we become blood brothers. I don't know who is gonna kill me or how I'll die or how long I have to live. But every day from here on out will be spent with you. The people of the east and the west are under other world leaders. What I'm saying is, it's your calling to be a boss weather you want it or not. I'm the bishop over every crime boss in the world. You're suppose to be voted in but my dream tells me they won't go for it. So, I'm gonna appoint you to be the "unannounced" boss. It's your job to make them fear you. I know you are not weak, but I know you have a weakness. . .your dick. You got to learn to control yourself. You can't keep jumping into every good-looking woman."

"Nikko, I've been watching this future show. It's this man out in Utah who cloned a sheep and a bull. Get cloned and go somewhere and live. You know I got you, you know I'm gonna keep it real with you."

Nikko stood and pulled a knife out of his pants pocket, he opened the blade and sat beside him.

"Rav, there ain't no escaping death. When it's your turn You're gonna die. That's why I like you, you're gonna try until you can't try no more.

He rolled his right sleeve up and extended his arm and cut his wrist. Rav closed his eyes and extended his right arm. Nikko cut it and used his towel to band them together, and then he prayed.

"Father join us this day into brotherhood, just as you and your son are equal, join us as equals. In the Name' of the Father and the Son, and the Holy Spirit, Amen."

They stayed joined for 5 minutes then Nikko put his left arm around Rav's neck and helped him up. He took the bandage and white tape from the nightstand and walked them to the bathroom.

Before they unbanned each other, Nikko said, "Let my blood be your blood, let my thoughts be your thoughts and let my life be your life."

He unbanned their wrists and put the bandages on them. Then he hugged him and kissed him on the cheek.

"Rav, I always knew you'd be the one, my father had the same dream but it never happened. So now that the dream has landed on me, I know it's gonna happen. Just do me a favor when I die, cremate me, don't bury me. Light candles around my vase every day, that way I'll be with you always. I'm going to Africa in a week or two to try to get this curse off me so I can soar the skies. That way I know I'll forever live with you."

"That's deep my guy, it really is and I promise I won't let 'em kill me, because I can't let you down. Nikko, I didn't know you believed in God."

"I don't, but they say there are two kinds of religion; death bed and jailhouse. I guess this is the death bed kind so He's got to honor my prayers now."

They laughed and Nikko helped him back to his bed. Nikko gave him a pair of black silk PJ's from the dresser in front of the window. Nikko sat back down in the chair and looked at Rav.

"Rav, I've had all kinds of pussy in the world, but pregnant pussy. Man, I really adore your girl Sonya. I know it's wrong to lust over your best man's lady but she's all I've thought about. It's her wicked ways and her dedication to the underworld. You know, I once saw a movie where a man paid a million dollars to be with a man's wife. What's your price, Rav? One billion, two billion, you name it."

"Whatever she's worth to you Nikko."

"Two billion," he replied.

Rav smiled and called Sonya in the room. When she opened the door Rav told her to put on Prince's song *"Beautiful"* on. She was kind of startled but she did as she was told. He held his hand out to her as she walked over to him. He told her to raise her arms. As she raised her arms he told Nikko to pull her gown off.

She looked in his eyes with disappointment while Nikko was behind her with his face in her cheeks. Nikko was pulling off her panties then he pulled off her blue lace bra. Then he went and started the song over and put the player on repeat. Rav looked at her and told her to dance for Nikko. A tear dropped because she knew where this was heading. He didn't even care about her being pregnant. She wiped her face, took in a deep breath and started dancing.

Excitement filled Nikko as she sat in his lap, fell to her knees and then kissed him through his pants. Rav just smiled as she was doing her magic. Then she slowly made her way to him, pulled his cock out of his pants and placed it in her mouth. With her left hand she signaled Nikko to come and watch. He leaped up to the bed and watched her pull Rav slow and the deep throat him. Deep down inside she didn't want them to have a threesome, so she took her time sucking Rav's dick. Using both of her hands to lean him backwards. She took her titties and put his cock between them, she then made love to him with her mouth and titties at the same time. Nikko's eyes didn't move until she climbed onto Rav and began fucking him to the beat. She knew how to lower a man and she knew Rav. She knew every man was a trick. So, she leaned over and kissed Nikko.

Nikko told her, "Not here." He wanted to take her somewhere special for a week, so he asked Rav if he could have her for a week.

He said, "Yes."

Sonya climbed off of him and went into his bathroom for a shower. She cried the entire time she was in the shower. When she came out Gloria was massaging Rav's back. Nikko handed her clothes to her. She dressed and walked over to the other side of the bed, kissed him and told him she loved him. She kissed Gloria and told her to take care of him while she went back to the States. She didn't want her to know what she had to do in the name of love and then they left.

"Nikko wants to sleep with her cause she's pregnant?" asked Gloria.

"Yep," replied Rav. He's been trying to find a pregnant girl that was worth something for a long time, I guess Sonya is the one." Then he asked Gloria to sing him to sleep.

CHAPTER 2

Sonya

The look on Sonya's face was the look of disgrace and hatred. She hated Nikko and she hated Rav. In his blue stretch Benz, they rode in silence. Nikko couldn't see the tears on her face for the darkness in the car. She faked a smile and showed her fronts every time he thought she was looking at her. She thought to herself, *"99 ways to kill a rich man."*

She hated rich people because they always found a way to devour the middle class and the poor.

She thought to herself, *"Yeah, you Son of a Bitch, you'll pay for this pussy, I'm gonna work it on you so goddamn good."*

She didn't finish her thought because Nikko kissed her on the side of her face. She rubbed his left thigh, she was in too deep to turn away now. This was the price of wanting to be a millionaire. She had already acquired 7 million but now her sight was on hate for them both.

She wanted this over with fast because she didn't want to think about Gloria making love to Rav all by herself. On top of that Nikko thinks he's gonna die but he doesn't know how. She didn't want him to die on top of her or inside of her. But she knew, with all of the money he had she could get anything she wanted. Through her baby she could even get Rav.

She smiled, finally things were going the way she planned. To keep him willing and ready she turned her body to the right, leaned over and gave him the best head he had ever had.

She wanted everything to be better than Rav. She wanted Nikko to lust after her for the rest of his life. As she pulled up and down she made popping sounds with her mouth.

Nikko was so far out there, all he could do was close his eyes and put his head back on the head rest.

When the car stopped at the airport and the driver stepped to the door, that's when she raised her head up and kissed him. She didn't swallow him, she just let it ooze down his cock.

He put himself back in his pants and asked her where she would like to spend 7 days and 6 nights?

She replied, "Athens, Greece." She wanted to see a part of the world she had heard so much about.

The driver standing tall in an all-white Tux with the matching gloves, opened the door and Nikko stepped out. He rushed to her door fussing at the driver

"You're supposed to open her door first, she's a guest, don't ever disrespect me or her again!"

Nikko opened her door and she stepped out with her left leg first, raising her gown up to her thigh, then her right leg with her gown still up. As she stepped out of the car and stood up the gown fell back into place.

They walked together, discussing their trip. He stepped on board first to check it and then invited her on board.

He then told the pilot, "To Athens, home of the 2004 Olympics."

They sat across from each other, staring into each other's eyes. They tried to break each other's stare, she didn't blink, neither did he. He loved the fact that Sonya was a cold-hearted Bitch. The bitch he needed on his team.

"How could that damn kid get so lucky, to have you Sonya?" Nikko blinked when he asked the question.

Sonya still didn't blink, she just smiled.

"We have the same dream, Power! I'm his better half, I know him better than he knows himself. I know how to push him and control him. But the control I speak about is love. I have his life in me and that's the only control anybody could ever have over him," Sonya said.

"If it was that much control, then why did he sell you to me for 2 billion dollars?" Nikko asked.

She almost choked on her spit. She had to blink twice on that one and then ended it with a smile. That made her feel better because she wasn't just a trick, she was a high-priced Bitch. She knew then that she could get paid behind this also.

"Nikko, the understanding that me and Rav have is beyond money, money is love. He put me up on the game. It's my job to charge you 2 billion dollars for the time of your life. Since you're fixin to die. See Nikko, there are two kinds of tricks in this world, one kind is me and the other one is you. Me because I have a pussy and you because you have money. Rav made me who I am and he gave me to you out of loyalty. The same way you told him he ain't got no dick control. I heard you when you told him you're fixin to die. That's why I pulled you to me because I heard the whole conversation. Is this really your reason or have you wanted me ever since I was sucking your brothers dick?"

The plane had taken off and that meant there was no turning back now. Nikko knew why his brother said this was the best bitch ever to walk the earth and understood why Rav said, "she was his rib" because she thinks just like them and talk quick like them. She was prouder of Rav now, then she could ever be. He always told her she had it in her to get herself to higher places. She now understood life as he explained it, life as he lived his, always on the edge with no worries.

Nikko called one of the guards to bring a computer so he could make the money transaction.

A muscular Cuban, dressed in a black suit handed him a Dell laptop. He transferred the money into Rav's account.

"What name do you want me put the money in Sonya?" asked Nikko.

"Sandra Anderson," replied Sonya.

After Nikko told her that the transaction was completed, she looked at him with a smile on her face. She put her hands in his lap and looked him eye to eye. She leaned towards his lap and kissed him and then and licked the left side of face, towards his ear and whispered, "You might as well turn the plane around, I'm a Federal Agent. The only reason I'm still living is cause I'm smart. During my training session I learned to count the keys on a keyboard. I know you transferred Rav's money but you put mine on hold. A cheap thrill isn't in me. You see? There is a bitch and a stupid bitch. A bitch is always two steps ahead of her trick, just like chess. A stupid bitch always ends up with a worn-out pussy and a mouth full of cum and I sure as Hell ain't gonna leave Greece with a mouth full of cum."

The more she talked, the more Nikko wished she was his and on his team. He knew no one could stop Rav but her besides the fact that he was a lot deeper than she was.

Nikko answered and said, "You're right Sonya, it is on hold. You remember the saying that, "you can't mix business with pleasure?"

Knowing that she was the boss of all bitches he'd met, he transferred her money. He knew then that she was gonna go all out for her money.

The plane landed and they were escorted off the plane by four of Nikko's bodyguards. Nikko walked out behind the last guard holding Sonya's hand.

Three black Rolls Royce's were lined up beside each other waiting for them. When they got within reach of the first car some red pumps came out of the car along with some black stockings leading up to her red dress.

The golden skinned arm reached out and joined hands with the head bodyguard, then he helped her get out the car. It was Relena, Nikko's sister, wearing a Red Tommy strap dress with a matching jacket. Standing all of 5'5'' inches tall, with the pumps, straight black hair, with red lipstick, and pinkish blush on both cheeks. She had a small baby face with a figure that would make any man drop to his knees. She ran and hugged her big brother. She was only 22-years-old and going to school to be an architect and a Greek theologists.

"Nikko, I came as soon as I heard you were coming here. I plan to come to Cuba in a week, so perhaps I will leave when you leave." She stood back and looked at Nikko and Sonya.

"Nikko, she's beautiful and she's expecting, is it yours?" Relena asked.

"No," replied Nikko, "she's just a friend, her name is Sonya."

Nikko introduced them to each other. Then he told Sonya that she had been in Athens for five years.

They hugged and kissed each other on the cheek. They entered the first car while the last car came around in front of them.

Relena went on and on about how excited she was about coming home. She hadn't been home in five years. Then the question of questions that they both feared came out.

"Who is Ravenion?" Relena asked, "everybody is telling me about him and I hear he is very handsome."

She pulled a picture of him out of her pocket. It was a picture of the first time he had left Cuba, he was dressed all in black.

"I want to meet him even though I already know him," she said.

They both asked at the same time, "What do you mean you already know him?"

"It's hard to explain, I don't know him in person, only in Spirit. Anyway, I hear he's a very fair man and he's for the people. I also hear he paid off the people debut. Is that true?" she asked.

Nikko dropped his head in worry because he knew she'd go after him no matter what. Sonya was more concerned because she was beautiful, younger and smarter.

Sonya looked at Nikko and said, "Yes he paid the debt but he's not the type you want to get involved with. He's my baby's father and he sent me here to sleep with your brother; so, what does this tell you?"

"It tells me you're weak and you have your own motives for being here. You could have easily refused but you're walking on your own free will. I know a lot more than you think I know Sonya. It also tells me you don't know how to force love on your man. Love is consumed emotions called money to you. Don't worry you don't have to feel threatened by me, I'm just asking questions. Believe me, I already know him sexually and if I wanted to sleep with him I have enough control to make it just a one-night stand. I don't have enough time for a man right now."

Sonya smiled at Nikko and said, "Yeah, you sound strong as an ox. Those are the kind Rav likes. I give her two days and he will be in her panties or she will be trying to find a way into his drawers. What's your color Relena?"

"Red," she replied.

"Your second day back, wear them, and when he, no when you throw yourself at him he'll leave you in the bed with a wet pussy. Hand them to me so I can frame them and date them, because Rav is very powerful. Nikko, don't you say nothin cause she disrespected me first."

Nikko held his peace because this truly would be a sight to see and a good test for Rav because she was a 22-year-old virgin.

The car stopped in front of the Hilton Hotel. The door man was there in a fine blue suit. A White man opened the door and they stepped out. Nikko made a phone call to a designer to meet them in the hotel.

They were escorted to the elevator. When they were all inside the door man entered his key and pressed the button to the Penthouse. It was only three rooms, Nikko's, her room, and Rav's. Under the floor was the Hilton's family floor.

When they reached the 21st Floor the door slid open and there were four armed guards waiting. They all walked out and one of the guards opened Relena's door.

Entering the living room, Sonya was so surprised because she was only 22, and her living style was much more mature. Plus, it was so clean. She had a lot of blue prints and sculptures of the past. Lots of pictures that had to be worth millions. There were wooden chairs, sofas, and tables with shining surfaces. Sonya turned to her and asked her how she obtained all of the art.

"See Ms. Sonya, you under estimate me. I designed all of this with my very own hands. This is why I am here, so I can build and create. All of this is my own work."

"Where is your TV?" Sonya asked.

"I don't watch TV, my mind is my TV," she replied.

The fight was over between the two. Sonya thought to herself, *"You just might be a challenge to him."*

She showed Sonya the rest of the apartment. The upstairs had three rooms. One of the rooms had all of her work in it and others she couldn't believe. Her bedroom was dated back to the early 1700's as was her Spiritual room. Her bedroom had a bed made out of stone, with rails and silk sheets hanging from the top. There was a painting covered up but Sonya took a peek at it. It was what she didn't want to see. It was a painting of Rav making love to Relena.

So Relena had a plan after all, was to take Rav away or was it just to make love to him? That sent Sonya back to the Spiritual room to examine some of the work she was praying over.

Relena was walking behind her and said, "Yes, your thinking is right."

She lit the candles that were in each corner of the room, then she lit the candle in the middle.

Sonya quickly asked, "Are you a Devil worshiper?"

"No, I'm a goddess," she replied, "when you made love to him yesterday, I was making love to him also. It's been prophesied, Rav is the one. When he died I visited him and gave him the kiss of life, so we could make love and conceive life in each other. My life will join his life only for the Gods to protect him. Rav will fall in the grave but the dirt will never touch him. You girls may have him now but we stand eternally."

"So, if you can see his life tell me what is he doing right now?" Sonya asked.

Relena sat in front of the lit candle in the middle of the floor chanting, "Oolay Oolay Hum Hum!"

Then she went silent. She reached towards a bible that was on the floor to her right and it opened itself to *1 Cor. 12*. She quoted the verse with her eyes closed. When she finished quoting her eyes opened again. Sonya was trying to leave because the sliding of the bible freaked her out. Relena reached out and grabbed her left hand. Sonya sat with Relena, both sitting Indian style. She closed her eyes and saw Rav sleeping with Gloria in his arms. The she saw Natasha coming in a storm, then there was a great boom and from there she didn't remember anything. When she came to she was in Relena's bedroom, laying in her comfortable bed.

Relena asked her, "Are you alright, your knees must have gotten weak or something?"

Sonya would never be able to figure out what happened no matter how much she strained her mind, so she didn't even try. All she knew was the bed she was in was the most comfortable bed she had ever been in.

"Relena, please make me one of these beds, I never want to get up." Sonya laid down under the silk cover wanting to go to sleep.

Nikko peaked his head in the door and asked, "Sonya, are you alright? I heard a loud noise."

"I fell or something but I'm alright," she replied. Then she asked him, "Do you have one of these beds in your apartment?"

"Yes," he replied.

She hopped up and said, "Let's go straight to your room."

CHAPTER 3

Back to Cuba

Sonya, Nikko, and Relena flew in the jet back to Cuba. It had been a lovely week for everyone. Now it was time to return to their normal lives. Nikko thought about what the future held for him and Rav. Sonya was thinking about him also and she wondered how he would look at her. Relena was just happy she was gonna finally meet him.

"There's an uprising going on in Cuba," said Relena, "something is wrong with him, I can feel it in my heart."

Nikko called one of his guards and asked for a cell phone. He dialed Vanquella's number.

"Vanquella, this is Nikko. Where is Rav?"

"He's missing Sir!" she replied.

"What do you mean missing?" he screamed into the phone.

Sonya heard the reply and spilled her white wine on her dress.

"What the Hell did you just say, Nikko?" she asked.

"How in the Hell could he be missing?"

"Vanquella, I'm not sure I heard you right, you said he's missing?" Nikko asked.

"Yes, he's been missing for seven days. Everyone has been looking for him. All I know is that him and Gloria got into a fight. When she went to check on him, the front door and the gate were open. Nobody saw him leave, they waited until you were gone and kidnapped him. We've been looking everywhere for him. He had to have been kidnapped because we've searched North and South Cuba."

"Tell everybody we know that if he's not found by morning, I'm taking

Cuba to war!" Nikko stated.

"I told him he was helping a bunch of ungrateful people that they don't give a Damn about him!"

Nikko had tears in his eyes and Sonya was up pacing. Relena was on her knees praying in Greek.

"Everybody is here now, Alex and Gloria just walked in," Vanquella said.

Nikko heard Gloria ask in the back ground, "Who are you talking to Vanquella?"

"I'm talking to Nikko and I've just told him that he's missing," she replied.

"Vanquella, tell everybody to meet me at the airport!" he commanded and then hung up the phone and said to Sonya, "fucking with you, I've allowed the boy to get kidnapped!"

Sonya didn't move at all for a moment, then she joined hands with Relena and began to pray. Nikko had leaned back in his seat with his hands over his face.

"Relena, that Greek shit you've been studying ain't gonna help us find him." She didn't answer him she just kept on praying.

He looked out the window as the jet started to land, he saw a sea of people and miles of cars. All the people of Cuba had come with candles to mourn the loss of Ravenion.

When the jet landed he jumped out of his seat and headed out the door and rolled up his sleeves. He walked right up to Alex and Gloria and slapped Gloria to the ground and screamed at her, "How could you let this happen? I left you in charge of him! The boy couldn't even walk on his own Gloria!"

Deep down inside Nikko knew it was his fault because he should have taken the boy into training. All of the sudden he pulled his gun out to shoot her. She just bowed her head and sank to her knees. When she looked at him she spread her hands and said, "My soul is one with his, so go ahead and shoot." She knew she would die for nothing, she had been praying all day and from the looks of things he hadn't been listening.

Nikko handed Alex a 357 to make sure it killed her. Everyone was upset because they were supposed to protect each other. Alex grabbed a hand full of her hair and pointed the gun at her forehead.

Relena came down the steps towards her with Sonya behind her and at the same time hollering, "Nikko! Nikko! He's not really missing. I just spoke to him, he's training himself to walk again, I just spoke to him and I know where he's at!"

Nikko grabbed Gloria and put her in the trunk of his black Bentley then he told Relena to lead the way. She dove into the passenger seat and told the driver to pull off.

Nikko and Sonya sat in silence while they traveled until they pulled in front of a green house.

When they got out they let Gloria out of the trunk and when she saw the house she told Nikko, "He's not here I searched here last night."

But Relena jumped in and said, "He's here Nikko, I can feel it!"

Alex walked up to the front door and kicked it in. Terry and the kids screamed as they walked in holding guns.

Bob came running down the stairs and said, "I thought I told you last night that he wasn't here!"

"The basement Nikko, he's in the basement!" Relena screamed. They all rushed to the basement and found nothing.

"Relena, he's not here!"

Nikko just stared at her, then said, "He is here, open that door because this is a training facility, right?"

Sonya walked in past the exercise equipment and smelled the bed and said, "He's been here!"

Gloria looked at Terry and said, "I ask you if you had seen him last night and you said no! I didn't know if you were trying to kill him or not. I don't know you, the only one in this room I know is Nikko, and anyway Rav told us not to say anything," Terry replied.

"Where is he now Miss Terry?" Nikko asked.

"He's out jogging on the path behind the fence," she replied.

"Miss Terry you've done a good job, you are trust worthy and he knew he wasn't gonna get better with a bunch of people around him anyway."

"He's with Mary, she's older and she's been working him," she said.

"And fucking him!" Sonya added.

Sonya opened the back door and saw it was fenced in, then she turned and looked at Terry, "What are you trying to pull. There ain't no path back here. There's nothing here but solid fence."

"Yes, there is an entrance, you just have to look closer to see the latch," she replied.

Gloria ran past everybody to the fence, found the opening and opened it. As she looked through it she saw the red, white, and blue jogging suit coming towards her.

"Ravenion! Ravenion!" she cried out then ran to him and threw her arms around him.

"I'm so glad you're alive!" she said.

"They were gonna kill me if you didn't show up by sundown! I promise I'll never do anything to harm you again."

Mary walked up with tears in her eyes, she hoped the sweat would hide her tears.

"You must be Mary?" Gloria asked.

She wiped her face with her hand and said yes.

"I'm so happy you got him up and walking. I'm Gloria and everybody is up at the house Rav. Relena told us where you were, I'm so glad you're alive!"

He stood there looking at Mary who couldn't control her tears any longer. He sent Gloria back to the house to tell Nikko he would be at the palace later on and to leave Terry a check for 1.5 million and to find the cab driver Torrain and bless him well for keeping his silence. He put his arms around Mary and brushed her tears away with his lips and said, "It's gonna be okay just be strong."

"No, it's not I'm gonna lose you and I'll miss you."

"Just stick to the plan," he replied.

He kissed her and took her hand and led her back up the path.

"Oh, Hell Naw Bitch! You've had him for seven days by yourself, them fake tears your given him ain't gonna work!"

"This must be the Sonya you've been telling me about."

He smiled and said, "Yes." They turned around and saw Nikko, Sonya, Alex, and Relena. He smiled at them and turned and walked back up the path.

"Rav, you must didn't hear me!"

"Nikko, control your Hoe, I said I'd see you guys later!"

Mary was stung because she knew Nikko was the boss, but Rav carried no fear and stuck to his plan. They walked up the path leaving them behind.

He heard Alex tell Sonya, "If she would have taken one more step forward he would have put one in her."

They walked and talked about the new memories they now shared. When he felt like they were long gone he led her back to the house. He explained to her he didn't want to mix her in his life style and prayed she would understand. She accepted it and told him to just stick to the plan.

When they entered the house, Terry stood there waiting. Her kids ran up to him and hugged him. Terry told her about the money Nikko had left. They all let out screamed and thanked him for his generosity. Him and Mary went upstairs. Terry told him that his driver was waiting.

They showered together and made love. He took off his necklace, a herringbone he always wore, and put it on her neck, then handed her a note that said, *"stick to the plan."*

He took another shower and got dressed and grabbed his gun. He walked back to her room and kissed her on the cheek and left. This time when she woke up he really would be gone.

He hugged and thanked Terry, then walked outside where he saw his black Bentley. His driver opened the door for him. He sat in the car looking out, hoping she would come out after him but she didn't. The driver got in and started the car and pulled away. The driver told Rav to look back and when he did he saw her standing in the doorway wearing his blue silk robe. She was flipping the necklace with her fingers smiling. He thought about all the fun they had had together. She was older than Sonya, Gloria and

Tasha and she knew how to trap a man.

He laughed at his next thought, "How could an old woman trap him?"

The more he thought about it the more he realized just how much he had enjoyed it. He doubted he could ever get that feeling from Sonya or Gloria. He was thinking hard about everything when they came upon a family selling oranges. He told the driver to pull over and buy all the fruit they had to sell and to pay them double for it and tell them it was from Ravenion. The driver did as he was told, but when they heard who they were for they refused the money saying they would give everything they had for Mr. Nalls.

That's what he wanted to hear, that the people appreciated him. At that moment two little boys approached the car and worshiped him saying, "We thank you Mr. Nalls."

He stepped out of the car and told the driver to give them everything he had in his pockets. The family members were all dressed in what looked like plain sheets. The mother held up the little girl showing her respect for him the same as the two boys.

He couldn't understand the little girls tears so he picked her up and asked, "Why are you crying little one?"

She replied, "Because my daddy is in jail for killing a man that raped me. I'm only 11-years-old. He had a job at the cigar plant and my mama worked at the coffee house until the foreman found out my papa killed his cousin."

Rav asked the mother, "What kind of work can you do?"

She stepped up and bowed down and said, "Anything to make sure my family has food and a roof over their heads. Mr. Larry gave us the oranges for sex. He let me pick 13 cases out of the warehouse but I have to sleep with him again tonight."

I can't do anything about your agreement for tonight because a deal is a deal, but I'll have your husband home tomorrow and he'll have a job for you. I trust you can read and write?"

"Yes Sir!" she replied.

"Then I have a job for you teaching children to read, what is your husband's name?"

"Raymond Hasson and my name is Vera, Sir."

"Well," Rav replied, "the only reason he's coming home tomorrow is because of your affair tonight. A real woman does what she has to to take care of her family and he will understand that too."

He looked at the driver and told him to take him to the jail. Rav asked Vera how old she was and she replied that she was 36, the same age as Sonya. She was very beautiful and he wondered what she looked like under that sheet. The more he thought about it the more he wanted to know. His driver knew his thoughts and said, "The same thoughts as me, huh?" They both laughed.

"Vera, how much does a case of oranges cost?"

"6 dollars, Sir."

"That's 78 dollars, would you step around the car please?"

She stepped around the car and the driver opened the rear door.

She started to get in but Rav said, "No! No! Nothing like that but tell your kids to turn their heads for a minute."

He sat down in his seat with his driver behind her. She bent down as if to give him some head but Rav said that wasn't what he wanted, he was just curious as to what was under the sheet.

The woman said to him, "Sometimes a woman has to do what she has to."

She asked the guard to open his coat real wide. He spread his coat real wide and she pulled the sheet up over her head. She had the smell of nature and a body a man would die to protect. She was the perfect female.

"Mr. Nalls, I would be more than happy to share myself with you to show my appreciation."

Taken by her beauty, he said, "Your husband is a lucky man."

She put her sheet back on and returned to her children feeling like a million dollars. Rav and the driver pulled away.

"Sammy, I don't know about you but I want that!"

"Rav, my daddy told me a long time ago that everything that looks good ain't always good. Sonya, Gloria and Mary are built about the same anyway. Besides, that's a man's wife."

"You're right my dear friend I bet that cat is old."

They pulled up to the jail, it didn't look anything like the U.S. jail. It looked like a jail out of the fifties. They walked in and told the deputy that they wanted to see Hasson. While they were waiting Rav recognized the deputy as a close friend of Nikko's father.

"Sir, may I call you Billy?"

"Yes Mr. Nalls, and I'm very happy you've returned." Rav smiled.

"Why would you arrest a man for defending his family? His baby girl was raped and you locked him up. Rape of a child is the worst crime you can commit because the child has to live with it for the rest of their lives. His wife is sleeping with the fruit man for survival."

"Mr. Nalls, I understand what you're saying but he killed him in front of thousands of people. I had to lock him up, I haven't even put it before the court yet. It's been over a year, I was trying to give it plenty of time so people would have a chance to forget."

"Would you do a special favor for me and let him go home tomorrow? He's paid for his crime. Have you seen his wife?" Rav asked. Raymond the woman's husband was standing behind him.

"She's wearing a sheet over herself and the kids also. Let him go and on his days off he can come by here for lock up or to do work for you."

"Have you slept with her Mr. Nalls?" Raymond asked.

"No, and my word is my bond. I damn sure want to but she's under enough pressure. Your little girl told me what happened. Billy, she's got to sleep with the fruit man to seal their deal tonight. He gave them 13 cases of oranges and I can't blame her for that when no one was helping her."

"Raymond, this is Ravenion Nalls. He's worked a deal for your freedom. You're going home tomorrow but you have to come back here one day a week to help out and pay $20 a month for 10 years. Thank your wife and little girl for this. I'll call the plant and let them know you'll be coming back to work."

"Mr. Nalls, thank you and I'm not upset with Vera for her actions."

He was young also and was well built. He put his arms around Rav's neck.

"Go take care of your beautiful family before the fruit man snatches them away because he's sure trying."

They left and went to the palace. He didn't care what Sammy said, he wanted to touch Vera somehow, some way, some day. When they entered the gates, people were everywhere clapping and cheering. Nikko, Sonya, Gloria, and Alex were at the entrance. The car stopped and Vanquella opened the door.

"Mr. Nalls you had the whole country on alert," she said. A news reporter was there to welcome him and his staff back.

"Mr. Nalls could you please tell the people where you were all last week?" he asked.

He turned and looked at the camera, "I've been at the Mary and Terry rehab clinic where they took real good care of me. If you ever need rehab it's a great place. I thank everyone for looking for me and there concern. We will be having a celebration, a parade, cookout with arts and crafts and a talent show. If you have a special talent I urge you to come and be a part of our celebration. We call it Cuba day and its one week from today. The most incredible exhibit will win 100,000. Remember, we want peace, no violence, so come and have fun." Nikko came out and spoke next.

"Yes, we want to show the people of North Cuba that freedom is here in South Cuba but you must want it. Most of you didn't know I'm from the U.S and there we have clubs where men and women strip naked and dance for you. We are going to build the same kind of clubs for the adults and clubs with no nudity for the young ones. It's time to live!"

They went in to the palace and gathered in the dining room. A great fish dinner was being served.

Relena came down the hallway wearing a white see through dress. She had on red panties and bra. Everyone stood when she entered the room.

Rav looked at her wondering whether he knew her or not. He sat and started to eat. He was really hungry and everyone laughed.

Nikko seated everybody and they all ate.

Rav noticed how close Nikko and Sonya sat but he didn't let it get to him. He finished eating and left. He got in his car and drove, thinking about all them women in his life; Sonya, Vera, Mary, Gloria, Tasha, and Erica. But the one he missed the most was Blue. He really was in love with his sister. He drove up to a house, beautiful green grass on both sides of a long driveway. It is the one he wants to live in and its empty. He had called the real estate agent and asked her to meet him there. He walked the yard, it was the size of a football field split in half.

The back yard had a pool in the center and a play area for the children. He could vision Nodiya and Juan running around playing there.

He still believed he would find Juan alive one day. There were still people looking for him but so far there were no clues. He thought about getting Gloria and Mary pregnant. He just wanted more children. He didn't want to be like Nikko.

"Mr. Nalls! Mr. Nalls!" a female voice called from across the yard, "are you alright?" she asked.

She sat down beside him and he looked at her attire, a brown skirt with matching stockings, white blouse and brown jacket. Then he looked at her face, she was beautiful.

"Why do I feel like I've died and gone to Heaven?" he wondered aloud, *"this land is filled with beautiful women."* She informed him that she was married and suggested they look at the house.

As they got up he noticed her ass through her skirt, he didn't say anything but just followed behind her. She opened the back door and into the kitchen. It was the type of kitchen you would see on Home Makeover or Cribs. She explained that the house was owned by a big star out of the U.S. that had gone bankrupt. So, he was selling it to stay out of the public eye.

After she had shown him the house he decided he would buy it. He noticed that she had taken off her wedding ring or she never had one on in the first place.

So, he asked her, "Carmen, why would you lie to me? I thought you were married?"

"I'm married to myself so I didn't lie to you. You have hundreds of girls like me so I know it would never become serious."

"Well, but I don't have hundreds of girls like you because there's only one of you."

Nothing else was spoken, they said everything with their eyes as they got in their cars. He followed her to her office. She was driving a white Camry.

Thinking about what she'd said he thought to himself, *"I guess that's how a true woman would act or she's playing hard to get. Nikko is right, my hard dick is gonna get me killed cause I don't have any dick control."*

He parked in front of the building and went into the glass fronted office. He agreed to pay 1.7 million for the house and gave a $200,000 fee for the sale. She refused it because she thought it was a bribe to get her in bed.

He knew she was willing and ready but he let it go and got his keys and left.

She was watching him as he got in his car. He smiled because he knew the power of money, it would and could change any body. Now all he had to do was wait on her to show back up.

He went to the phone company and all the utilities, even got the satellite TV hooked up. He wanted to live like he lived in the states, not like Nikko with hundreds of people around him all the time. That shows fear.

He went back to the palace to get Sonya. She was at the door waiting when he arrived. He opened the car door and she stepped out of the house and asked if it was safe to get in with him.

He told her, "A guilty conscience was her problem, not his."

After she had gotten in the car and they had pulled away she asked, "Do you want to know what happened?"

"No, cause I know you got paid."

"Yes, that's true. I got 220 million and, in the morning, I'm transferring 110 of it to your account."

She was leaning towards his zipper but he stopped her, she knew something was wrong.

"Look," she said, "you made me do it because what ever happened you ordered it." Her tears came full force because she knew he didn't want her to go.

"Sonya, I told you to go. That's your job so I'm not mad at you. We have an open relationship."

It had gotten dark by the time he turned into the driveway. She saw the high border grass so she threatened to jump out but he had locked the door. He pulled the Glock from under the seat.

"You can't kill me for sleeping with him, you told me to do it. I did it out of love. Everything I do for you I do out of love. I've been jailed, raped and almost killed. I've murdered for you and sold my body for you. I made you rich. I'm the one who got you all your dope. You're only where you are because of me!"

The car was going real slow. He cocked the gun back and she saw a bullet eject, now it was pointed towards her head. He hit the gas and screamed "You Dirty Bitch!" and pulled the trigger.

She screamed and the car came to a stop. She was holding her head in her hands. When she looked up and saw the house and looked at him.

"Why would I kill you? You're very stupid. You just feel bad for going. I know y'all stayed in my room and I know you saw the rings. Now tell me why I would kill you and our baby? I love you." She tried to fake a smile, but she was scared as Hell.

"Who lives here Rav?" she asked him.

"You do Dummy. I saw how close you and Nikko were becoming so I had to get you out of that environment. You're having my baby not his. I don't want to wait to have sex with my baby's momma because she got some nut pussy whipped! You did a good job Sonya, I'm very proud of you. If you ever need me to sleep with a female let me know and I'll do it. Now let's go have sex in our new home. Sonya this is what you wanted for us, to move away. We got money and a big house. I guess I'm ready to get married." He kissed her hard and got out of the car.

She was so afraid a minute ago and now she was fixin to get married.

He went to the front door and opened it when he heard her blow the horn and hollered out to him, "You scared me so bad, my legs don't want to move!"

He hustled back to the car and picked her up. He carried her in and closed the door. He laid her in the bedroom. It was huge with black marble furniture, two walk-in closets and a 69-inch Plasma TV

Since her legs wouldn't move he spread them for her, playing with her but her legs still didn't move.

"Sonya, do I need to call a doctor," he asked.

She said she just wanted to eat something and go to bed. Deep down inside she knew she had never been so scared. She didn't understand what was wrong with her.

"Guess what? I remembered everything except food!" Rav laughed.

He called Nikko and told him what was what and to send someone with some food to the house. He told Nikko how bad he scared her and that she couldn't move her legs.

Nikko said just because she could talk didn't mean she wasn't in shock.

He hung up and thought about what she said when she was scared. He saw she was still crying and her nose was running, he didn't know what to do. So, he laid down with her to cuddle her.

"Dammit Rav, is sex all you think about? I didn't ask for all this pain, I just wanted to be loved by you. I've been beaten raped and whored for you and all you care about is yourself. I would have never scared you like that. I can't even move my legs and all you want to do is put your fingers inside me. Sex ain't everything. It's plain to see you don't love me, all you care about is yourself. I felt so bad when I saw that prayer in the Bible, and I saw the rings. I didn't want to sleep with Nikko but you told me to. Tasha wouldn't have ever done that for you and you would have never told her to do it, so why me Rav? You better answer me and you better be sincere because if you don't I won't be her when you wake up, I'll be back in the states. Dammit! Answer me Ravenion!"

"Hold on Sonya, our food is here."

He went downstairs and opened the door, Gloria came in with the food, gave him a kiss and left. He put the food on a silver platter and carried it upstairs. He put it on the floor and laid Sonya beside it. He kissed her on the cheek and surprised her when he started to pray and asked the Lord to give him the right words to say.

He opened the tray and there were two wine glasses, lamb chops and a chilled bottle of wine. He poured them some wine and cut her food for her and began to feed her.

The attention made her feel better but she wanted to hear him say he loved her. She asked him to say it.

"Sonya, I'm not gonna lie to you. I don't know if I would have asked Tasha to do the same thing or not. She's dead now. For all it's worth Sonya, I'm scared of you. Emotionally, what I feel for you is deeper than what I feel for Tasha. I worry about you every day even though I know you can handle yourself. The reason I've never told you I love you with sincerity is because I didn't want you to go soft on me. I do really love you but I know your gonna leave me. Yes, you and Nikko were a power move and a test of your love. I know you'll walk through Hell for me. You're the girl I want on my team. Ain't no other bitch would have done half the things you have. So, know I know what I got; there ain't no me without you. But I can't let my opponent know you're in my heart. So, I do little stuff to throw them people off. You see how you attacked Tasha? I don't want that to happen to you. I do crazy shit and I know what I asked you to do was stupid but I knew you'd thrive off of it. You know I'm gonna break you off. I did, so if you have to fly, you'll be strapped for life. Sonya, listen to me! If don't know body love you, me and Nodiya love you. I love you! I love you!"

He stopped talking and picked her up and carried her to the tub. He ran some water and bathed her. Her legs moved but he didn't see it.

She just played it off because she wanted to see if he would try to sleep with her. If he did he didn't mean a word he said but surprisingly they slept peacefully through the night.

Gloria brought a classic American breakfast, eggs, bacon, grits and toast. When she knocked he answered the door reading the note Sonya had written. She had left before he had gotten up.

"Gloria what's up?"

"Sonya was at the palace this morning saying goodbye to everyone and left, what's up with that?"

"She didn't feel loved by me so she left."

"Do you want me to stay and keep you company?" she asked.

"That's alright, I'd like to finish reading her letter. It's six pages and to get a good understanding I need to be alone."

He put the tray on the table and ate. After he finished, he went upstairs and laid on the bed and read the letter.

"Dear Juan, at this time my heart is bleeding. I'm so confused. Leaving you right now is the best thing for me to do. I feel I am doing what you would want me to do. You trained me for this knowing I wasn't gonna fuck him for free. You said it last night, I'm gonna leave you. Nothing under the sun last's long, life included. But love does. Some people say love doesn't live here anymore. Every time someone dreams they are in a state of remembering something dear to them. You are my first love. You are the first man I've ever loved and the only man I'll ever love. I believe everything you said last night. I wanted to see if you were gonna sleep with me. I knew that if you did then your words didn't mean Shit. I know your love is scaring me. If it takes me getting beaten, burned, and raped then I don't need it.

When you took me to the park; did you know that's the most fun I've ever had? I wish we could start over. I don't want Nodiya's father running from the law and popping in and out of her life. I want you home with me, I love you more than life itself. I just can't compete with your life style.

He turned the letter over then decided to put it in the drawer. He went to sleep thinking of his life. He remembered his promise to Gloria and that meant he had to get his life in order. Dick control is all he needed.

Someone knocked on the door. He went downstairs. He was still in his PJ's and without a shirt.

It was Carmen. She walked right in with some papers in her hand. She was looking good in her white jeans and a tight T-shirt.

"How may I help you?" he asked.

"You forgot your deed," she said.

She handed him the deed and a home rental contract. She explained to him that it was an agreement that the previous owners had so a tourist was welcome to stay in one of the rooms for a short period of time. Her company supplied the maids, gardeners and maintenance people.

She told him the land was a total of 1500 acres and she knew of a contractor that could build more homes if he wished.

He asked her to take a seat on the love sofa. She smiled and assured him that no love making would be happening on that sofa today.

Since he had described the sofa as a love sofa, he smiled and said, "I like a nice strong defense but I wasn't hitting on you that's just what they call it in the states."

She took a seat on the corner of the sofa and crossed her legs and asked him what he thought.

He smiled but he wasn't feeling her on the rental or home building. That's how he almost got killed the first time. Plus, he wanted to hire his own workers. So, he turned all of it down but told her if she came up with more land that he would buy it and let her manage it.

She smiled politely and then frowned because she had already rented some time to one couple and two other males. They were due in today at 3:30. She was known to be the most dependable agent around and she was highly recommended. She was on the up and up and for the first time she found herself in a tight situation, one that would make her bend the rules.

There was no way the company could refund the money, she had made big money on her commission. Most of her money was helping her family open their own tourist company and that would be backed by the real estate company. The extra 200,000 was put into a house and a school. She was only 19-years-old and she was in a panic.

She had a chance to live at the palace but she wasn't a whore nor did she believe in combat or trafficking drugs.

Her and Gloria were best of friends until she went on that land full time. She thought about calling Gloria and asking for help to get him to do it but she hardly ever talked to her anymore.

She was thinking about telling him the truth and the thought of it got her heart pumping.

He got up and went upstairs to the bathroom. She watched him go up, she liked him but all of this was against her belief. A tear rolled down her cheeks, everything she stood for was over. If she slept with him she may as well have slept with everyone else. The more she thought about it the more she thought she should tell the truth. She decided to go to the palace and she prayed to God to make a way for her.

He came back down and saw her bent over and rushed to her. He asked her what was wrong. When she didn't answer he went to the kitchen to get her some water. By the time he got back she was standing and her eyes were dry. Her mind was made up she was going to do it for her pride and a little pleasure.

She took him by the hand and walked him up to his room. She didn't want to do it in the living room and feel like a cheap whore.

With a smile on her face she stood in front of the bed and took the cup of water from his hand and set it on the nightstand. Her mind remembered the money he gave her yesterday and she realized he had paid good for it. She kissed him hard on the lips and on the neck. She started to unbutton the PJ's and kissed his chest. She helped him out of his boxers. She dropped to her knees and made love to him with her mouth. She swallowed all of him and then she stood and undressed.

His mind was more surprised than ever. She laid down and spread her legs to show her shaved pink clit. He laid down beside her and asked her what all this was about? In a squeaky voice she asked him the favor she needed of him.

He looked her in the eye and kissed her and told her, "All you had to do was ask and I would have said yes. But since you lowered yourself the answer is no. I just wanted to see how far you'd go, all you had to do was be honest cause I knew you couldn't get the money back. I could've grudge fucked you and made you hate me for the rest of your life. I just can't allow myself to stoop that low. So, deal with your problem the best way you can. All you got out of this was a stomach full of Cum! Now get out!" She was crying as she got up and got dressed and then ran out in shame.

He was so mad at her or was he just hurt behind Sonya? He laid there thinking about what he just turned away, now that was dick control. He covered himself and went to sleep.

When he woke up there was a beautiful Black female standing over him. Her green and yellow dress fit her perfectly. Her breasts stuck out and her hips spoke to you.

"Mr. Ravenion, my name is Glenda and I'm from the United States. I'm one of your guests. I'm married to Dr. Gerry Brown out of New York. I just wanted to thank you for letting us stay for two weeks."

He closed his eyes in disbelief. He forgot about his nakedness as he got out of the bed.

"My Lord!" she said as she bit down on her lip.

"Please forgive me," he said as he was putting on his boxers.

"Are all of the guests here because I have something to tell y'all."

"Yes, everybody is downstairs." He walked passed her to the steps and there John Adam greeted him.

"Are you one of the guests?" he asked.

"Yes, I am."

"Then y'all are lucky."

He felt safe with him being there because you couldn't tell he was Federal. But John knew all about people. So, he phoned Carmen and told her she owed him big time because he didn't have the heart to put his own kind out in a different country. He hung up before she could say anything.

He called Mary and told her what had happened between him and Sonya and told her she was number two, so get ready to be known. Before she could say anything, he hung up on her too. Then he went and showered and dressed.

He was so angry with Sonya that he wanted her dead. He was even angrier with Carmen because he couldn't have one night alone so he could gather his thoughts. He looked at the phone. He was used to people leaving him. He just hoped she was strong enough to hold up during her debriefing; would she tell or not?

He got a long sleeve red shirt out of the dresser and put it over his tank top. Put his gun in his waistband, then put on a black and red Fubu cap on to hold down his beehive weaves. Finally, he slipped on some low-cut snake skin shoes and his shades. He counted out 20 grand in cash and walked out of the house.

He jumped in the Bentley and called Nikko to ask how everything was going toward Cuba day. He told him it was all gonna be righteous. Not really wanting to talk he told him he would be there for dinner and hung up.

He pulled into the driveway of the training camp. The camp was on 5000 acres and was built in a country club style. There weren't many cars in the parking lot and when he got out Gloria met him.

"How did you know I was here Gloria?"

"The camp has a lot of cameras and you have a big tag on your car that says Rav.

There was a pavilion top and a red carpet at the entrance. Two armed guards stood at the door. They went inside and she took him on a tour of the club. She showed him all of the shooting teams and she explained how they were set up. The other rooms were for hand combat training such as martial arts and arts. She showed him the swimming pools and the water torture tanks. Next, were the tear gas and pepper spray training rooms. Last, she showed him the computer training center and asked if he would like to see the training fields?

She showed him the advanced shooting range and the mock mine field and how when you stepped on a mine you were covered with purple paint.

He laughed and said, "I don't need any of this stuff I just need pistol and shotgun training because bullets can stop everything else."

She laughed at that and took him to the gun room. She gave him some safety equipment and showed him the 306 and how to hold it properly. She demonstrated and when she was done, she hit a red button to retrieve the target.

His goal was to become a sniper, he knew that was the only way to get Smokey and Leo out of jail. He had thought of many ways to get them, going over the top was the best way. He just had to hope Sonya would stay true and find out where they were. She had enough money to make sure her and Nodiya were taken care of. She wouldn't need him because she would get in and get what she wanted, and then get out. He just had to hope she wouldn't be a jack in the box and pop in and out of his life.

She handed him the gun after she made sure it was loaded. He leaned forward as she had showed him and she put some padding on his shoulder until he got used to the kick. He counted to three and fired. She asked how it felt and he said there was no pain.

After a couple of tries he was still missing. He was upset with himself but she told him to not worry about it, it would come in time.

He fired for nearly an hour before she realized what he was doing wrong. He was sighting it wrong so she reloaded for him and showed the correct way. This time he was on target and she loaded full loads and shot at full body targets.

She was happy now that Sonya was gone and not in her way. She didn't know about Mary. Mary was a secret that no one was going to know about. He hated that John and the other guests were in his house. He wanted to spend time with her alone. He guessed he would have to take her somewhere else.

Gloria stood by him smiling. He couldn't leave her like that, so he took her in his arms and rocked with her. She was very surprised and smiling. He kissed her and told her to maintain and to not be afraid. They walked to the car and she sat on the hood. He stood between her legs went down and kissed her between her legs.

She laid her head on top of his and grabbed him by his face and said to him, "I'll die loving you."

"Know that shit gonna get ruff and can't no hoe walk in your shoes," he said.

"If I'm with someone it's just a power play and you got to maintain. OK?"

"OK," she agreed.

He got in the car and phoned Mary and asked where she wanted to go. She was so happy, she said she wanted to go to the pathway and she told him their business was jumping. She told him just to come and she would be waiting.

When he got home, John and some others were playing cards and the women were cooking. He went and took a shower and dressed in some Jabo pants, boot and a little Issyme cologne.

When he went down the steps John was sitting at the table. He handed John his key and got the key to his black Maybach. He wondered why everybody traveled in black cars. The back gate was open and he didn't let Terry and Bob know he was there he just went straight to the path way. He could hear Toni Braxton's song, *"Spanish Guitar"* playing and saw the candles burning. They were surrounding a colorful quilt. There were plates with steak and salad and potatoes. She was preparing his food for him to eat when she saw him she stood. She was wearing a white blouse and matching slippers. She kissed him and held him and he ran his hands through her wavy hair. When she turned into the light he could see she was naked underneath everything. She fed him and herself.

"Mary, you're like a blessing to a man just coming out of a coma with no friends and as he looks in your eyes he sees a bright future. He no longer cares for his past life he just wants to be with you. That's what I want to do is to build a place for you and allow your new home to be here in my heart."

She cried because those were heartfelt words, like a husbands vows. She took the bag with the pillows and the quilt. She took off her blouse, laid back, and pulled the cover over herself. He took the gun, his phone and put them under his pillow and then made love to her. They spoke about the love they were feeling. She told him with tears in her eyes that she feared she would never see him again. She held him while he slept, protecting him with her Spirit. When he woke up she was coming to him with breakfast.

CHAPTER 4

Tears, Both of Joy and Betrayal

Tears, both of joy and betrayal, rolled down Sonya's cheeks. She couldn't understand why she had left the man she had devoted her life to. He gave her so much including pain. He only did it to make her stronger. She told herself she was doing it for Nodiya, but as she looked out the window she saw the shadows of betrayal. She was wearing a black dress with a white collar. Her reflection was that of a widow. She let Gloria and Mary win. She left him after he told her the truth and that he loved her. She thought about telling the pilot to turn around but what was done was done. She knew by leaving was the only way to protect herself the baby and him.

She would learn Smokey and Leo's whereabouts and tell them he was alright and that he was coming to get them. She thought about the debriefing and all the questions they were gonna ask. She wondered if they knew that was her in the barn shooting. If so, she was gonna have make him the prime suspect in something.

They finally landed, but she didn't see anyone waiting for her. She got up and exited the plane, the Atlanta air felt good and she walked through the airport smiling. She finally hailed a cab and went home.

When she got home she was careful to stay to the side when she opened the front door, everything seemed alright so she went in and closed the door. She looked out across the street to the other houses, no one seemed to be watching the house. She searched the house and there were no taps and nothing seemed to be disturbed. She couldn't believe they hadn't been in the house. She checked the phone for messages, there weren't any so she called headquarters. There was no voice when the other line answered so she put in her code, 814370 followed by the star button. Another tone came on so she entered 338329 followed by the # key, it rang three times and then the soft sweet voice of her captain came on the line.

"Sandra, how were your trips to Greece and Cuba?" he asked.

"Great," she replied, "I got a chance to relax from the last case. How is it going by the way?"

"After you come in for debriefing we will talk about your next case." He told her.

He told her she needed to come in as soon as possible and she hung the phone up.

She went upstairs and grabbed her neck badge and her ID from the nightstand. She went outside and gave another check for security then locked the door and left.

As she pulled away from the house she begins to feel panicked and the same reaction that her legs wouldn't move again. She knew it was the thought of Rav with the gun and she wondered to herself why he had to torture her.

She picked the phone up and heard a tick and closed her eyes waiting for death to come but it didn't. She called the office and told them to send someone to check the car for bombs. She was so confused she begins to cry and beat on the steering wheel with both hands and wondering how she could be in so much pain and be so much in love with someone. After about 15 minutes she begins to calm down.

A black truck pulled in behind her. It was the bomb squad and all six of its members.

The sergeant approached her window and asked, "Ms. Anderson are you alright? He was the one who recruited her. He had tried to hook up with her but she didn't show any interest. He had saved her life when a drug deal had gone bad. She was under cover with some bad dudes smuggling drugs and weapons and they found out she was an agent. Another female agent had exposed her because she couldn't make it and accused her of fucking her way through the program. So, when the failed agent saw her at the drug meeting she quickly told the thugs who she was. The leader had just smiled at her and opened fire. That's when Agent Gann came through the window and stood in front of her and took a couple of bullets to the vest as she escaped.

Afterward she dated him a couple of times, but she wasn't feeling him. She couldn't be with someone she didn't love because if she could then she could hate the world. Her own mama had watched her stepfather rape her and her excuse was that he had taken them in when her father had died and that if he hadn't they would have been whores so she should just take it. Her mother said she had suffered a lot for them and she had finally found someone who wasn't just interested in her but all of them.

So, she acted like she was mad because Gann tried to sleep with another agent and he still hadn't forgave himself because he was in love with her.

He got her out of the car and sat her in the F150 with her legs hanging out the door. She just laid back and cried. He couldn't understand her pain but he tried his best to comfort her. When the ambulance arrives, they checked her vitals and she told them she couldn't move her legs. Her blood pressure was high and she was running a light fever. They loaded her in the ambulance and transported her to the hospital.

As they were in route one EMT looked at the other and said, "We have a problem, she's pregnant!"

They arrived at Grady Memorial Hospital and she was fine in a few hours. They had put her on bed rest so she didn't hear Melissa when she came in to the room. Melissa read her chart and saw she was just in shock and that the baby was fine.

She was having a dream and was saying out loud that she was sorry to Rav and that she never meant to hurt him. Melissa woke her from the dream and told her everything was gonna be alright.

When everything came into focus she realized she was at Grady. She wanted to use the phone and check to see if Rav was okay and mad at her.

After the call she told Melissa that he had been found and that he wasn't missing and for her to call him and tell him that she loved him.

Melissa smiled and said she would and after she left Tasha and Blue walked in.

"So, where is he, Sonya?" Tasha asked.

She looked from Tasha to Blue and asked, "How did you know I was back and in the hospital anyway?" Sonya asked.

"Bitch, we followed your scary ass from the airport now where the Hell is my brother?" Blue demanded.

"How much did it cost y'all to make those up? Maybe I can get the same "Keeping your memory alive Juan" outfit since he fucked all three of us."

What the Hell is she talking about Blue? He's your brother!"

"Tasha the bitch is drugged up, I don't know what she's talking about!" Blue answered.

"Sure, you don't! You thought I didn't know you was fucking him?

What I didn't know was that y'all was brothers and sisters. You ain't his damn sister Erica! I know his whole family history and ain't no white bitch in his family!"

"That goes to show what you know, I'm named after my mom because my dad was on a mission and couldn't sign the birth certificate Bitch! Now answer my question!" Blue slapped her.

"Ok! Ok! I'll answer the question. Yes Tasha, he fucked her. In the mountains when they went on a hiking trip. Go on now Erica and tell her how good the dick is. Tell her he took your virginity. You see Ms. Tasha you hate me but you keep her by your side. They say keep your enemy's close so I must be your enemy.

She closed her eyes and slid deeper into the bed.

"Oh no bitch! You ain't going to sleep!"

Tasha bent down and started choking her, "You remember when you tried to kill me bitch, you thought I was really in a coma didn't you bitch?"

Sonya was so weak from the sedative she couldn't even fight back. She just laid there and closed her eyes, she knew Tasha wouldn't kill her.

Blue stopped her and said, "Stop it Tasha, if you kill her we will never find out where he is!"

"I see how y'all do it now. Beat a bitch when she's down. Y'all would make really good agents, you really would. For the life of me I want to find him too, I'm pregnant with his little girl. Nodiya is the name he gave her. For all I know he could be dead. By the time I got here he was already gone. I thought you were dead any way."

"The doctor said you flashed your badge and said we needed him alive."

"Yes, I did flash my badge but his people got bigger badges than mine.

He works for the government. He's an agent just like Blue's father. You should call him, he can give you all the information you need."

"If my father knew, we wouldn't be here. And he's not no damn agent! Bitch, you're full of it and you know where he's at because the nurse said she gave the letter to you. So, you left with them!"

Sonya sighed and closed her eyes again trying to throw them off because she wasn't gonna tell them. She just wanted to sleep. And where the fuck was Melissa's ass?

"Tasha, I need to stay in touch with you because I don't want Nodiya fucking her brother in the years to come. Ain't that right Blue?"

Blue wondered for a minute should he tell her? Then it came to her, nobody knew they were fucking except the people in the mountains. They could've all been agents.

She smiled at Sonya and told her, "Everybody ain't sick or processed like you're trying to make me spending time with my brother wrong. Yes, I was in Paris, because he needed to get away. He took me there because he didn't want to get me killed. Yes, I was in the mountains with him but because we slept in the same tent don't mean we was fucking. Only a sick person would think like you. I know you know where he's at because if you know where he took me then you know where they took him. You're a stalker and your obsessed with my brother. And you think he's fucking every female he comes in contact with. What you gonna do try to kill me next?"

Sonya laughed and said, "Okay, I've had enough!"

Then she picked up the phone and called the nursing station and yelled, "Send some guards! I've got some people in here trying to kill me!"

They looked at her and said it wasn't over with and left. Two guards came in wearing black uniforms.

"Where have you two been? Two females came in here and attacked me! Luckily, I was able to fight them off, I thought I told you there was a threat on my life?"

"Ms. Anderson, You probably did but we didn't know because we are APD not Federal. The only reason we are here is because we were just relieved from our post. I advise you to call your captain and find out why your protection detail isn't here. As of now everything looks secure so we are outta here, have a nice night."

"What's your name since you want me to have a nice night?" she asked, "as a matter of fact give me both of your names and badge numbers. We gonna see who has a nice night by the time I get off of the phone! I'm a Federal Agent who was just attacked and y'all tell me to have a nice night! I'm gonna see about this shit!" As they wrote the information down Sonya mumbled a few more words and fell off to sleep.

"She must have dreamed the whole thing Mike."

"You might be right Jerry but let's lock the door or she might say to white guards were in here fondling her!" Jerry locked the door as they left and they wrote a statement in case she remembered.

Sonya sat in her pool naked with the waves going away from her dragging her hands back and forth through the water. The sun shined down on her, her belly sticking out of the water as she back stroked from one end of the pool to the other. When she looked up guards were surrounding the pool armed with automatic weapons.

The one who appeared to be the leader spoke to her, "Sandra Anderson this is from Rav, you've been ordered to die!"

Before she could say anything all of the men fired at once. She was screaming, "No! No! Please Help Me!" She jumped straight up in bed sweating and touching herself allover.

Melissa and the nurses ran into the room and leaving the key in the door.

"Sonya, what's wrong with you? Melissa asked seeing the sweat on her face. She checked her temperature. It was pushing 106! She reached into her pocket and gave her some codeine for pain and to help bring her temp down.

Melissa stayed by her bed side because she knew that's what Rav would want. Plus, Sonya had helped her through all kinds of shit and she owed her. She held her hand stroking it.

"Sonya we've been friends for 9 years now so talk to me. I've never seen you so afraid, then again, I've never seen you pregnant either. Sonya, what's wrong with you? Why are you screaming for help and screaming his name? What have you done to make you so afraid?"

"Do you have your phone?"

"Yes," she answered quickly and then she handed her the phone and she called him.

"Rav, I'm in the hospital. I'm running a high temp and you know that's not good for the baby. I keep having these dreams and in all of them you keep sending people to kill me! I'm afraid to even crank my own car or go into the house! Ever since you put that gun to my face I've been afraid. I knew you'd kill me and I'm even more afraid now that we're apart."

"Then come back! I don't know why you think I'd hurt you because I won't! I love you so you're just fighting yourself. When you get back in the field again you'll be your old self. You need to find out where there hiding Smokey and Leo and you're gonna be alright because you're tough! I love you and I'll never do anything to hurt you. You're the mother of my child, so think like her and you'll be safe. Do you need a bodyguard?"

"No, I'll be alright now. I just needed to hear your voice because the way I left was messed up. I know you love me and you're willing to take on the world. I love you Ravenion!" She smiled as she hung up the phone.

"I'm fine now I just needed to hear him say he loved me."

"Well, I'm just gonna stay here awhile and make sure you're alright," Melissa said.

"Thank you, Melissa, I owe you Girl."

Melissa flipped through the channels and found Shrek and they watched one and two and she fell back asleep. Melissa left and locked the door.

The next morning, her captain was sitting in the chair next to the bed. He just sat there hoping she would say something about Nikko while she slept. He just sat there in his finely tailored clothes and waited, but she said nothing. He decided to go get a bite to eat. As he was leaving she rolled over.

"Captain, why are you leaving?"

"I wasn't leaving, I was just going for a bite to eat. But since you are awake we can go over somethings."

About that time a slim well-dressed woman walked in carrying a briefcase. She opened the case and inside was all the debriefing material. The woman took out a small machine to test her answers. She hooked some patches to her forehead and one to each side of her hands.

When she turned the machine on a series of lines appeared on the screen.

Then the woman began speaking into a small microphone.

"This is agent Patricia Fields, I'm sitting with captain Paul Bryant and Agent Sandra Anderson. Today is Saturday, April the 6th of 2002. Agent Anderson, would you please state your field name and your assignment?"

"My field name is Sonya Ramon and I work international drug trafficking between Cuba and the United States. Also, the multiple murders between Atlanta and Detroit tied into gang violence, and their connections to the Cuban Cartels. I'm investigating Raul Escobar who is in hiding and has left in power his brother Nikko. They are doing business with BFM. I have an informant by the name of Juan Ellis. He has become Nikko Escobar's right-hand man. He reports to me and I report to Captain Bryant."

"Where were you on the 8th of March around 11 p.m.?"

"Home," Sonya replied.

The lines stayed even but Sonya didn't even look at the screen. She knew she had to answer direct and fast. She knew how to get through this. She had done it many times before. Her old partner had taught her how to handle everything. All she had to do was ask them to repeat the question and, in her mind, if she had ever fucked God and say no. She had passed them all and this one should be no different.

"Did you leave home for anything?" the agent asked.

"Yes," Sonya answered.

"Why?" she wanted to know.

"I was called by one of the gang members, him and Juan were in a shootout with the Feds. So, I went to the estate only to find the street filled with gang members and an agent that had been shot. So, I came in through the back and showed my badge and we took the agent to the hospital. After the surgery, they put both of us on a plane. He stayed in a coma for 8 days. When he awoke he told me to go to Greece with Nikko. When we returned he was missing, that's when they sent me back. I'm here in case he pops up or someone wants to make an exchange." She never looked at the screen and her captain was smiling.

"Sandra, do they know your pregnant and do they know who the father his?" the agent asked.

Sonya decided this was a good time to end the session before too much was exposed. So, she pretended to be angry with the agent and asked, "What do you mean do they know? It's none of their damn business! I'm not a slut or hoe! I know who my baby's daddy is! What you got? 3 or 4 kids? Do you know who their daddy is? Juan Ellis is Nodiya Ellis's father. Everybody in Cuba knows who I am. Don't ever dis respect me with a question like that again!"

The agent responded by saying, "I think that's enough questions for today. She needs her rest. You did good Sandra." Then she took the patches off and left.

Sonya did her homework and knew that after a dealer was busted the drugs were put back on the street. She knew about every agent on the force. All of them were dirty one way or another. Even her Captain was waiting on her to slip. She was good but she didn't know she had already slipped. He knew about the money.

"Sonya while you were Greece, 220 million dollars showed up in your account. I didn't know God was putting money in peoples accounts now. He must have skipped me. But as soon as you left Greece 120 million disappeared. All I ask for is 20 million. I know you can do it, your baby's daddy is a billionaire. I know you set the two gang boys up to take the fall. He's moving up too fast Sonya and your moving with him. You must have forgotten I have people on the street too." He rubbed her legs with both hands, this was the moment he had been waiting for. The best agent in the world had slipped.

"So, what, you gonna try to fuck me next, right?" Sonya asked.

The captain acted offended and said, "No, I'm just trying to comfort you! Do we have a deal or what? Because you were still on the case I know you were in that estate that night. I know you went through that tunnel and I know you fired. I also know you fucked Nikko for 220 million. You gave Juan 120 million yesterday, why can't I have 20 million? You could never spend that much money in a life time. I'm fixing to retire and I have something you need. I know where the gang boys are being held. Let me in and I'll have your back just like I've always had it."

"So why are you hustling me now?" she asked.

He dropped his head and answered, "I'm in trouble Sonya. They came in with internal affairs while you were gone. I had to cover your ass and I had to let one of my men get hit for 15 million. I had to make the call. They think it was a set up for us to get the dope and guns back. There was a diamond in them somewhere. It's worth 15 million and I don't know where their holding it. The other money I want for myself for my family in case something happens to me. Sonya or Sandra, whoever I'm talking to, they sent me pictures of my kids and grandkids. My one-year old granddaughter was kidnapped 3 days ago. That's why I'm so glad you came back I was about to go ask Nikko for a job myself."

"How do I know you're not lying?" she asked.

"Let me make some phone calls and I'll let you know what's up later. I need a secure phone." He smiled and kissed her on the head and left.

She ordered breakfast and it came while she was in the shower thinking about Paul. She could help him but she had to make sure he wasn't setting her up first. When she came out of the shower the tray was sitting on the bed. She saw that it was a full meal with all the fixins. So, she dried off and prayed, thanking God for everything and the meal she was about to eat.

While she sat and ate wearing nothing but her bra and panties she called for Melissa. When Melissa came in she pushed the tray away from the bed.

"What do you need Sonya? I'm off duty right now."

"First, I need your phone and then I need you to investigate something for me. I think my Captain is trying to bring us down, including Alex. Don't forget I put you on him. Didn't I promise you a man with money? Haven't I always taken care of you? Aren't you supposed to be in jail for all those robberies you set up?"

"Yes, but why are you bringing all of this up? You act like I'm not gonna help you. I'm just tired of you calling me. People already don't like me here. They think I'm trying to steal their man and then some shit got stolen and the finger got put on me. Since you're the Feds they think I'm talking to you about them. I feel like you're trying to blackmail me for a telephone!"

"Listen, I'm gonna give you an address. I need you go and see if a kid is missing. And I want you on Tommy Capes, I want you to fuck him good and you'll get 2 million out of the deal. After you fuck him I need you to find out where their keeping that diamond at and get back to me with the information A.S,A.P."

"Sonya, I'll bring you the diamond and you bring me the money."

She handed Sonya the phone; she called him and told him about the diamond. He told her it was her call because he wasn't big on jewelry he just wanted her to keep protecting him and to remember Nikko was the head man. She couldn't believe he was letting her do her thing her way. She asked him why the change?

"I guess you don't get it, I read your letter and realize everything you've done for me. You've helped make me a billionaire and I know you'll protect me. Bring your captain in and once we've gotten all we could from him, kill him."

As she spoke to him tears rolled down her face. He told her no one was gonna feed his child but him. She wanted to go home; she wanted to go back to Cuba. She hung the phone up and laid back and relaxed, she could finally get some sleep.

Melissa saw the joy in her eyes and covered her up without saying a word. Melissa had never seen her cry before, all she ever saw was the dirty side of her. But she knew she really loved that boy, everybody knew. She just hoped he really loved her. From all she had just heard about love she wanted to call Alex and hear him say it, so she called before she left to tell him she loved him.

Sonya laid there and imagined all the life they would have. Nodiya would have everything. Then she thought about Juan, she had to get him from her even if she had to kill her. No one was gonna get in the way of her family. She could love Juan Jr. better than Tasha could. Her family was her new focus, she let those words roll off of her lips and loved the way they sounded and then fell asleep.

She slept better than she had in a long time. When she woke up she felt well rested. She thought about her Captain and about the story about a missing grand baby. She wondered why he wouldn't go into funding and get the money. Something wasn't right about all of it, she felt it in her heart.

She got out of bed and washed her face and brushed her teeth. She didn't check out when she left because she needed a cover. When she felt the wind in her face and heard the noise of the people she had a little pep in her step. She was back on her own turf where she knew every thief and every hooker and pimp.

She didn't have to signal a cab because one was waiting for her. She knew him, he was one of her informants. His name was Felix, he was facing life in prison for a heroin bust. She had helped him escape out the back window when they came through the door. Now he used the cab to set up the dealers and he never had to testify. If anything was going down Felix knew about it. When she got into the cab she checked all around to make sure Felix wasn't being followed.

"Okay Felix, my captain says a bust went bad and he got some of our people knocked off and a diamond is missing. He owes them 15 million and now they've taken his grandson. Talk to me Felix." He looked at her through the partition and told her all he knew.

"Damn Boss, you've been gone for a month! You've been to Cuba and Greece. I know your pregnant and you got 100 million dollars. I can't understand why you left Cuba after he bought you a 2 million-dollar house? Now why are you so scared?"

She smiled, "So that's the word on me. I'm not scared, just tired. You know a bitch needs a break too! I sure don't want to harm my baby." Felix filled her in.

"His granddaughter is alright. The deal is that he busted Que, they were dealing between here and New York. The Mills and Shepperd family, there into laundering the money but nothing heavy. But he gave up both of the families. Together their worth about 90 million. The diamond itself is worth 100 million. It's been in the Deluma family since the 1600's. It was stolen from Europe and the reward is worldwide. The two families got together with cap and found it. They were gonna get 5 million apiece and cap was gonna get 20 because he set it up.

Cap has a connection with an Asian gang here in Atlanta. How they got the diamond I have no idea. He set the whole deal up for guns and 5 million in cash. He was in the Hyatt Hotel when they came in and made the bust. One of the Feds shook caps hand and the family all got out in two days with no charges pending and then his grand baby went missing."

"Do you know where the baby's being held?" she asked.

"Yes," he replied.

"She's being held at the old Jefferson County Jail. Remember when they said they were gonna make a club out of it. But the best headquarters would be an old county jail, lots of cells and no one can enter without them knowing. They are smart but hurting in other areas at the same time."

"How much money do you have Felix?"

"Why, what's up Sonya?"

"I need that gang down with me, I got the money to own them but my account is being audited. I can get the money in the US, but I don't have anyone I can trust. I'm gonna make you my big man. We gotta let them know we don't need any heat. You gotta convince them that's our best interest."

"Sonya, you see that Chinese right there? He's Noky and he's second in command to Mr. Chin."

"He don't look like no general he wears glasses and he's skinny."

"Remember he's Chinese," Felix said.

They pulled up to the curb and Noky swung a pump up into Felix's face. He looked at him real hard and Felix tilted his head back. Noky twirled his finger around in the air and signaled his troops to follow and walked around and got in the back seat. They both just stared as they pulled away from the curb. This wasn't exactly what she wanted but it was done now.

She spoke to Noky and said, "My name is Sonya and I'm a Federal Agent, but I don't roll with my job. I have a proposition for you that will be very prosperous for you. I work for Nikko and Ravenion. We want that diamond and we need you to work for us. We have the drug money and the weapons. That old jail is a death trap. I can help you if you are willing to take orders from me. I don't care about your gang and I don't even want them to know about me. I'm giving you 10 million good faith money so you know we are about business. I really don't have time to negotiate so you either accept or I will kill your whole clique in front of you. So, what's your answer?"

"You're giving me an ultimatum and I don't even know you. You sound like a desperate woman. Me don't fuck with desperate people cause desperate people get you killed. One mistake and it's over." She told Felix to let him out they pulled over.

"Now get out and I'm gonna show you how desperate I am!"

After he got out and the cab had started to pull off he waved for them to come back. Sonya told him to keep going because she had made her offer out of good faith. He didn't accept it and he called her desperate.

Felix's phone rang and it was Noky. The caller said they didn't notice who she was until they had pulled away. He said he understood and would take the deal. Felix relayed the message but she wasn't hearing it, all she was hearing was the disrespect to her man.

When they got to the office she went to her captain and explained what had to be done and Nikko wanted to conversate. She told him to get a game Warden, not Local or Federal and they could put all kinds of charges on them and hold them without bond. They would all get life. She kissed him on his bald head and told him to go and get his grandbaby. She had no time for thank you's, she had to go right in to action. Felix took her back to the hospital and this time she was heavily guarded. She sat on the bed and turned the TV to Channel 11 and waited to see the bust. When they showed it on the news she knew something was wrong. There was no resisting, no gunfight; something was wrong. It had to be staged. She called Melissa and told her to forget the diamond it was a set up. She wondered how stupid her captain thought she was. Normally she would kill anyone who crossed her. But she had to play it cool in order to find out where Smokey and Leo were at. Nikko didn't care about his men. Laying up in the hospital wasn't that easy. She needed something to do so she asked the nurse for paper and pen. She was going to write a book for Nodiya so in case something happened to them she would know who her parents were. They would know they would never need anything. Quinn was always too busy keeping them safe, and she was dirty. She used Sonya for so many licks. She taught Sonya the I don't give a fuck about country or job attitude because your own country will treat you like a terrorist. When she started the book, she decided to name it, "Money is Everything," and the first Chapter started like this:

*"It was a stormy night around 9:30, I waited patiently in the shadow of a dark house, shaking because I was scared. Quinn had me posing as a call girl who had gone astray. The only time I could pull a trick was between * and 12. Mainly because Mrs. Hannah Anderson brought her 16-year-old daughter in after midnight. She didn't care who I was with, I could've been out with Jesus. She didn't care, if she had known Quin had her turning tricks to set up robberies she would kill her. There I stood in the living room waiting for the black Limo. They didn't know the house was empty because Quin had furnished it. I had a tracker in my shoe. And let me tell you what I had on, A black body dress with no bra and no panties. I didn't even have a gun all I knew was that I was some man's date for a party. And there would be a lot of important people there. The car pulled up and the door was opened. I got to the car and saw that my date was a woman! My first thought was that I'm not gay but she came out of her purse with10grand for the night. I needed that money real bad. I needed my own car and Quin wasn't about buying me my own wheels. Now that I think about it that bitch still owes me 5 grand! Anyway, she knew I was 16 and all she talked about was all the fun we were gonna have. She said all the men were gonna love my red ass. She made me lay back and she licked me once and said sweet. I looked at the White lady and smiled."*

CHAPTER 5

A Lonely Night in Georgia

He laid in bed listening to a radio station out of the U.S. He had satellite radio because he couldn't understand Spanish. He looked at the mirror above his bed, he had put it there in case one of his dates tried something. He looked at what he was surrounded by, all of the silk and satin and realized he had tucked himself in like his grandmother use to do. He was afraid of being alone. He was full of mixed emotions about Sonya, Mary, Tasha, and Gloria. He realized all four women had confessed their love for him, one was dead and the other three were out and about. Maybe Sonya was right about this life, nothing comes out of it but pain. She confessed that to him in the letter she wrote to him. He thought about everything she had done for him and all he had put her through, and she was still there breathing his life.

A lonely night in Georgia was blasting out of the speakers and the DJ said it was dedicated to all of the Georgia troops fighting there and he added that a female had called the station and dedicated it to a man named Juan and that if he was listening that her heart would be raining for him and that he needed to make it home to that lovely lady. His heart leaped and cried at the same time. That sounded like something Tasha would say. He closed his eyes and before he knew it he was asleep.

The sound of horns and music woke him and he looked outside to see and there was nothing. So, he went and washed his face and did a little work out. He did this every morning so he kept his body tight. He dressed in a black warm-up suit and black Adidas, grabbed his money and went and had some breakfast. He had gotten use to April cooking for him and he looked forward to dinner. He grabbed some power bars and called Nikko because he didn't want to drive. Nikko told him to just walk to the end of the driveway and have a look.

He smiled and saw that he had forgotten about Cuba day. He went into his garage and got on his 650 Kawasaki and rode away. He saw people walking and laughing. He was about to pull off and then he saw Mary waving to him. She jumped on and they rode to the palace.

All the grills were fired up and they were giving goodie bags to all the kids. It was a great day, everything was free and not once did he think about Sonya or Tasha.

Mary was with him and they were running and playing. She grabbed a picnic basket and a sheet. He went to talk to Nikko at the entrance. Nikko was all smiles because he had never seen his people so happy. Hate and envy never crossed his mind about Rav because he knew he was the chosen one. He was just sad because he had to leave his young friend. Rav walked up and said, "What's up Nikko?"

"Just enjoying life while I have it," he replied.

But deep down inside he was asking God why, why did he have to leave? Why didn't he bring Rav much sooner? Then he admitted he was scared, not of death but for Rav.

He looked at Rav and stated, "No matter what happens in this life or what you get yourself into remember the same God that shines the sun on the just also shines the sun on the unjust. Stop being afraid of him stop being angry with him. Have you ever heard of King Tut? He died when he was 19. He was the youngest King in the world and he ruled for 5 or 6 years. He went down in history as one of the fairest and most modest Kings and nobody ever knew his color or cause of death.

I compare you to him because no one knows you're a King but me. Look at these people Rav, they'll die for you. You've made them free and you've made them believe in a new life. Look at how fast they've adapted to the life you gave them. Every man must be a good follower to be a good leader. But I've never seen you follow any man so when you see me looking to the sky I'm praying for to keep our King intact safe and respected. I never had to go out and put in work, but you'll have to continue showing these people who you are and show them you'll never quit."

Rav looked at him with honor and said, "Don't worry I'll stay alive no matter what."

By that time Mary and Helen walked up. Helen is a dark-skinned Cuban with raven black hair. She had nice round tits and a perfect ass. She was dressed in a Gucci dress, heels, and jewelry. Nails perfect and her makeup.

She was speaking Spanish, a language he didn't understand. He was hoping Mary would interpret. This was an example of why he couldn't be a leader or a chosen one. He couldn't talk to his people and couldn't understand them.

Mary ran behind him with the picnic basket, with her arms swinging she had to wait for people to stop saluting him before she spun him around. She locked his eyes and gave him her best smile.

"She only said hello Ravenion, that's Nikko's wife."

About that time Helen and Nikko were approaching and this time they spoke in English.

"I'm sorry I offended you but as we spend time together I will teach you to speak Spanish," said Helen.

They gathered under the trees and laid out the food Mary had brought. They had some of the red wine Helen had chosen. Nikko looked at all the people walking about. He had cut the field down low and put up small tents, so the families could stay together with each other. All the kids were playing ball and running about and the teenagers were sneaking off to do their own thing.

A small girl ran up to them and said, "Ravenion! Ravenion!" She jumped into his arms and kissed him on both cheeks. It was the little girl whose family was selling oranges.

"My Daddy's home!" she said excitedly.

Then her father spoke and said, "I know we are indebted to you and I know how to do lots of things. The first thing I'm gonna do is clean up your house for you every day. Thank you for getting me home." He looked at the smile on her face and a tear dropped from his eye. He thought of Juan and Nodiya and knew they would be the same way.

"Where is your mom and pop?" he asked.

"In our tent," she said.

"Tell me something, you gonna tell me something right?"

"Right!" she said.

"How would you like to stay at my house? I have a swimming pool and a big yard and I will fill it full of toys!" he told her.

"Yes!" she exclaimed.

"How about your brothers?"

"Yes! Yes!" she exclaimed again.

"Go and tell your mom and pop that y'all gonna stay with me until y'all get on your feet. You gonna go to school, right?" He put her down and she took off running.

Nikko looked at him and told him, "You gotta have dick control, I told you."

"I'm not gonna fuck the man's wife!" he said.

"But you want to keep her near, right?"

"It's the little girl Nikko, I swear," Rav said.

"I bet you sleep with the man's wife, I know you man. You can't control your dick, you're a Black young man with power. Women control you mentally," said Nikko.

"So, you're saying I'm weak. You don't know how it is to have your child hood stripped from you. I had no one and on top of that I made all kinds of promises to myself. When I became a father, I swore I would be better and give my kids everything and then to have them snatched away for no goddamn reason." As tears rolled down his eyes he got up and walked away. He truly wanted his son.

Mary got up and went behind him because she knew how much his son meant to him. In his sleep he would call out to him and she would cradle him like an infant while he slept. She wanted so bad to give him a son. She promised herself she would conceive if it killed her. She was just waiting on the right time to ask him and tell him that her life belonged to him and she was willing to do whatever it took to conceive his child. She wanted to make love to him but it wasn't the time or the place.

He had his head down looking at the ground as he walked. She raised his head so she could look into his eyes and wiped away his tears and kissed him. She told him that she loved him.

"Rav, I'll do anything for you. I'll lay down my life for you. I know your heart and I know your intentions are good. I want us to have a baby no matter what it takes. Promise me you won't hurt me or let me get killed."

"I promise," he said. They kissed and when they looked up and the Hassan's were walking up.

"Mr. Nalls, my Baby tells me you have offered to let us stay with you in your home."

"Yes Mr. Hassan, I have a job for you and your wife can be my housekeeper. I'll explain better tomorrow and you don't have to come in for two weeks. As for now, go and enjoy your selves."

Nikko noticed how Vera looked at Rav. She lusted for him. He only hoped Rav knew what he was doing. A Cuban will kill because of betrayal.

He watched her walk away and noticed that Rav didn't watch her. She was trying real hard to get his attention. Nikko had seen earlier through her Gap shorts what she had to offer. The whole family wore the same outfit so they could keep up with each other.

Mary and Rav went back to the picnic and talked about a better tomorrow. When they were all together again Mary shared their plans for a baby with them. Helen looked at Nikko and said they too were trying to have a child. Nikko smiled looked at Rav and winked.

Ravenion didn't believe in being different from lower class people. He believed everyone was equal.

Helen pulled out ham and cheese sandwiches cut into triangles and a big bag of sour cream and onion chips. He smiled because he thought she would pull out something fancy. He decided to go and get a plate from one of the workers.

Him and Mary smiled at each other and said, "All this free food out here."

And she smiled and waved to get one of the cook's attention. When the cook looked at her the elderly woman started to turn her head. Nikko and Rav stood and her eyes got wide. She told the other cooks that Nikko and Ravenion were here and they were hungry and to get them a plate quickly. They were all smiling because they never would believe someone with their power and fame would eat with the people.

Helen looked insulted and said, "Y'all mean I made all this for nothing!"

Nikko rushed to her side and assured her they would eat everything. He looked at Mary and wondered how Rav was always so lucky with women. He had never been lucky enough to have a woman do for him like his women had done. He thought about Gloria's dedication to him. He thought it was Rav's money that bought it but it was the size of his heart. Rav was one of those people that could never forget about the less fortunate.

Nikko started to think about Mr. Hassan and how he use to be a famous chemist and humbled down after he chose to have a family. He left money and fame behind.

He looked at Rav and said, "I figured it out, you didn't help the family because of the little girl." Helen and Mary stopped and looked at him.

"I'm not gonna sleep with that man's wife, I already told you!"

"I know that, you're after her husband," Nikko said.

Everyone looked puzzled. Mary looked at Rav and asked, "What's he talking about Rav? I know he's not saying your gay!"

"I don't know what he's talking about so let's let him explain himself," said Rav. Nikko smiled and apologized.

"I'm sorry everyone. I didn't think about it until it came out the wrong way. Mr. Hassan used to be a chemist and out of the blue Rav decided to help him and his family. First, I thought it was because you wanted his wife and then I realized you wouldn't take a chance like that. If you wanted his wife you would have had her first and then gotten her husband out. Am I right so far?"

Rav just smiled then said, "My man you are so right. Mary has some good stuff between her legs, I wouldn't take that risk."

He slapped Mary on the ass and they all smiled.

The evening went well. Everyone was pleased except Gloria. She stood away looking at Rav and Mary. He jumps from woman to woman she thought.

A messenger approached her with a note from her mother. She read it and walked over to Nikko. Mary complimented on her clothes and shoes. She nodded and said thanks. She bent over and told Nikko they had the location.

Nikko signaled to Rav and they excused themselves from the group. Alex, Gino and Niger all saw the play and they all met up in the dining room. Once they were all seated Nikko took over.

"First, I apologize for interrupting y'alls evening. But we have a problem. There is a Russian by the name of Darrian Sandovitch. It seems he has come up with a new drug. It's a mixture of crank, ice, and heroin. The drug keeps you up for 96 hours and it will kill you. He's also come up with a disease that will kill you in 10 days. It's called the new AIDS and it will shut down your immune system within 10 days. He's from Moscow but he's been hiding in Koslov in an old army hospital. It only has three buildings and at this time we don't know which one he's in. But what I do know is the Chinese Mafia are trying to buy them both. Once they get it they can knock us off. They have a gang called the Teaki 3 that's been scoping him out. Mr. Sandovitch stays on the move, so we got to act now. The jet is already fueled up. Gloria, go and pick our best men for the job."

She stood and said, "I don't need nobody but Rav with me. I've been training with him and I want to get in and out before they know what hit them. If we show up in a jet with a bunch of men they're gonna know what's up and move before we can get there. All I need is Ravenion. I'll come back with everything. Just watch my back Rav." She pushed a button and the TV screen came down and was replaced by a satellite picture of the site.

"From what our information tells us, he's in the first building in the basement in a small concealed corner. You see that tree Ravenion? That's the tree y'all be in and you'll have night vision goggles on with an AR15 with a grenade launcher on it. With the goggles on you'll be able to see the body heat through the building. All you got to do is make sure I don't get killed or shot."

He smiled and asked, "Why me?"

"Because this is what I been training for, I trust you Ravenion, I don't trust Alex and them, we fought while you were missing."

He looked at Alex in disbelief. Alex only raised his head higher. Because in his heart he knew she felt vengeance and it wasn't over. Rav just looked on and asked when they were leaving.

She smiled and said, "Right now! Our gear is on the jet waiting."

They left and went straight to the jet and she didn't say much on the way. They boarded and sat across from each other. He wondered how long the flight was gonna take. He looked at his watch, it was 5:30. He figured the flight would take a day.

He watched her, trying to read her. She had a good poker face. He went to gear up and get some rest. She told him to sit back down.

"What's your problem Gloria?" he asked.

"You're my problem, you've been playing me for a fool. You don't care about me. I'm supposed to be by your side not Mary. I was the one who threw those grenades on that chopper not Mary. I been loyal from the jump. I slept with another bitch just to bring peace and you ask me what's my problem. It's you Rav and your too blind to see who loves you and who's out to kill you. Alex is gonna kill you before it's all over. Can't you see it in his eyes or is it that you don't care? Now Sonya, as bad as I hate to say it, that bitch loves you and you're disrespecting the both of us by being with that bitch Mary. What's she got that we ain't got? I know you want a child, I can have a child. Talk to me Rav. I'm not talking about making love to me. This is why I want you here with me now. Do you love me? I need to know right now!"

She had tears in her eyes, she stood in front of him demanding an answer. He lifted his hands to her and she took them. He knew she needed to be comforted and that was what he was gonna do even if he had to lie. He didn't know how to love anybody but Natasha Middles. She sat in his lap looking for sincerity.

Without blinking he said, "Yes, I do love you, you're a part of me. I just can't let it be shown because I don't want to get you killed. If I show you my heart it will make you a walking target. I don't care about Mary. I can't let none of these people know where I stand in my heart. Nikko and Alex think it's because I don't have dick control but I do. I just don't want them to get fixed on one person like they did to Natasha. Look at what that got her, death and a missing son. I don't know if my son is alive or not. I got to play it like he's dead by now because nobody's tried to get in touch with me about his whereabouts."

He dropped his head hoping she bought and she did. Every word of it. Her face lit the whole jet up. She lifted his head up and she wiped his fake tears away and kissed him hard. Inside, he hated he couldn't feel love but he knew he loved her but not the way she desired.

He thought about what she said about Alex, she could be right. So now his focus was on Alex. He wasn't afraid of nothing but deep down inside he knew he was in too deep. He just wanted a family and now he had a country that loved the ground he walked on. He had never been a soldier but now he was a leader of them. That's what scared him the most because leadership brought on enemies.

He reached in his pocket for his phone and called the only person that had the brain to pull this off. Sonya. The phone rang and rang, finally the voice mail picked up.

He left her a simple message, "I love you and I miss your company."

He knew she would love to hear that. Finally, he fell asleep. They awoke when the wheels touched the ground.

She went in her pocket and gave him a stick of gum. Due to the time difference, it was in the wee hours of the morning so her timing was right.

A white BMW with dark tinted windows was waiting on them. Their driver was a heavyset White male, who only nodded as he opened the back door. She got in first and grabbed the black tote bag. He changed into blackface and some good black hi-tech boots. She handed him his black ski mask and goggles. Then he fixed his gun and transmitter. She kissed him and made sure he could hear her.

He nodded, "yes" and then she said, "let's do this!"

They drove passed the entrance and passed some woods, the whole area appeared abandoned. Trees and grass were taking over the road. The entrance to the old fort was brick and about 8 feet high on both sides. It looked like an old prison camp.

They got out and headed towards the woods. They put on their goggles and walked in parallel lines. As they went they looked for traps and guards. He threw his hand up signaling a trip wire. He had learned sign language in the hole at Valdosta State Prison, in Georgia.

They stepped over the wire and noticed many more around it. So, they turned sideways, stepping over them together. She stopped and signed to him to take 30 steps backward, so they could be ready for an ambush.

He stepped foot by foot and she watched and counted the 30 steps. Then it happened. They fired one shot at the same time dropping their ambushers. He made it to the tree and saw he couldn't climb it because he didn't have any spikes on.

She walked over to him and pulled out a 223-crossbow with a wire, attached to a grappling hook. She shot up the tree and it wrapped around the trunk. She watched him climb the tree and once he was in position walked away with the bag over her back.

Through his mic he heard her say, "I love you Rav."

"I love you too," he replied.

She smiled as she put on her gloves and climbed the pole. At the same time, he saw a guard come out of the first building, he told her to hold up before she finished snipping the wire. He wanted to see if he was gonna walk around the building or go back inside.

He stood there with his weapon and then went to the front side of the building. As soon as he made it to the front, so he could get a shot he fired and took him out.

As she scaled the wire she saw two at the entrance. She pulled the gun from her shoulder, locked her legs and fired. Both shots hit their mark dead center, one in the front of the head and one dead center of the back.

She scaled her way up the first building and released the strap from her shoulder and pulled the bag around to her stomach. She opened the bag and removed the rope and held it in her teeth and zipped the bag back up. She slid down the building and placed a C-4 charge on each corner, jumped down and rolled sideways.

Rav smiled because it all looked like a James Bond movie, she was doing a fine job. She didn't need to go in the building, she already knew where the target was. She ran to the last building and planted the C4.

She said she was going in the window. He told her not to, that it was a trap and to go in the door. It had to be unlocked and there were no bodies around the door. She looked around and saw there were men all around the building.

"They'll kill me before I can get through the door. What do I do?" she asked.

"Come back and blow the buildings and wait till they move out. Call for more back up too. No time to play hero and I ain't no action figure."

She came back out and walked back towards the woods. She climbed back up the pole and pressed the button on the remote and blew the buildings.

Men came out running and they started picking them off. She told him there were six more men inside and he said to meet him around the front.

At the front gate, they regrouped and posted at the front door and kicked it open. They didn't go right in they stood to the side and saw two men standing behind a beam in the back. They ran to the back and shot them both and then ran back to the front.

They didn't see or hear anything and assumed they had to be in the basement. He grabbed one of the dead men and drug him to the basement entrance. He knew there would be at least two men at the stairs waiting for the door to open.

When she opened the door, she threw a body down and a smoke bomb behind it and began to speak Chinese.

Rav had no time to be impressed, he took a gas mask from her and ran down the steps shooting. There were four in all, they took out the first two and the other two were with Sandovitch. Guards were posted at both sides of the door. As they rushed through the door they shot the two guards. Sandovitch threw two darts and missed.

She shot him in the shoulder and he just laughed. The CD in the computer was burning. She pulled it out but it was badly burned. The Russian just laughed.

She had to think. They had to have paper work to back up the disk. She checked the garbage.

Rav looked in the other rooms and found nothing.

Sandovitch was laughing and said, "You two are stupid. Everything you were looking for you blew up."

Rav looked at him and just shot him in the head. Gloria looked at him. They weren't giving up yet. She looked through the desk and found nothing.

"Something has got to be her, I know it! Help me move the desk!" she ordered.

"Forget it Gloria, there's nothing here," he said. His phone rung, it was Sonya.

She asked what was wrong and he told her about the disk burning. She asked if the computer was still on and he said it was. She told him to look at the screen and tell her what he saw.

"A lot of codes and molecular breakdowns," he told her.

She asked him who he was with and he said Gloria. She asked if Gloria had her laptop with her? But she didn't.

"Look for a disk!" she commanded.

He found some in the desk and she told him to put one in the computer.

She told him to press F-5 and hold the A button down and then said, "Now press A2 and A5 at the same time, then press 10."

The screen went black and then ran some kind of test pattern. She told Gloria to hold her hand over F1 and enter and wait for the count of three and press down.

At first, Rav thought she had erased the disk but she told him that she hadn't but she had down loaded all the info onto the disk and erased the password. She told them to get out of there and to meet her in New York.

"I'll be expecting you in two days and I've got some shit to tell you. I love you Juan!"

He didn't say anything and she said to him, "Oh! You can't tell me you love me because your bitch can hear you!" He signed to Gloria to go on ahead.

"Why do we got to go through this? I called you earlier to tell you I was thinking about you. Our ride is here I got to go, I love you Sonya."

He hung up and they walked out the front door, got in the BMW and rode away.

She handed him 2 darts and a disk. He thought he remembered seeing 3 darts but wasn't sure. Once they left she looked at him in a sexy way. He smiled because he knew where her mind was but he didn't want to have sex right now, his mind was on Sonya. She was always in the right place and had even saved his life and now they were a thousand miles away from each other.

He smiled because he had finally figured it out. She thought he was smiling for her so she kissed his neck then lowered her head to his dick and put it in her mouth and stayed there until they reached the airport.

The car came to a stop and she raced up the stairs to the jet and did a security check. Once she saw everything was clear she motioned him inside. He walked in smiling at her because he knew he hadn't paid any attention to her body in a while and she at least deserved that.

She was waiting in the door way with her top off, her breasts stood firm and high. He picked her up and sat her in the seat and kissed her breasts.

As the jet took off, he laid her in the aisle and kissed her down to her navel. He helped her kick her boots off and then her pants. She put her legs over his shoulders as he kissed her through her pink panties. He slid those off of her and began to make love to her with his tongue and fingers. She moaned out his name as he squeezed her spur tongue, licking it hard and slow. His tongue started moving faster and he rubbed her G-spot she started speaking Spanish. He undid his pants and went inside of her.

She knew he loved kids so she prayed for a child in Spanish while he was going in and out, going deeper with each stroke. He really didn't feel it but he went with the flow. When he finished he went to get her a blanket. He used the bathroom and cleaned himself. He looked in the mirror and was very surprised at what he saw.

He didn't recognize himself any more so he said, "Fuck it! I'll find myself later!"

He made them a pallet on the floor. They laid there kissing and she was so happy when he told her that he loved her and made love to her. Sonya was out of the picture and Mary didn't even matter. They made love again and fell asleep.

The co-pilot woke them up and told them they were having some trouble and to prepare for an emergency landing. There was a bad storm and it was forcing them down. Gloria smiled because that gave them more time to spend together.

"Where are we landing?" Gloria asked.

"Spain," the pilot said.

She asked him how long they would need to be there and he told her only as long as the storm lasted and they should be out of there by morning.

Rav looked at her and smiled and asked her if they had people over there?

"Yes" she answered him, "we have people all over the world. We are the mob and we are everywhere. Inform our people that we're here because this is our time together."

He smiled as the co-pilot walked off, they were both naked and she was fine to look at. He knew their relationship couldn't go anywhere because of Mary and Sonya. He took a deep breath and told himself that if anything happened to Mary and Sonya he would devote himself to her.

When the jet landed a black Jag was waiting for them. He thought she wasn't gonna tell anyone they were there but she just smiled at him.

"I guess the pilot informed them because this is one of our cars," she said.

It was very windy and he just wanted to stay on the plane and wait the storm out but the airport laws wouldn't allow that.

The man that stepped out of the Jag wore all black and had a pencil thin mustache. He had very broad shoulders. He greeted Gloria with a hug and a kiss.

"Hello Bartel, it's nice seeing you again. How did you know we were here?" she asked.

"Your pilot called and informed me you would be landing due to the storm and that Mr. Nalls would be with you. Excuse me Mr. Nalls, I meant no disrespect, I'm Bartel Tarrelli, Gloria and I go way back. We've had our times and when the pilot called my heart jumped."

Rav looked at Gloria with a slight grin on his face and then turned and shook his hand.

Before another word was spoken Gloria spoke up, "It's not what you think Rav, we've never slept together we're just old friends. I saved his life when I was 16. I wasn't supposed to go on the mission but I snuck on the plane."

"If she hadn't snuck on there we would've all been killed. Me, Alex, Giovanni and Martinez. We were in Brazil, Nikko sent us to collect money from Earl. He had told Nikko he wasn't paying any more and had hooked up with the Chinese. We went out there to talk and it was an ambush."

"So, you're saying Nikko set y'all up?" Rav asked.

"No, they out smarted us. We thought meeting in a café was smart but they set it on fire with us in side. Gloria saw them setting the fire and opened up on them. She saved all of our lives!"

Rav clapped his hands and smiled, "Well done Gloria, I know that's some Bullshit!"

"What do you mean, bullshit?" they both asked.

"I mean some bullshit man, I don't care about some fling you two had, that's on y'all."

They both looked at each other and smiled and laughed. It really wasn't a lie, everyone who heard the story thought the same thing.

They got in the car, Rav sat in the back and she sat in the front. It didn't feel right because she was showing disrespect by sitting up front. Rav just pulled out his 9mm, chambered a bullet and rode in silence.

When they spoke, it was in Spanish. She looked at him in the mirror and he looked tired. As they rode the streets and Rav wondered as he looked at all the people "were these common people?"

It was 3 in the morning and the streets were packed. Gloria noticed the confusion in his eyes and told Bartel to stop the car. She apologized to Rav for the disrespect and she felt herself something wasn't right. He saw lights approaching real fast, so he jumped out and ran across the street, she was behind him. They went into a store and looked out the window. They didn't notice all the people staring at them. It was a black Jag and it stopped beside Bartel. Rav turned and looked at all the White people looking at them and realized, "This isn't a store it's a Red Neck bar!"

He looked closer and saw 5 pool tables a jukebox and the bar. Then he asked where the back door was. The bar tender pointed through the double doors. Gloria was still looking out the front at Bartel. He called to the jet and asked if everything was straight? They said it was.

He looked out and saw Gloria coming and jumped the fence and walked up the alley to the front of the street. He seen Bartel and another man with guns out. He called Nikko and asked him was this the way it had to end?

Nikko assured him he was safe and Bartel was his number one man. He wondered about the second gunman. He still didn't believe anything.

A crowd came walking up the street and he blended in with them. He hailed a cab and went to the airport. He got a ticket under Jones. He went to the coffee shop and had a cheese cake and a coffee. His phone rang, it was Gloria. He just looked at it. He looked around for a security check. It wasn't long before they called his flight and he walked to the plane checking his surroundings carefully. His phone rang again and it was Nikko. He still didn't answer.

He was seated in first class next to beautiful Black female with an enormous rock on her finger. She was looking out the window not bothering to notice him. He heard her sniff but couldn't tell if she was crying or was sick because her face was buried in the clouds. When she finally turned toward him, she was crying. He told her everything would be alright.

She asked how he knew that when he didn't know her or her people. He asked her how she could have so much pain built up inside. It was bleeding from her eyelids.

He told her to, "Let it go and it couldn't be that bad and that a stranger was the best listener."

She smiled and told him her husband was married to another woman and to top that he has a family. I came to Spain just to see it for myself. She became very angry and he calmed her.

"I walked to the door and peeked through the glass. I rung the bell but he kept going upstairs so I rung it again and a child of 8 or 10 opened the door. Before I could speak two more came out. He has two boys and one girl. I acted like a salesman and I wanted that bastard to see me. When him and the woman came downstairs I couldn't believe the bitch was pregnant with his fourth child. When he saw me he nearly fainted. The woman invited me for a cup of coffee. I told her I was selling insurance and guess what came out of her mouth?

Out of respect Rav said, "What?"

"She said that was something me and her husband Frank should discuss Frank!"

When she went back upstairs I asked him, "I thought your name was Patrick Hanberry? Does your name change in every country? Guess what the bastard had to say? He said please don't do this Gail, I have a wife and kids and I'm on Government business. I'm a spy! Please don't blow my cover."

I looked at him and said, "Get the Fuck Outta Here! He had the nerve to say he would explain it to me when he got home! He told me Rhonda wasn't really his wife and the kids belonged to the state. He said she wasn't really pregnant! That's one nigga that's been reading to many books! I just got up and left! Oh! I'm sorry. I've just been running my mouth, allow me to introduce myself. Martain is my maiden name since I gotta get a divorce now."

"My name is Ravenion. Why are you going to New York?"

"Our home is in Manhattan."

"What do you do there?"

"I'm a novelist and I bet I have a best seller now, don't I?" she said.

"I guess maybe I'll get to write my story one day," he said.

"And what will it be?" she asked.

"I don't know yet but I will get with you, I promise you that. You wouldn't believe who you're sitting by."

She smiled and told him in due time.

He looked into her brown eyes and smiled. He extended his arms and comforted her. He told her God had her back, not to worry. He promised to keep in touch with her if she wanted. What she wanted was a good fucking to ease her mind, but she didn't tell him that. She did give him her number to her home in Sandy Springs. She fell asleep in his arms and he just watched the clouds and everything was fine. No signs of death and no faces.

After the plane landed and they parted, he checked into the International Inn and called Sonya. She said she would be right there. He just laid and waited because he knew she would be on time. She knocked on the door and when he answered it he saw she wasn't all that big but she was carrying a basketball. She wore a beautiful T-Boz Blue maternity dress and her hair was in a ponytail. She walked into the room and said she loved him and demanded he make love to her. He kissed her and held her and finally made love to her, she sat on top of him smiling.

"You know I love you, right? That new drug you went to get is a new ice called "fish tank." It supposed to take 24 days to make but they can make it in 12. That CD that you gave Nikko has the formula on it. That chemist you have in Cuba can make it. He told me you asked him to stay with you. He knows I'm Federal because I saved his life. The U.S. had been kidnapping chemists and giving them better lives and in return they were building bombs and weapons of destruction, Hassan is the best in the world. They hid him when they got word. They locked him up for murder, but in Cuba the laws are different. If a man rape or try to rape, he's killed and looked at like a hero. But Hassan was locked up so they could keep him. Now there's a Chinese Mafia in New York I know will deal with you if you supply them. I also have my captain, I can send men to snatch his grandchild back on your command. I also have my hands on a diamond that's worth millions, it alone will get you connected. You can build your own army, you don't need Nikko. He's working with the U.S. and before this is over you'll get life in the Feds. No lie!"

"Juan, leave him and come with me or allow me to run everything over here in the states. You know I'm capable and you know I'm protected. I got the government; how can I fail?"

"Oh My God! Oh My God! My Stomach!" She climbed off of him and grabbed her stomach.

"The Baby's Coming! My Water Just Broke! HELP!!! CALL 911!!!"

He called the front desk and asked them to get an ambulance. He dressed and helped her get dressed. She laid there panting and squeezing his hand.

The ambulance came and they counted her contractions. They knew the baby was coming in the next 30 minutes.

They rushed her to St. Joseph Hospital and while they were waiting on the doctor she screamed at Ravenion, "This is all your fault!"

He just smiled at her, for the first time in his life he was gonna see a baby born. Not just any baby, his baby girl.

A Black female doctor came in and rushed her into the delivery room. He helped her push and held her hand.

Nodiya came out on the third push, she was crying so that meant she was alive. . .Sonya laid back and reached for her child. This was her first and last baby.

She looked at him smiling, "It's over Baby, were a family. Here's your little girl! Oh My God Help Me, I'm Fixin' to Die! Help! Help!" She raised up and the doctor told her to push another baby was coming.

"Ain't No Baby Coming! I Would've Known if I was Having Twins! I'm Fixin' to Die!!!"

"Push Sonya, the lady knows what she's talking about! She's down there looking at the baby right now! So, push God Dammit!"

She pushed and pushed finally another baby came and he named her Nidiya. Sonya looked at him and said she hated him and they weren't having no more babies. When the nurse handed him both babies Sonya looked at him in confusion and asked which is which?

The nurse said Nodiya was wrapped in the pink blanket and Nidiya was in the red blanket. The nurse took both babies to the infant ward.

Sonya asked him what last name and he said Ellis, he was signing the birth certificate. He signed Juan so he was signing theirs. He looked down on her and her pretty green eyes just stared at him. He kissed her and asked where she wanted to stay. She was everything to him. He asked her to quit her job and she asked him to leave the streets and he smiled and said soon.

They took her to her room and she went to sleep. He signed the birth certificate and kissed her. That sealed the deal they were family. He thought about his life, he thought about Tasha and Juan, he'll never forget them. He looked at his girls and promised to love all three of them forever. He promised to find their brother.

She said they would stay in the hospital for a few days and made him to promise to be there every time she woke up. He smiled and gave her his word. To prove it he turned the phone off. He told her to call her people and get her captains grandchild back. She called and told him where the child was. She called the Teky Mafia and told them to move they were going to get hit and told them to leave the child. She told them to trust her. She patted the side of the bed and he smiled.

CHAPTER 6

Pay Back – Gloria Goes to New York

Gloria set on the jet waiting on him to show up but he never showed. She called Nikko and told him he was tripping out and left. Nikko asked did he have everything and she said no! She had it. She didn't want to leave him because he would think she left him to die. Nikko told her to come on home because Ravenion left Spain early that morning. He wasn't in Cuba either, but he wouldn't tell her where he was. His people said they saw him walk into three tunnels. They knew that New York was one of them. She dropped her head and told the pilot to take off. Rav left on another flight.

"How could you tell me you love me and trust me Ravenion?" She thought to herself.

She wanted to fight with him because he was fucking with her head and emotions. She paced the jet thinking about him; how he held her and whispered in her ear that he loved her. Her thoughts jumped to the dart she cuffed to kill Sonya with. It made a lot of sense now, he thought she was gonna kill him for Nikko, that's why he was so paranoid.

She called Nikko and told him what happened and Nikko told her not to tell him the truth because Sonya was carrying his child and he would kill her if he knew.

Then she thought about the truth, the dart wasn't for Sonya, it was for him. Her people needed new leadership because they didn't have any ties with other countries. She didn't want to stay in the underworld she wanted to sing and hold her head high and be proud of herself. She wanted friends and to meet someone who would really love her. She had to leave and she was gonna leave soon.

The plane landed and there was only one car waiting. When she got in Hassan was in the back with his laptop. She handed him the disk and he quickly made a copy of it. She told him about the dart and he said to give it to Nikko because he had everything on the disk.

They drove to Rav's house, dropped off Hassan, and went on to the palace. Nikko was sitting in the dining area waiting. Gloria noticed his clothes that he was wearing, he had on a blue Rocawear outfit and some blue AI Reeboks. Rav had taken his toll on him, they dressed just alike. Plus, Nigeria, Gino, Arod, and Alex where of the U.S. now. They didn't wear the suits of Cuba anymore. They came home happy and alive.

She walked over and kissed him and gave him the two darts with the disk.

"Rav has cut off his phone, I guess he is done with us. Alex is trying to locate him and tell him that he was just paranoid. He's been all over with a badge and hasn't found a clue. He knows how to survive, so don't worry about him. He just needs time to think; Alright?"

"Nikko, He told me he loved me and he don't even trust me. How do you know he's in New York?"

"Gloria, you got to do something to let him know you mean business and we tracked him to New York through Cambra. And you got to have faith that will move mountains." *(Mark 11:23-24)*

So, if they found her she'd throw that back in his face. She landed in Miami and got a ticket to New York. When she got off the plane she didn't look new; she looked like she belonged.

She hailed a cab and went to the Hilton Hotel and registered under the name Gloria Nalls. She paid in cash, got situated, and then hit the streets of Manhattan. She went to a club called Favors and sat at the bar. She ordered a club soda and checked out the setting. The club was very spacey with big booths along the wall. There were a lot of stars there and then she saw who she was looking for, Kelvin Kelly the President of A-J Records. He was a pecan tan fellow with a goatee, black wavy hair, and 6 feet about 180 lbs. He was sitting alone, so she told herself that this was her chance.

She walked to the booth introduced herself as Gloria Nalls and got straight to the point. He seemed very interested in her and gave her his card. He told her to be at the studio at 9:30 and if she was late to not bother to come. She thanked him and left.

She went to St. Nicholas Street and 147th Avenue and found the number to a one-bedroom apartment. She checked her watch and so it was 9:25.

She saw a prostitute standing on the corner. She walked over to her and asked where she could get an I.D. at. She gave her name of a man named Warren on 125th Street and Lenox Avenue. She knew the streets and knew how to act in the streets. All the years of training were playing off; she fit right in. She left smiling and caught a cab back to the Hilton.

She felt good about herself but deep down she missed him. He would always be the love of her life. She just wanted to show him she could go out and make it. She sat in the tub and thought about if she made it big, what would he say? She knew what he would say, "Gloria you did it! You did it Baby girl! All by yourself, I'm so proud of you."

She washed herself, dressed, and went down to dinner. She saw so many famous people. They were all drinking, smoking and seemed very interested in each other. She looked at her blue J-Lo dress and she definitely looked like a female out on the town. Nikko had taught her well. She sat at a table in the middle of the room and looked around. The room was so full yet she was so lonely. Out of nowhere, Kelvin kissed her on the cheek. He wore a black Sean John suit. He took a seat without asking.

"I just couldn't get you out of my mind, you're so beautiful. You won my heart with your beautiful smile. Please allow me to pay for our dinner tonight?"

She smiled and said, "OK."

They talked about the business and how risky it was. She assured him that she had her own money to back herself and some very wealthy people to back her if it was needed. When she said that his face lit up.

CHAPTER 7

Will We Find Him?

Then Blue sat up and asked for the phone. She called the number he gave her as if she felt something was wrong with him. She had called it before and Nikko had put her through. She explained to Tasha who and why she was calling so Tasha pressed the speaker phone. She told her not to say anything because he would hang up. Nikko picked up himself.

"Nikko, this is Blue, I'm looking for Rav he hasn't contacted me in a while and he told me to call like the last time."

"Blue honestly, I don't know what to tell you, I don't know where he is myself. He's not answering his phone. He thinks I'm out to kill him, so he left us also."

"So, he's in more trouble?"

"No! I just want to know he's alright. His neck hasn't healed completely. The bullet may have messed up his nerves. Please call him, his new cell is 226-783-2212. He needs to be found he's at risk."

She dialed the number, on the 5th ring the operator picked up and said the number was no longer in service. She thanked him and hung up and looked at Tasha.

"Tasha, I don't think we'll ever find Juan. He doesn't want to be found. You heard what the doctor said."

"All I ever wanted was to grow up around him. He's so cool, we got real close after you left. He said if you were alive you would finish school and he would leave the game and raise the baby. He wanted to move out of Georgia to a small town where y'all could live. It hurts because he hasn't even contacted me. He use to call me every week. Tasha, my brother is dead!"

She sat on the end of the bed in Tasha's condo. The condo she bought for her and Juan. She didn't want to admit it, but she thought he was dead too.

Blue laid across the bed holding her stomach. You could tell something was seriously wrong with her, or she really missed her brother. Lil Juan laid at the top of the bed, he looked so much like him. She would talk to him like she was talking to Juan. She looked at the phone and stared.

"Well, it's over. If they can't find him, then no one can. They are connccted all over the world."

She stood up holding her stomach looking in the mirror to see if her face was getting fat. Her face was pale, and she looked sick and she felt sick. Her jeans felt tight around her hips. She thought about her period and if she was late or not. She looked at Tasha, strange wanting to be happy. Wanting to be pregnant by the only one she ever loved.

No one really knew they were sister and brother, so it would be easy to pass. She smiled at Tasha because she knew she could hide it from her because of Ron, her new boyfriend. She used protection when they had sex. She wouldn't give him any head or ass, that was Juan only.

"Tasha, I think Ron got me pregnant!" she said excited.

"Blue, you ain't pregnant, our cycles are a week behind each other."

"Damn Tasha! You sure know how to tear down a bitches dream quick." They laughed and she walked down the hallway telling her she was going to Wendy's.

When she turned to go out she fell down the stairs. Tasha jumped up to see if she was alright. She cuddled her and Blue looked at her confused.

"You know I'm clumsy as Hell of course I'm alright. I think I just peed on myself."

"Well get your clumsy ass up before the pee hits my carpet!" She helped her up, but Blue fell back to her knees.

"Tasha, something is wrong I have pain everywhere!"

She begins to cry and curled up in a ball. Tasha called 911 and explained what had happened. The operator told her to get warm rags for her until the EMT's showed up.

Tasha didn't want to tell her what she knew was happening. It would hurt the strongest person in the world. She knew Blue had just lost her child and her brother was missing and her family wasn't there to help.

"They said you may have a kidney stone, not to worry and I've got you a warm rag to make you feel better until they come."

As soon as Tasha left, Blue began to cry she knew what was happening she was just trying to comfort her. She had just lost her only child, a child that would have been more than just Juan Jr.

"Damn! The EMT's are taking forever!" Tasha said as she held the rag for Blue, trying to keep her comfortable.

"Tasha, I know what happened. God just took my child!"

"Blue, you don't know that! Just know that God is gonna take care of you."

The EMT's finally showed and they got Blue ready for transport. Tasha smiled at them while tended to Blue. On the way to the hospital she followed behind them in her Benz.

She waited in the hallway. As always Grady was packed and people were waiting all over the hallway.

About an hour later. the nurse rolled Blue out and said she was ready to go. Out in the lot she put Juan in the car seat and strapped Blue in the passenger seat.

"Blue everything will be alright. God does everything for a reason."

Blue told her, "Everything's straight. I just had my period but I'm four months pregnant and I'm going home to Washington to be with my family. This is Johnny's child anyway, I added up the months. He's the only one I never used protection with and I've only ever been with three people."

"You are a Damn mess! You just said it was Ron's and now I'm hearing it's Johnny's baby!"

"Remember, I told you about Johnny, the candy licker?"

"Oh Hell! Ya the one who ate your ass and thought it was your pussy?"

"Ya, ain't that some shit? I told him he would be the last bastard I'd grow old with and that Bastard busted me!" They both laughed.

She hated to lie about the baby, but she was going home. She had to put the baby on a sucker to keep people out of her business. She loved Tasha, but the dead needed to stay dead. She would stay in Washington with her mom and dad."

She had already told them about a guy named Johnny. Truly she was talking about Smokey but she would just tell them she didn't know he was a gang leader. When they pull him up and see his charges and see he'll never get out of prison and won't say nothing else about it.

She had Tasha drop her at her apartment on campus. She didn't want to go to Tasha's she wanted to pack her bags and leave.

As she got to the door she smiled. For the first time, she had someone to care for and protect. To love and be loved. But then she tripped and thought what if he wanted to take the baby. She figured that whoever he was with would just have to accept both of them.

She sat down and imagined and remembered how he felt and touched herself. He felt so good. She willed the phone to ring, willed him to magically appear. The phone didn't ring and no one appeared. She finally fell asleep.

CHAPTER 8

I'm Writing a Book

"**I**'m writing a book in case something happens to us, so the twins will know who their parents were and what they stood for. I've been thinking about what you said and I'm gonna leave my job once I get the info you need to get Smokey. What are you gonna do about Nikko and your Cuban family?"

"Sonya, Cuba is where I stay. I've got to house you where your safe. I'm not walking out on them and I'm damn sure not walking out on y'all! Look at Tasha and Juan they haven't been found yet. My son is gone. I failed them. I've been thinking, I really want you to go in a safe house when Smokey and Leo get out. They already know you're the Feds, who knows what they'll try. You know how God can drop shit on you in the spur of the moment. You're going back to Atlanta, an environment you can feel safe in, you know how to work the city anyway. Then I'll meet with the Chinese."

"No! That's my deal. I'll call them and tell them it's going down in Atlanta and that'll give me enough time to get on a treadmill and lose some of this baby fat!"

They laid in the bed and she watched him while he slept and she thought how proud he would be when she got Lil' Juan. She prayed God would protect them and keep them safe and together.

The next morning at the hospital, he took them all over the hospital and bought matching bears and laughed because the nurse had picked their colors and he was sticking to them. He opened her door and she was on the phone talking to the Chinese and setting up the deal in Atlanta. She smiled at him and Nodiya started crying. He took her out of the stroller and handed her to Sonya. She pulled out a breast and began to feed her.

She handed him a bottle from the table and he asked, "I thought you were gonna breast feed them both?"

"I can't feed them both at the same time. That's breast milk. Nidiya is gonna be your responsibility so feed her!"

She finished her call by telling them she would have 5 million up front and hung up. She called the captain and made sure he had his grandchild. He got the child back and she told him about the deal with the Chinese. She had set it up well and he knew it would be very hard for them to bring her down.

"Ask him about my boys."

"He's telling me now." She hung up and told him they had Smokey in Florida and Leo in Virginia.

"How, when they haven't been to court yet?"

"They don't want no one to pin point them so they're moving them every 30 days and they'll switch them in about 10 days and you'll have about 3 weeks to figure out a plan to get them back," she said.

She leaned over and kissed him. The door opened and it was Alex. He looked at him in his suit and he was looking more American every day.

Alex looked at them in the bed one holding the bottle and her breast feeding the other and both wearing red silk PJ's.

"So, this was your reason for leaving? I would have done the same thing. You have two kids now, what are their names?"

"This is Nidiya and that's Nodiya," he said lifting her up, "how did you find me?"

"It was very hard. I put your picture all over town and a woman walked up and said she had just seen you here in the baby ward."

"We have a bigger problem. Gloria is missing and Nikko's on a rampage. Everyone figures y'all are together."

"I'll call Nikko and tell him I'll be back in Cuba with my family. We are hooking up with the Chinese and getting more info on the drug and the disease. Have you spoken to Hassan?"

"All we've done is worry about you!"

Alex called Nikko and told him the news about the twins. He said not to worry about Gloria, she would pop up. Nikko didn't want to agree with him, but he had no choice. He just wanted his brother to return back to Cuba.

Alex looked at Sonya with a concerned look and wondered how you could expect a man to walk away from his family to a family that's not his blood. You couldn't because he knew Rav, he would do it for their safety. He knew Sonya wouldn't allow him to return to Cuba. Now he was looking at Sonya with a look of pleading. Hoping she would come back to Cuba with him.

"Rav, do you think Gloria will be alright?" he asked.

"Gloria isn't looking for me, she wants a life of her own. I use to give her money when I came to Cuba, she has that hidden and I'll give her some more. She wants to sing and I know she can protect herself. She's in one of three states New York, GA or Cali. Trying to get a record or a modeling job. If she's happy then let her fly."

Sonya looked at Alex, then she looked at Rav, she knew she couldn't get him away from his family. She had to accept it, it was the only way the girls would have a mother and a father.

The phone rang, she answered it, "Yeah, Sonya here."

"Sonya, this is captain. They're moving them in three days. Their taking them to the Washington air strip then by train for three days. There all together; Eduordo, Mandi, Smokey, and Leo. The others are informants so leave them. You need to stay in the hospital with Rav so you won't be suspects. That's an order!"

She hung the phone up and gave him a serious look because she knew he wouldn't let them do this by their selves. She didn't want to tell them but she had to. He would've went on a real dummy mission and he would have sworn she set him up. So, she told him everything her and the captain said and begged him not to go. She said to let Alex over everything and send the Chinese. That would be a way for them to prove their loyalty. He smiled and looked at Alex.

"Alex, if I died would you take care of my three girls?"

That puzzled Alex, but he quickly answered, "Yes."

"The next question is if I was wounded and asked you to leave me so y'all could get away, would you do it?"

"Rav, if I didn't drop you last time what makes you think I would this time? Since you got hurt you've been acting kinda scary. Running out on us and hiding from us and now these questions about my loyalty. What are you really trying to ask me?"

"Why do you want to kill me, Alex?"

The question I asked you was from my heart. Your answer was from some shit you've been programmed to say. He laughed at Alex because he looked hurt.

"Hell Alex, I'm just Fucking with you. I watched the Godfather and he asked his men some of the same questions. I just wanted to see your expression."

Sonya knew he was lying because he ain't watched no Godfather. She'd been slipping sleeping pills into his juice so he could get some rest. She was beginning to understand some of the wild dreams. He was afraid to die.

She looked at Alex and thought, *"If something happens to him there's not enough earth to hide you!"* They both looked at her like they had read her mind.

Alex had to say to them, "Why all the hard looks and questions? I really need to know what's going on."

Sonya looked at Rav and said, "You might want to let me know what's going on because there ain't been no Godfather on. If you don't trust him then let him know and let him go."

"I'm going off something Gloria said before we split up she was like you're to blind to see Alex wants to kill you."

"Rav, listen no man wants to be under another man. Yes, I would like to be in your spot but I'll still be under Nikko, you're under no one. I'll never be free like that, but being under you is like being free, free to decide what I want to do or say. I don't have to worry about you reporting me or something happening to my family. Yes! I'm free over here but I still have to answer to Nikko. See, I can give you a lay out and you'll tell Nikko that's how you want it. So why would I want to kill you? If you die I'll still be established here in the States. But I'll still have someone watching me. Just like Poco, you see why I love you so much? Nikko told me to stop looking for you because you would come back when you were ready. He told me to find Gloria but I kept looking." Alex's phone rang.

"Hello"

"Alex, this is Mary. I know Rav just had twins but I got to talk to him. I got to hear his voice please! Let me tell him I love him."

Alex smiled because he knew Nikko had put her up to this, to bring him home. He handed him the phone.

"What up Mary?"

"How did you know it was me?"

"From Alex, I know Nikko put you up to this didn't he?"

"In a way, plus, I told him that I miss you and love you. I just wanted to hear your voice. I know you're with Sonya and the twins so I'll go." She hung up the phone and he laughed then looked at Sonya.

"Nikko be tripping, Mary is my therapist also someone I sleep with. So, don't be in the blind or think crazy. When you were with Nikko, I was with her."

"I know I'm a woman. I knew it when you stayed over there. So, what's your plan on Smokey and them?"

"I was hoping you had a plan."

"Let me sleep on it and then I'll tell you. Alex, it's your job to protect him. I can't raise the twins by my lonesome."

"Alex, you need some rest You're gonna be here all night." He laughed and went to get a blanket.

Rav and Sonya burped the twins. Alex was envious because he wanted children too. Before he knew it, it was 8:00 p.m., he walked with them to the nursing station and when he got back he saw her putting the pills in the juice. Rav was in the bathroom and she didn't see him when he came in. She stirred it up and he watched. When Rav came out of the bathroom she went to hand it to him.

Alex jumped up and pulled his Glock and said, "Rav, don't drink that! She spiked it with pills!"

He looked at Sonya and threw it in her face and yelled, "Bitch! You Stupid Bitch! Kill her Alex! Put the pillow over her head and kill her!"

Alex grabbed the pillow, Sonya showed no fear. She remained calm and said, "Go ahead Alex and kill me. I was putting antibiotics in the juice for his infection and pain pills for his pain. The doctor said you had an infection and Keeflex would control it. I've been doing it for a week and you can't tell me you don't feel better. You don't trust anybody and you wouldn't have taken them if I had been straight up, would you?"

"You're right, I wouldn't have taken them. Where are the pills?" She handed him the pills, he saw she wasn't lying and took 3 of them and was asleep in 15 minutes.

"Alex you know he left the hospital to early. He needs an MRI and you know he won't go on his own."

About that time, two male nurses walked in with a wheelchair. They hooked him up and took him to X-Ray.

They did the MRI in 45 minutes, Alex and Sonya watched. When it was over they were on their way back to the room and two agents were at the door.

"Agent Young and Algood, how are you?" Sonya asked.

They went in and Sonya got the IV out of his arm and then called the agents in and asked, "What's the house arrest for?"

"It's not, we got a tip Juan was gonna break his boy's out tomorrow and were here to make sure he doesn't use the phone."

Sonya looked at him and smiled, she was happy. He was safe and would be protected. But her captain had lied to her. She went over their conversation in her head, 3 days and 6 that's 9: Leo, Smokey, Mandi, Lovy, and Erundo: that's 5, plus 9, that's 14 subtract 6 leaves 8. Tomorrow is an 8-letter word.

"I'll be damned, how could I slip and now he's asleep. Alex call your people and get them to the Washington airport. What do you think?"

"The train would be best if they are gonna travel 3 days. We can go in quick and get them without anyone knowing. We need to know their route or the airport."

"The Feds always use Ronald Reagan. It's gonna be too late to go to Washington. Get me a phone!"

She called Melissa and told her to find the route by 9:15. She was about to hang up when Melissa told her she had the diamond and didn't know what to do with it. She told her to keep it she might just need it. Melissa told her that the captain had his granddaughter back and hung up.

She told Alex to get some rest and as soon as they were on the train the two agents would leave. She cuddled Rav with Alex watching over them. She didn't trust the agents. At 4:35 a.m. Alex phone rang, it was a woman he didn't know.

"Don't talk, just listen, get Juan Ellis out of that hospital! Don't wake Sandra, I don't want her to be involved. Just get him out! Go to the fax machine at the nurses, station and I'm gonna fax you some info. Please do this for me Alex!"

"Blue is this you?" Alex asked.

The phone went dead and Alex got up and left the room. He found a nurse and paid her $3,000 to get a wheelchair and wheel him to the nurses' station to get the fax and then take him to the 1st Floor. The nurse did as she was told and Rav was still asleep when they got there. Alex got the fax and it was a picture of Lil Juan standing in front of Underground Atlanta. He was standing by himself.

At the end of the page it said, "Sonya, where do you want him housed?"

Alex told the nurse to bring the twins to him. He called and got the jet fueled up and waited for the twins. He moved down the hall with the twins and the nurse, he saw the two agents by the door and slipped into the elevator. The nurse asked if she was involved in an escape?

"No! You just helped get him out of danger. He's in Federal protection. If they ask just tell them his neck started bleeding and you took him to the ER."

"Mr. I just don't want any trouble."

"I tell you what, just sign out sick."

"No! Because I don't work this floor but them guys might recognize me!"

"Even if they do, I rolled him down the stairs and you just fixed his neck, OK?" He pulled up his shirt and showed her his gun.

"You know what? Sir, I ain't seen nothing and I haven't even been on this floor!"

"That sounds good because I know your names Elaine Jackson and I'll have your whole family knocked off!" The door opened and she stayed on as they got off, he was calling for her to help but the door closed.

He thought to himself, *"How in the Hell am I gonna carry him and two babies?"*

He tried to wake him up and get him to hold the twins but it was no good he was still out of it. He was startled when a Black female nurse walked up and took the twins out of his arms saying, "I'll help you Sir."

They walked out and he hailed a cab. She helped him prop Rav in the back seat and put the chair in the trunk. He gave the nurse everything in his pocket minus what he needed to pay for the cab and told the driver to take him to Reagan airport. 45 minutes later they were there.

The driver helped him with Rav and took the twins and made them a pallet in the rear of the jet. He only hoped he had done the right thing. He knew Rav would understand once he saw the picture.

Sonya was still sleeping when the agents came in an hour later. The agent told her something wasn't right because a Cuban nurse took him out in a wheelchair.

She jumped up and told him that, "No one should have taken him anywhere!"

They ran to the nurses' station, "Where did y'all take Juan Ellis?" The nurse looked at the roster and told her they didn't have a Juan Ellis registered.

Agent Young flashed his badge and said, "Ma'am, I just saw a Black nurse bring him down here now where did they go?"

"Sir, I don't know. All I saw was a man come and get a fax and leave then another one came in after he left!"

By that time, some more agents had shown up. A tall slim agent pulled out his badge and said, "I'm agent Dwight Railford, we've come to take Juan Ellis into custody. Now, where is he?" Agent Young just dropped his head.

"He was tipped off with that cell phone and then he left with the Cuban."

"Hold up! Y'all was here to take him into custody?" Sonya asked.

"He's wanted for drug trafficking and murder. Eduordo and Mandi told us everything and he was headed here to the U.S."

The nurse handed Agent Young the second fax. When he read it, he took off running towards the baby ward with everybody behind him.

Sonya was screaming, "My Babies! My Babies! No! No! Y'all were supposed to be watching them and y'all let them take My Babies!"

She fell to her knees crying and picked up the fax and read it, "Oh Hell Naw! Somebody want to play some serious games! OK! I'm ready to play! Let me see your phone!"

She called her captain and told him, "You used me. You made me keep him here so you could lock him up! Well, guess what you failed. He's long gone and so are my daughters! You got four days to get them back or I'll bring this whole department down on you! As of now, I'm off pay roll, you wanted war and that's what you got! This is a war I got to win! A war I will win!"

She gave back his phone and went back to the room and got her clothes and walked out. She hailed a cab in her night gown and went to the airport. There she caught a plane to Atlanta. She was a woman on a mission!

CHAPTER 9

She begins to Sing

Their conversation grew beyond the money to the business. He told her about management and a tour he was planning. He kept mentioning how empty his life was. She just smiled.

After they ordered she explained to him that she was involved, she enjoyed the info but that was all.

After dinner, they walked to her room and she invited him in. They talked on the couch. She lied and told him she was from Fairburn, GA. He was born into money and went to Harvard and later changed his studies to music. His father owned the recording company and he had recently taken over.

She begins to sing a hook and a half of a verse: *"How could you, how could you leave me without no excuse. You leaving me boy. How could you leave me, how could you leave me? I gave you I gave you everything and you let me go. When you was locked down boy I was there for you."*

He put his finger over her lips and said, "You had me from hello, your voice sings a tune of its own, you just got to be there at 9:30." He left.

She fell asleep thinking about her future. She was making it on her own. Her dream was of the fans shouting her name. She was on her own and not in his army any more.

It was 7 a.m., she showered and dressed and hit the door. She took a cab to St. Mary and 16th. She was there on time. There were gold and platinum albums all over the walls.

She walked up to the desk and gave her name to the receptionist. She pointed towards the elevators and said 3rd Floor.

When the doors opened she took a deep breath and thought, *"God, this is my future and life in this bag."* Before she could say amen the door opened and he was standing there waiting for her. She looked at the black fur coat tank top and blue Tim's and smiled. He looked like a real New Yorker.

He pointed her to a both. Then he asked her to sing a song without the music. He told her they would bring in a beat to match her rhythm. She begins to sing, *"Love Take this Pain."*

It was the song she had sung for Ravenion and she sang with all of the love she had for him. They made her sing the song three times then called her in the main studio to listen to her voice. DJ Real and a dark-skinned, Dred were mixing on the board. They came up with a nice beat but it wasn't the beat she felt. She took the head phones from Dred and began to work the board herself. Finally, she stopped and told them she was ready to record.

They were amazed, she told them to take it down 1, 2, 3, and she started to sing. DJ Real didn't want to mix he just wanted to listen. Her vocals were ham.

"Love take this pain from me, love take this pain from me. Look in my soul and watch the pain grow."

She stopped the beat and told them to start over. She begins again and this time it was more than alright. They loved her voice and believed she was the next Mariah Carey. The session went fast. In five hours she had recorded seven songs. Kelvin called her to his office to discuss her contract. His lawyer was at the end of the table when she walked in with her bag. She sat between them.

"Gloria, we want to discuss a contract, we understand you have your own money and can probably produce your own album. We're your distributor and label so we'll get a small percentage. We offer a split since you can dub your own music and do your own thing. For 50 grand this is what your contract will be, he handed her the contract. There will be no advance money and we will go 50-50, album to album."

She smiled and handed them the money. They smiled real big when she went in the bag and handed over the money so freely. They both knew she came from money.

Kelvin told her that was enough for the day and that they were going shopping for clothes and somewhere for her to stay. No more hotel for her.

As they were leaving the office he announced, "Everyone I give you Gloria." They all clapped, she had the whole package and would sell.

DJ Real turned on the news and she was astonished to see a shot of the nurse rolling Rav out and Alex carrying the twins.

Her reaction told everyone she was mob connected and Kelvin looked at his lawyer and said, "I knew this was too sweet!"

The reporter said reports were they had fled back to Cuba. It showed Sonya storming out of the hospital with two Glocks in her hand carrying a black tote bag. She had Dred hit the mic so she could hear her conversation so she would know how to handle her. She called her best friend Angel who lived in the palace.

"Angel, this is Gloria."

"Gloria, where are you? There going crazy looking for you! How could you abandoned me like that?"

"Angel, how is Rav? Did he get shot? I saw him in a wheelchair, what's wrong with him?"

"Nothing, he had an infection that's all. He's in surgery now for nerve damage. Nikko said Rav said let you live. You're not in any danger and your free. You're not a slave any more. I want to come to the U.S. How are you surviving?"

"Rav gave me a quarter million and told me to live my life. I think he's testing me, he'll never love me. He just had the twins with Sonya so I'm out the picture."

"No, you ain't, Sonya killed Tasha and took his son so you might have to come back."

"Tell Alex I'm in New York and I'm recording my own record. Rav said I could do it. I'm gonna live my own life. I promise I will send for you when I get situated."

She sat at the table and pulled out a pad and pen and began tapping a beat in her head. She didn't cry or feel anger or guilt. She didn't want the first song she wanted this one. This would be the song the street would hear.

"Your love left stain,

Your still causing pain,

So hard to survive,

These tears that I cry you hurt me, your love left stain, and still you causing pain.

So hard to let go these tears that I cry, you hurt me, hurt me why.

How could I be so blind and easily led in to this love?

You really don't love me, no signs of wrong. So much happiness in this home, Until I said I do.

Not one time but two, what cause you to tick the way you do?

"You hurt me hurt me why?"

She was amazing and watching her drew Kelvin closer. She was a Mafia Queen.

She finished the beat and rushed everyone into the studio. She realized they didn't know the beat but she didn't care. Dred could make the beat later.

"Testing 1, 2, 3."

"I got you Gloria." She closed her eyes and took in a deep breath.

"Your love left stain, and still you causing pain.

So hard to survive, these tears that I cry.

You hurt me, hurt me why."

"One more time from the top Gloria!" Dred asked.

She started from the top while Dred listened on the head phones and moved the buttons. By the time he finished, he had the entire beat all the way to the bridge. He pointed at her with three fingers up and counted down then music filled both sets of phones.

She sang the song with more feeling; listening, you would have thought she was s crying on this track. It was so soft and sincere. It brought tears to the crew and the song was better than the first.

Kelvin knew he had the next American Idol and her beauty and her voice would take America by storm.

She came out with tears in her eyes and they all hugged her. They all went to lunch and discussed promoting the record. They decided on the first and the rest would follow.

They left the restaurant and when they turned the corner they saw two guys trying to break into the Benz. One was prying with a Slim Jim while the other stood watch.

Gloria had already sized them up by the time Kelvin hollered at them, "Stop! That's my car!"

One of the guys pulled out a slim, black automatic and said, "Good, you come on out with those keys and turn around! Don't try anything or I'll shoot!"

The other guy came to his aide with the Slim Jim in his hand. After she saw he wasn't armed she told them to do what they said.

"Go check their pockets, Fats!"

Fats began taking the items out of Jenny's bag, she was the production manager. Then he went to get everything out of Johnny's, then Dred's pockets. The gunman stood behind them to get a good view of them all. Fats made DJ take off his shoes and Gloria dropped her tote bag. Everything she had in her life was in that bag, the past the present and her future. The money Rav had given her was in there also. She wasn't giving it up without a fight.

She saw the gunman's face out of her left eye. He was smiling as he took the money and the jewels out. She spun and kicked the gun out of his hand and followed with a kick to the throat. He was out cold. She pointed the gun at fats. With a calm voice she told Fats to wake up his buddy and get the Hell outta there. Kelvin wanted to call the police but she told him she couldn't justify sending them to jail for their way of making money. After Fats woke up his partner they left running. They all thanked her and hugged her to show their gratitude.

After they loaded up he couldn't say anything because he was so ashamed she had to save them, he couldn't do anything to help them. He broke the silence by asking about the guy on the news.

She smiled and told him that was her heart and her reason for living. He saw that she wasn't going into any detail so he changed the subject and asked her what were her plans for her album. She said she wanted it released in both the U.S. and Cuba.

He told her it would be in every country and she smiled because she had people in every country, almost. She didn't care about being rich she just wanted to be free and be with Rav. They went to Mannies, an Italian shop in upper Manhattan. They sat in a cozy corner booth.

Dred started the conversation about the robbery and wanted to know how she learned to fight like that, she told them she had trained very hard and they were in good hands, like Allstate. Everyone laughed.

Jenny asked if she would train her. Gloria said sure and Kelvin suggested they turn one of the rooms into a gym and they all agreed. He told her he didn't want her in that hotel. She explained she had to return to Cuba to check on Rav. Kelvin frowned and everyone laughed.

They finished their meal and went to the studio to record two more songs. Afterwards Jenny took her back to her hotel. Gloria noticed how much Jenny liked her so she told her she wasn't gay and Jenny told her she wouldn't try her if God told her to! They both laughed.

CHAPTER 10

Lying Lifeless in Bed

The twins cried as if they could sense the separation of their parents. Nikko came back and told Mary the infection wasn't that bad and Rav would be ready to go as soon as the medicine wore off. Mary said she was glad. They all sat around his bed and they placed the twins on each side of him.

Nikko looked at him lying lifeless in the bed and remembered when he was first shot. He said the same prayer he said then, *"My Lord take my life instead of my friend. There's no greater gift than a man that lays down his life for you."*

He now understood the prayer. Rav was supposed to kill him and take over everything, his family, and everything he had worked his whole life for. It would be easy to kill Relena, she is in love with him, she studied him with the stars.

His thoughts were interrupted by Relena, she said, "I never thought I would see you in a jogging suit, when did you start wearing them?"

He smiled and pointed at Helen and told her Helen had gotten him jogging every morning. Looking at his attire she saw that he was living his life instead of the cartel life their family had left them.

Mary had on a black sundress and Helen sported a blue Baby Phat suit, they looked at Relena and saw she was wearing a red dress that she had made herself. She made her own clothes mostly. This dress was one full shoulder with a strap on the left, her slim waist and thick thighs curved the dress nicely to her red pumps.

As they sat and talked and looked at the pictures of a young Rav. Nikko didn't understand but Mary, Relena, and Helen understood perfectly. "Kill the love of his life, save the son all in hopes of bringing a family together."

They explained it to Nikko from their point of view but he still wasn't buying it, Sonya was too smart to slip like that. It wasn't her, he couldn't explain it but he knew it wasn't. He'd been with her and he knew she was at the top of her game. He defended her honor not because he cared so much for but because of her record, her life, how she infiltrated his family and to believe it was love and, in the end, how she infiltrated the Feds to cover Raul death. He always wanted Sonya from the first day his brother had brought her around. He knew they would never get involved, so he dropped it. Then Rav brought her back into his life, it wasn't a fetish, it was love. Rav was his right-hand man so he accepted they would never be together. It angered him to be in love with her and she was in love with Rav and Rav don't care nothing about her. He exhaled and smiled, cherishing the days he'd had with her.

An hour later, Rav woke up not knowing where he was. He felt the twins under him. He raised his head and it was feeling heavy. He laid back down and closed his eyes, when he opened them Mary was kissing him.

"My prince is alive, I love you Ravenion." He thought he was dreaming, so he just stared at her with a puzzling look and then he noticed Nikko and Helen and knew it wasn't a dream.

"How did I get to Cuba? Where is Sonya? Is she alright?"

"My friend, the two guards at your door weren't there to make sure you weren't going to break Smokey and them out. They were there to arrest you for murder and drug trafficking. Mandi and Erundo told them everything about you. I spoke with my lawyers and they said it was nothing concrete because they ain't place you in the corn field. I already had them dug up and the bodies burned. When they come they won't find anything, so your straight. We got pictures of young Rav with Wednesdays time on them."

"Nikko, what day is this?"

"Today is Friday, you've been in surgery again. The first doctor didn't clean the wound properly so you got an infection. You're alright now, you just need to keep it clean. Anyway, the picture came by fax with a note on the bottom asking Sonya where she wanted them housed. Here's the picture."

He handed him the picture, he looked at it and said, "My boy, you're a fighter and you don't look afraid so I know your safe."

Then he looked at Nikko "This ain't right, Sonya's not that sloppy. Whoever she's working with ain't getting paid. Hit Nina up and check her account."

They called Nina in Switzerland and checked Sonya's off shore account. It was missing 5 million withdrawn three months ago. He was puzzled so he called Sonya. When she answered he handed him the phone and he said, "Bitch, explain the five million you took out of your account three months ago. What's goin on Sonya, where's Juan? If you want to see these twins you bring Juan back!"

"Rav, I don't know who sent that fax, I don't know nothin about Juan. That money was for you when you thought your money was gone. I still got it and can account for it."

"How did you know I thought my money was gone?"

"Nina called me Rav, I been dealing with her for a while. Rav I love everything about you I know hurting your family would push you away from me. Rav, please come back with the kids, we're a family. Since we know Juan is alive we can get him back. You know I won't rest until I get him back!"

Nothing she said made since to him, all he could make sense of was that she said, "If we can get Juan back we can be a family." He stopped her from pleading her case.

"Sonya listen to me good, you got 72 hours to get Juan on a plane to Cuba. If he's not her then I'll have so many Cubans on you you'll kill yourself." He hung up the phone and handed it to Nikko and then picked up Nodiya.

"Nodiya is always to wear blue and Nidiya is always to wear red, it's the only way I can tell them apart. What time is it?"

Helen told him it was 5:45 in the morning. He looked at Mary and told her to sign him out and take them home. Mary got up and walked out to get him a wheelchair. Relena step beside his bed and said it was time. They were all confused so he asked, "Time for what?"

She leaned over and kissed him and Nodiya, "It's time for our family to come together. I've stepped aside long enough only to see and feel your hurt. Mary won't last and Gloria isn't coming back and Sonya must die." Mary came back with the chair.

"You're all signed out. The doctor was coming with the medicine. He'll come around once a week to check on you."

Nikko and Helen got the girls. They sat Rav in the chair and wheeled him out of the room. They took a left and looked out for others, but there was no one. Nikko called Alex and told him to have everyone at Rav's house.

"This won't be like the last time Alex."

When they left the hospital, the car was waiting. They helped him in the car, Relena and Helen comforting him and Nikko and the girls sat across from him. He only hoped there were no visitors in his house. He went to sleep and dreamed about Cindy. He missed her, he missed a lot of things. He opened his eyes and looked at Nikko, he wanted to ask him if he could get out of the mafia for the twins' sake. They sure needed their daddy because if Sonya didn't have little Juan in 72 hours she would be dead. He saw the way Nikko held Nodiya, he held her as if she was his own. He had to snap out of it, it had to be the medicine.

"Mary, I guess I got to go at it again, this time I'll get the equipment and you stay at the house with the kids," he said as he smiled at Relena.

She didn't smile back but Mary did because she knew Relena had it out for him. It comforted her to see that he just chose her over Relena. Relena just rubbed his face because she didn't mean it like that. She wasn't gonna sit in the cut no more, it was time she got what was owed to her. What her God promised her.

They pulled into his driveway, the sun was shining on the lawn freshly cut. Relena looked at the house and knew this was the house the stars had shown her so long ago. She told Nikko she needed a copy of the blue prints so she could build an escape route. They were greeted by Alex and the rest of his men, they helped carry him in the house. Relena told them to take him to the bedroom. Then she walked around the house checking doors and windows.

When she was finished Helen looked her in the eye and said, "I guess you wasn't playing in the hospital."

"No, I wasn't, she'll soon find out."

Mary knew she was talking about her and couldn't depend on Helen to tell her she was right because they were about to be sisters. Niger walked downstairs and called Mary, she got up and went to him, he pointed upstairs. She went to his room which set next to the steps. The girls were up but weren't crying. They were lying next to Rav who was calmly watching them. They were his just like Juan, they knew they were sisters.

Relena came up the steps and took a picture of the three of them. She told Mary to lay beside the twins so she could get a picture of them. Mary cuddled under Nodiya facing them then they changed positions and she took another shot. Nodiya started crying and seconds later Nidiya started.

Relena went and fix their bottles and brought them up and they were both still crying. Nodiya had both fists balled up. Rav just looked at them and laughed. Relena threw the bottle to Mary and ran down to get the whole baby bag.

Alex asked Nikko what was going on because Relena never acted like that? Helen smiled and said, "Young Relena is in love, she's tired of being last and holding her feelings back."

"She says the gods told her it was now or never. You know how she is about her gods." They all laughed as she ran right past them.

She threw Mary a diaper from the bag and changed Nodiya while Mary changed Nidiya. It was funny because she had never changed a diaper. They both finished changing them and dressing them and they, both laughed because it was a Kodak moment and Nikko had it all on camera.

His little sister had changed her first diaper. Relena looked at Mary and told her straight up that her job was to take care of Rav and the girls. Mary looked at her and told her she didn't need her to tell her how to take care of her man and kids.

Before it got out of hand Nikko sent Relena back to the palace. Mary didn't let it phase her because she knew her position and she wasn't fixin to let some young powerful bitch tell her what to do. She bathed the girls while Alex went and bought two cribs. Then she cooked an old-fashioned meal of vegetables and corn bread.

Rav could walk so the surgery wasn't that serious. Mary told him about his therapy starting Monday. All of them were gonna chip in with his therapy and the girls.

Mary went upstairs and put the twins to sleep by rocking them. Sonya had three outfits for them and they were the special colors for each of them. They slept the same way and looked the same, it was impossible to tell them apart. She liked dressing them in the different colors cause she wanted them dressed in hard colors. When she walked down the stairs she saw everyone was out back.

It was a beautiful night and Rav was in the pool staring at the sky. He really couldn't believe Sonya was behind this. He knew she tried to kill Tasha once, so he knew she was the one who killed her, since she had Juan. But why keep Juan for so long, he was only two, why do him like that?

He knew the game, people kill people just to prove a point, move in closer or to prove a point. The mafia style of life consisted of everyone trying to get ahead. He knew it firsthand.

He was so lost in thought he didn't see her standing behind him. Mary leaned over and kissed him.

"It's gonna be okay Rav, it really is. I'm not going anywhere, I'm in to deep, so deep I'll kill someone. I'll do it! Just to take care of you and the girls!"

"Mary, can you shoot? Because your gonna need a gun running with me. Because I'm not gonna hide out I Cuba. I got a lot of shit to do. Plus, I gotta meet with the Chinese before Sonya. I need a phone so I can call Tam and ask him what's up. Tam is a cat that knows everything about the Chinese under world."

Mary got his phone, he went through his contact to reach Tam. He asked him about Sonya meeting with the Chinese. He told him that she had a meeting with the Teky Mafia this morning and presented the drug to them. "She got some chemist to hook it up, she also told them she just waged war with the Young Don of the Cuban Mafia. There's a hit on your head Young Don. She also gave up 50 million and she's now putting them to work. She's not looking for your little boy's."

"No! She's not looking for him, she's building an army of Chinese and Blacks, she's not playing! But I heard someone kidnapped her twins and she's posted a 5 million-dollar reward worldwide."

"Listen, I need a Chinese connection in New York, New Jersey, and the upper states."

"Listen Rav, my family is the Nusuk family, they just had ups and downs with promises to be the leaders of the yellow dragons. Right now, the dragons are under a lot of stress because of the Dawi murder. Their looking for a leader with major bread to back them. My family will be their leader under you if you back my family. Sonya got this chemist and we gotta be better. If her drug carries a 72 hour high it's going for four grand an ounce, we got to either lower the usage or add more for an even longer high."

"I'm gonna get with Hassan in the morning, I gotta plan up my sleeve that will target the rich and the poor. Let me talk to Hassan first. As a matter of fact, where is Hassan and his family? Let me get back with you."

He called Nikko and asked where Hassan was. Nikko told him he moved them to the palace because so he could work at the farm. So, he can have his own lab. Rav was happy to hear that. Just before he hung up he told him Relena was playing them tarot cards. He laughed.

He got out of the pool and she gave him a black silk robe and walked him to the shower. They showered together and went to bed and shared each other's bodies.

The next morning, Mary fed the twins and set up the equipment so when he walked downstairs he had breakfast. Arod, Niger and Gino played with the twins. They all looked more American in their Coogi suits. They walked into the equipment room.

He said, "I thought I was supposed to work out?"

There were five machines instead of one and Gino told him they all needed to work out. Mary had redressed his wound. By that time Relena had walked in and told Mary they needed to talk. Mary told her anything she needed to say she could say in front of everyone. So Relena told her to prepare to die. The tarot cards had told her of two deaths and one spelled out Mary.

Mary didn't back down she just told her, "We were all born to die!"

Rav grabbed Relena by the neck and took her upstairs. He threw her on the bed and snatched off her black dress and then tore off her bra and panties. When he saw her body, he was amazed at the shape of her body.

He told her to stay there and went to get Mary and told her to be naked when he got back.

They were both side by side when he came into the room. He told them to learn to accept each other and left the room. Everyone was gathered around the intercom

Mary had installed for the twins and heard Mary tell her, "It's okay to hate me but not over a man."

Relena told her, "Mary, I'll never wish death on anyone, I'm just telling you what the tarot cards showed."

"Well, who was the other death?"

"My brother has been having visions of death for 6 months or a year. The dreams have become more intense and he can feel it in his bones. I asked him if he could see his murderer. He says no but I can feel that he does know. He always say to make sure the Gods take care of Rav and that's why I turn these cards every day." Out of nowhere, Nikko ran into the house wearing black fatigues and a black skull cap and a Teflon vest, carrying two tote bags.

"Listen up, it's going down now, their taking them to court in 23 hours. Sonya is due to take the stand in their indictment hearing. They all filed paper work to face their accuser. Sonya's crew is planning to break them out and are talking about destroying some hard evidence. Rav, she's trying to keep the people off of your ass. I spoke with her last night, she says she's hitting the evidence room also. With all of this Alqueda stuff goin on it's gonna be a sweet lick. They just bombed the Twin Towers a year and a half ago, so now is the time since the threat came from Atlanta."

"Nikko, I'm not trying to help Sonya, really I'm not but I told her I would help get them boy's out, so we stay clear of her. If anyone has a clear shot at her then take it."

Alex asked him, "What about the girls?"

He ran up the stairs hoping to see them making out but they just laid there staring at each other. He told them to take care of the twins and to learn to live together. He grabbed his bandages and the cream and rushed out the door. 15 minutes later they were boarding the jet.

He put on the black fatigues and grabbed his CD player. At Charlie Brown Airport they switched to a helicopter. Nikko was the most eager to do this because of Mandi and Eurondo's loose lips. That was the only reason he was on this mission.

He had three more copters on standby to make their escape perfect. They were five minutes from down town Atlanta, they came up through the Pryor St. entrance. There were a lot of people on the street and barricades around the courthouse.

When they flew by they saw Sonya's people around the courthouse and snipers on the roofs of the surrounding buildings. He called his ground crew and relayed the info. When he called Sonya, she said to call the other three copters. Once they were in position the hit was called in and the first copter opened fire with 50 caliber guns. The snipers tried to take cover, but it was too late, they were already exposed.

The ground crew started shooting and walking towards the courthouse. The agents started shooting and all possible routes were covered so no one could interfere. They broke the barricades and ran up the courthouse steps.

Nikko yelled out to break through the barricades and when they scattered out the copter landed in front of the courthouse. Arod and Gino were shooting AR 15's with launchers on them. They threw two grenades through the door. They threw another at the agents by the steps. Once Arod said "clear" the rest of them jumped out of the copter, Rav ordered some of the ground crew to go in first. Once they cleared the way they waved him in and they went up the steps. Seven men went on each floor. Rav looked at the location board and saw that they were on the 7th Floor, Room 794.

One of Sonya's men walked up behind him, put a gun to his head and told him to put his hands up. He stepped off of Rav and called Sonya and told her he had Rav. By the time she could instruct him to kill or take him as a hostage, Rav round housed and unloaded his Glock into his throat. He called Nikko and told him to check room 794 on the 7th Floor while he ran down the stairs to the holding cells.

He opened the door and saw two guards standing side by side. He threw a gas bomb down the hall. The guards started shooting at the door. He ran out and dove on the floor and shot the guard on the far wall. The other officer took off down the hall so he followed.

Just as the door was popped on the holding cell, he shot the officer in the back of the head. He knew there were no guns allowed in this area.

Smokey had already taken control of the guard when he heard the shooting on the radio. He ran out and pointed at the last cell. Leo grabbed the keys and uncuffed himself and then locked the guard in the cell.

Rav turned and looked at the elderly lady in the booth and pointed his Glock at her and she showed her praying hands. He ordered her out of the booth. When she came out he went in his pocket and gave her a wad of money. Then he told her if she turned it in she would be dead by sunrise. Smokey told him the other three were upstairs getting immunity. Rav asked who the third person was and they told him Lucy. He called Nikko to see if they had found them yet, he said they weren't in 794. He told Nikko to try the judge's chambers and to get all the tapes and paperwork. As they were going in the judge's chambers they heard gunshots and went into find Nikko had killed the judge and the DA.

Erundo was pointing at the bathroom saying Sonya was in there. Nikko grabbed all the tapes and paper work and told them to get going. But Erundo kept insisting they go in the bathroom, Nikko knew Sonya was in there hiding. He looked up at the ceiling and saw she could be in the roof by now. So, he opened the door halfway, she was behind the door. He shot up in the ceiling, looking at her through the mirror.

"Ain't nobody in this bathroom, Erundo!"

"Nikko, she must have went through the ceiling. She's in the roof, shoot the roof up!"

"What, you give me orders now?"

"Damn that Nikko! Erundo does she have any documents?"

"No! Nikko got all the files right there!"

As they ran down the stairs Nikko told the pilot to be ready. The pilot told him the Air Force was coming, they had to hurry. They ran out and jumped in the copter. He told the pilot to stay ground level that way they wouldn't shoot. All of them hugged each other.

Nikko said, "Sorry it took so long for us to come get y'all. We're going back to Cuba by boat. We can't risk getting shot down. I have diplomatic immunity so they won't search the yacht."

Rav was cool with that and told Nikko this was his problem because they deceived them he would have to deal with it. Nikko looked at all of them as they began to plead for their lives and tried to explain why they did it. Mandi said they had always been treated like the help. Erundo told him to do whatever made him fell big because they would never be his brother or Ravenion. Nikko told Niger and Arod to tie the rope around their neck and that it was a test of their loyalties and they failed. With no questions asked or answered Nikko shot all three of them and hung them from the copter. When they got by the express way they cut them loose.

When they reached central Macon, the copter landed in a field and they burned it. A black Limo was waiting for them. A black suit each for Smokey and Leo with 20 grand in the pocket of each.

They rode to Savannah and boarded a Cessna with the words "Freelancing" on the side. Rav told them they had one stop to make in Florida. Nikko and Rav didn't talk any more, everyone could sense the tension between them.

Rav asked Nikko to step to the head of the yacht and asked him what the new beef was.

"Rav, there ain't no beef, I just don't want to be off course."

"I'm going to the Americas most wanted studio and I'm gonna blow it up."

"You see? That's what I'm talking about! You go off on impulse. You think about it and you do it. You must not have seen them jets coming at us. If we didn't get all the evidence there will be a worldwide man hunt for you." About that time his phone rang and it was Sonya.

"Are you alone?"

"No"

"Is Rav with you?"

"Yes!"

"I got all the evidence and the location they gave up. Their putting together a man hunt for Smokey and Leo, but it will be different. They're not televising them just the dead bodies. They are sending troops out searching for them. Rav can walk around free in the U.S., I really need your help Nikko. I really need to find his son because I didn't have anything to do with the kidnapping. As a matter of fact, Tasha them ain't dead, they're in witness protection."

Nikko handed Rav the phone, "Yeah?"

"It's me, just listen. Tasha isn't dead, the whole thing was staged to get them into witness protection. I don't know who sent the fax. I don't even know who staged the kidnapping."

"Well, how do you know they ain't dead?"

"Because I seen them with my own eyes when we was leaving the hospital the night you got shot." She didn't want to tell him about the picture and the letter, so she just pleaded with him.

"Sonya, if they're alive then you can find them and bring them to me. You have 48 hours and your time is running out. By the way, take the price off my head or the next death will be yours."

Rav hung the phone up and handed it back to Nikko, Nikko told him about the man hunt and the evidence was destroyed and he was a free man. They agreed they had to watch their step because they were on the U.S. most wanted list. They were being treated like Saddam and Bin Laden.

They sat back and grabbed a blunt and said, "We're all born to die."

Rav told them about Tam and his family and the gang the Yellow Dragon. Nikko told Rav he would meet with them. Rav told him to do it after he met with Hassan. He had a new plan about the new drug.

"You know the drug they give you when you have surgery? I want to add that to the drug, liquid as well as powder. The same way we cook meth is the same method. The new drug has to be cooked with corn liquor, I saw a lot of the info on the computer. From what I gather its pure heroin and pure coke mixed with some kinda downer. I have to talk with Hassan first, so we're going straight to the palace and then to the lab."

He was getting tired and sweaty so he laid down. Nikko studied his neck, it wasn't bleeding but he knew he hadn't used any of the medication.

Nikko called the studios of America's Most Wanted and told them they were under a bomb threat and not to air the Atlanta Courthouse escape. Then he called and activated a contract so the building would be blown up that night. Rav looked at him and asked him why he would warn them and then blow it up? Nikko told him when he called the studio all he got was an answering machine and now they can't say they weren't warned.

They all laughed and Nikko went up on deck he had to figure out how he was gonna get off of that boat and help his friend. He called Sonya and told her she had to come up with something to get him off of it. She told him to go to New York and check out the Yellow Dragon himself and then ease down to Atlanta to meet with Tam. He asked her how she knew about that? She told him nothing went down in Atlanta without going through her first. She was the queen of the city. They both laughed and hung up. The truth of the matter was she had spoken with Yysek, the co-leader of the Yellow Dragon this morning he had told her they had a meeting with the Young Don in three days. She asked him who set the meeting and he told her Tam.

Nikko went downstairs and told Rav he was getting off in Key West because he wanted to check on some business in little Habannah and check on the Dragons. Rav agreed and Nikko was gone. Everyone else chilled and drank some beer. A cook appeared and grilled steaks and fish.

After eating and conversating about the war against the Feds and how they thought he was gonna sell them out because they hadn't heard from him. They all laid down and fell asleep. Alex told them they would love the palace because females were everywhere. So, they all went to sleep with their own vision of Cuba.

CHAPTER 11

A House in Buckhead

There were plenty of yachts lining the shore. He looked for a ferry to take him from Florida to Savannah. He was thinking about taking a plane so he caught a cab to the airport. He really felt like a man. He was wearing real clothes, he was involved in an escape. A lot of his people feel like he should dictate all of Cuba. But he just wanted a simple life, he would kill to have been raised like Rav.

He was just trying to save one friends life and the son of another one. In the end everyone would be happy except him, he would just watch Sonya walk away with another man again. He got to the airport and went and booked a flight to Atlanta.

Ten minutes later he was in First Class looking at the clouds, He remembered Rav saying the clouds would warn you. He wondered if the clouds would show him falling to the grave or the Heavens opening up to him, like Rav.

The plane took off and he searched the clouds. It was 8:30 in the morning, so the opening would really be a sign. He called Sonya and told her to meet him. He stared into the sky but it never parted. He smiled and closed his eyes, he fell asleep without dreaming for the first time in months. He woke up and looked at the sky, it was the same. The plane had landed. He got off and walked through the tunnel and when he got to the parking lot Sonya was standing there with the Benz at the curb. There were four Chinese standing by her. He walked up to her and kissed her on the cheek.

She introduced her bodyguard, Kim was a tall slim 23-year-old. Mr. Wan was the same but older. Last was Tommy Nugen, he was 19 and very quick. Her and Nikko got in the Benz and the others got in the Limo, then she cried for her babies and her family.

"I don't know what's wrong with Rav, we're supposed to be in this together. Instead of loving we're worrying our kids are gonna grow up without a mother or a father because he ain't fixin to kill me!"

"Calm down Sonya, he ain't fixin to kill you. He just went into shock because of the fax. It's got amateur written all over it and he knows it, he's just acting stupid. It he wanted to kill you he could have already done it, he knows where you stay."

She pulled off and said, "No the Hell he don't! I don't stay in that house no more, I got a house in Buckhead with guards 24\7. I'm not fixin to let him kill me, I'm not Federal no more. I have a life now!"

"So, these four guys stay with you?"

"No, they just got out with me, they figuring you want to see the result of the drug."

"I do, but I'm in need of some rest first."

She pulled up to the home. It was large with black gates manned by armed guards. She pulled in and the men checked the car.

Nikko noticed the cameras and other security. They stepped out together and walked in the house. There were two doors to get into the house, your picture was taken while you waited to enter through the next one.

"Is all of this because of Rav?" he asked.

She told him this was the house they were all supposed to stay in before he went crazy. She took him up the steps, they passed the security room on the right and went to the room on the left. It was a guest room. He sat on the bed with his feet on the floor.

She closed the door and took off the white dress she was wearing. He went wild at the sight of her body. Even after the twins she was beautiful.

"How do you like my body?" she asked.

Her white Apex bra and panties turned him on, she stepped out of the panties and pulled the bra off. She walked over to him and knelt down in front of him and sucked his dick. He laid back on the silk sheets. She knew she had to let him think it was gonna be them, to get his money and aide. This was the best performance she had ever given.

She undressed him and laid on top of him and whispered in his ear, "You're the first since the twins so be gentle and promise to love me. It's us now not Rav, OK?"

"OK." He was so happy he finally got her, he finally got his girl.

"Sonya, I've been in love with you for a very long time. Rav doesn't really care. He will always be in love with Tasha and I'll be very gentle."

Nothing he said mattered to her, it didn't matter if he was gentle or not because she was gonna act like he was killing the pussy anyway. She slid under the cover as he kissed her and made his way to her secret.

He put the head in real slow, she took both of her arms and pushed him out with a loud moan, "Please Daddy, be gentle!"

She knew that would excite him and make him cum quicker. She let him put it in to see what he was gonna do, he stroked real slow and soft. She moaned like he was killing her. He stroked faster once she grabbed him and held him, he knew he was the man.

She whispered, "You the man Daddy." Three more strokes and he was cuming.

She faked it with him screaming, "Yes! Yes!" Really, she was mad because he got his and she didn't.

"Eat it freak! Eat it now!" she commanded.

This was the Sonya he loved, he ate her for 30 minutes, she came twice. She rolled him on his back and squeezed his balls and sucked him at the same time. She bit his nipples and rode him like a wild horse. He came and grabbed her because she was trying to keep going.

"Love me Nikko, Love me forever!" she said.

He laid in her arms and asked why they didn't hook up when his brother went away? She looked down at Nikko and laughed to herself, as long as she got him she'll always have Rav and the ups on him.

"Nikko, when is Rav coming out so I will know to stay clear of him?"

"Sonya, Rav hasn't even seen the product yet, he's not in a rush to put nothing out. All of his other drugs are worldwide now so he ain't sweating no money." Nikko didn't feel right talking about Rav so he grabbed the remote from the nightstand and turned the radio on.

A disc jockey came to life saying, "Welcome to the Quietstorm, I have a request that came all the way from Cuba." They both rose up in bed wondering if it was from Rav.

"This request came with a 5 grand bonus to play R. Kelly: Slow Dance and Hey Love every hour on the hour with a sweet message. Sonya love now war later, if love is war and war is love, what are we doing when pain is war? One love from Juan Jr., Nidiya, Nodiya, and the Young Don." Slow Dance flowed through the speakers and filled the room.

Nikko tried to turn it off, but she stopped him and told him, "He knows those are my favorite song's, that's why he's doing this. It's some kinda mind game." They made love again and fell asleep.

The next morning, they got up and showered and jumped in the Limo. They ate breakfast at the Hard Rock Cafe. Afterwards they went to a clothing store called Fashion Sense on Mitchell Street. She looked at a couple of out fits and him a couple of suits, but he wasn't into suits any more. After they chose the out fits and had changed the clerk took pictures and gave Sonya a copy and said she had never seen any mafia people before.

They smiled and walked out, it had to be luck from God cause she saw Tasha walking down the street. They sat in the Limo waiting on her to pass by. Nikko had never seen Tasha before so he wasn't sure Sonya wasn't just playing. When Tasha walked by the door Sonya opened it and pointed a Glock 9 in her face and told her to get in. She got in like a terrified little girl and sat in front. She knew this was about Juan.

"Listen Sonya, I don't know what's goin on, if this is about Juan, I don't know where he's at or if he's dead or alive."

"Stop lying Bitch, you wasn't kicking this scary shit while I was in the hospital, you got involved with the wrong nigga. Then on top of that you pull off this shit. I'm now at war with Juan. He's holding my children hostage because of a picture you sent me while I was in the hospital. So, I can't get his sisters from a madman of a father they got."

"Juan is in a safe house you should know more than me since your Federal."

She told the driver to take them to the warehouse and no one spoke on the way. Tasha knew she was gonna die but it wasn't gonna be sitting down. When they came off the Fulton Industrial exit the light was red so Tasha put up her praying hands. Sonya had the Glock pointed at her side. Sonya raised up and Tasha hit Sonya in the throat, and then opened the door and took off running. Sonya told him to go after her. The driver left the on ramp and went after her. She was running towards Bolton road and did like Juan had taught her and went inside a clothing store. She bought some men's clothes and went to the bathroom and changed and made a mustache with eyeliner.

She walked out and saw Sonya and them pass by. She had nowhere to go she was about to panic when a labor truck stopped and men started getting on it. She got on with them, not caring where it was going just glad to be out of the area.

Sonya went in every store and no one had seen the girl come in. She looked at Nikko and told him there wasn't no way she had just disappeared. She ordered her troops to search everything. She told Nikko that she had underestimated Tasha and Nikko said she hadn't but Tasha did what Rav had taught her and that was survive.

They went to the warehouse and she showed him the drugs. The warehouse was a huge lab with about 40 Chinese workers walking around. Sonya handed him a mask and they entered. Sonya went to the computer that handled all the security and checked the outside cameras and found what she was looking for. Tasha had gone into the men's clothing store across the street. She never saw her leave until Nikko pointed her out dressed like a man. Sonya didn't think she was that smart.

Sonya showed him the drug and told him it was a lot like meth. It had PCP and acid called Yeah baby in it. The acid had a high of about 10 hours and the meth was about 6 hours and the PCP was about 24-hours, once all of them kicked in you would be high for at least 2 or 3 days. She said it sold for five thousand a pound and dealers would bring down 8500 easy. He smiled at her, she had it all figured out. He told her to call her people and see if she could find Juan Jr. He felt in his heart that trouble was coming. He picked up the phone and dialed the number on the side of the truck that Tasha rode off in.

"Manson Demolition," a female voice answered.

"Yes, I was wondering the location of your site, I'm trying to get on there?"

"Yes Sir, it's 1652 Jimmy Carter Blvd."

"Thanks very much," he replied. He didn't write it down so she just looked at him.

"She wouldn't give me the address." She walked upstairs and got her laptop and Nikko stopped on the 4th Floor and called Rav.

"Rav, listen I'm in Atlanta right now. I ran into Sonya trying to find Tam. I seen Natasha with my own eyes, she's alive but she won't be for long cause Sonya is trying to kill her right now! She ran and jumped in this labor truck and she's on a site at 1652 Jimmy Carter Blvd. Your son is in Federal Witness Protection and I'm trying to get some info now."

"Call to that site and get hold of Tasha. Tell her to get to the Hawthorne Terrace Park and I will be there in 6 hours." He hung up and saw Sonya was on her laptop. He called the site and the crew manager described Tasha and went and got her to the phone.

When she came to the phone he told her, "Tasha, don't be afraid I'm calling you for Juan. He's in Cuba right now. He'll be at Hawthorne Terrace Park in six hours so go there and hang out." He hung up and walked into the spacey office Sonya sat on the desk on the computer.

"I got it. There at 1652 Jimmy Carter Blvd.! Let's Go!"

She called her troops and told them what they were looking for. Nikko asked her why she was so into killing Tasha?

"It's very simple. She's been a problem from day one. Ever since she was in that coma he's been praising her and her son. My kids deserve the same praise. Since that disappearing act has cost me so much pain. I might as well go ahead and make her disappear, for real."

She walked down the steps and out the door. Nikko didn't know what to do because she was fixin to kill the girl for nothing. When he walked out he saw she had a Mac 11 strapped to her shoulder and had put her fur back on she was ready for war. She could see that he was stalling and wondered if he had warned her. She knew he was soft and something wasn't right she just couldn't put her finger on it. She checked to see if he had used the phone and saw he had and the last number he called was the mansion.

They sat in the Limo, she asked him if he was up to this and he said, "No! He wasn't up to no killing on either one of them!"

He told her that because he knew if she killed Tasha that Rav would kill her. She just laughed and told him to stay in the Limo cause it was bullet proof.

He watched her and was impressed she didn't blink or waiver a bit she just stared straight ahead. When they got to the site she got out of the car and cocked the Mac 11 and rolled out a gangsta movie. She didn't look to see if any of her soldiers had arrived she walked right up to the foreman and showed him a picture of Tasha. He didn't see the gun but he did see her entourage and knew she was about business.

The whole worksite knew something was wrong when they saw all the Chinese pull up on the bikes.

There was one guy who was on the truck Tasha came in on and he walked up to Sonya and asked, "Ma'am, you're looking for that girl right? She got a phone call and left walking towards the park on Hawthorne."

She looked at Nikko, he didn't get out of the Limo so he didn't know what was said. She circled her hand in the air letting them know she wasn't there just in case she came back.

She got I the Limo and told the driver to go to Hawthorne Park. She checked Nikko reaction and didn't see one. When they got there, she asked around to see if anyone had seen her they said she had left.

No one had seen her climb in the trees with all the colorful leaves. She watched them as they looked for her. She prayed they didn't look up. She was praying for Juan to come and save her.

A lady was pointing towards the tree and Sonya started walking towards it. She looked up and Tasha nearly fainted because there was nothing she could do about it. But to her surprise she wasn't looking up for her she was looking up in frustration.

Sonya called Kim and told him she had to be warned by Nikko. Kim told her she was still in the park she just wasn't looking hard enough. She told him they had searched for three hours and hadn't found anything.

Her phone rang and it was Chin Li telling her five cars of agents were heading her way and he had seen Ravenion coming with 10 Hummers of men.

She clicked back to Kim and told him he was right about being in that park because the Feds and Rav was coming. She told him to get ready for war.

Kim called one of the troops named James and told him. James started yelling out the Feds and Ravenion were coming in Chinese. They started pulling their guns out taking position in the park. Nikko rolled down the window and asked what was going on? One of the men told him the Feds and Ravenion were coming.

Nikko got out of the Limo and called Sonya and waving his hands in the air and then she spotted him. She told him to get back in the Limo because she knew if Rav saw him he would kill him.

Then Sonya looked up at the tree and saw her. She pulled the Mac 11 out and pointed it up towards her. Tasha jumped to the other side of the tree as she started shooting. Nikko jumped back in the Limo as the Feds and Rav started shooting at Sonya and she took cover.

Tasha landed hard on the ground and rolled around to the other side of the tree. She stayed low and ran towards the oncoming cars and Hummers. Rav was in a bullet proof Hummer; Alex drove it straight to her and opened the door. She jumped in and when they got out they all had on the Kevlar body armor and were trying to trap Sonya behind the tree.

She started shooting and running towards the Limo. The Feds jumped out and she covered her face. The Limo driver met her halfway; Nikko opened the door and she dove in. As they went up the street the Feds were after them, but Rav made Tasha call them off. She was mad because she didn't understand so he explained she was an agent also and all she would do would pull rank. She was trying to trap Smokey and Leo and these agents blew her bust, but they had her outnumbered. She understood well once he explained that and they were sitting there holding hands when the Feds pulled up.

The head got out and a Black fellow that was well built introduced himself, "Hello Ms. Middle, I'm agent McCoy and were here to escort you back."

She looked at Juan and asked if she could go with him? He told her no because he was in the middle of a war and he would just get her killed. He told her to forget about him and he would follow her bank account. He promised to add money every year. He kissed her and turned her over to the Feds.

They got back in the Hummers and the Vics and went different ways. He called everyone and told them to meet him at the Lakewood Amphitheater. Lil Jon, Webbie, Boosie, Pimp C, and more was coming. He wasn't afraid of the Chinese or Sonya. He had one life and he was gonna enjoy it.

CHAPTER 12

Webbie on Stage Rapping

Hassan was hooking the anesthetic to the Ice to be a speed ball. He mixed it with every drug they had. He was gonna give you a high you were gonna chase every minute. He's supposed to have you so high and bring you so down. The trick was to make it an everyday drug, not a three or four-day drug.

They all met up at the Hilton Hotel downtown. They all walked out in the lobby in their colors Coogi outfits and all colors of Gators and Kango's. The whole lobby stopped and looked at the 30 man clique and some of the women licked their lips. Him, Smokey, and Leo tried not to draw attention to themselves.

They got into a white Jag with the steering wheel on the right side. He sat in the back while Alex drove.

Out of nowhere Alex asked, "Did they see Nikko point at Tasha?"

Rav told him he wanted to act like he didn't see that. He also told them it was Nikko that called him and the Feds, so they shook that off. When they got to the concert.

Webbie was on the stage rapping, "If it's my car or my clothes that make the hoes want to fuck fo sho."

He told them to drive up on stage and pop the trunk. When they drove up everybody thought they was part of the show. Webbie started pointing at the cars and rapping the song over and pointing at the cars, he smiled and they got out.

Everybody started yelling, "It's the King of the South and it's not T.I!"

In every trunk was a hundred grand and it all equaled up to a million dollars and they started throwing money in the air. The after party was at the Ritz, two Limo's pulled up for the women only. He knew they wanted to have fun, what good was it to hustle and not enjoy yourself?

They drank the best beer and wine. He knew Sonya didn't club much and as long as she had Nikko with her they weren't coming out.

He paid the hotel clerk to keep all the police out. He called Poco to have someone come and get the cars and send the Limo's.

He told her to call Nikko and to be at the hotel at 9 a.m. sharp. She told him that Helen and Mary were in Atlanta with the twins. He was too drunk to understand what she was saying. He just said the Hilton in the morning and kept partying. He wasn't into the sex part of the after party because he knew someone could take advantage of them.

Smokey and Leo were already upstairs with some girls. Out of the blur he spotted Kau, his African love queen walking into the ballroom. He quickly ran up behind her and took her into his arms. He rubbed the green silk dress down to her thighs. She knew who he was from his soft touch.

"I heard you were here and wanted to see you and talk to you."

They walked up to the counter and got a room on the 5th Floor. He made sure it was by the fire exit so he would have an escape. He called the front desk and told them he was in room 504, but he was really in 514. had a master key and she asked him how he got it and he said there was no hotel gonna turn down a hundred grand in an hour. She just smiled and called him a show off. He asked her about her schooling and she said it was all fine and made real good on the exams. He liked seeing his money was going to good use.

She pushed him down onto the bed, took his shoes off and slid his pants off. She undressed as he slid up on the bed. He never forgot her pretty body. She slid down and took him in her mouth. She took him in her throat, pulling back without using her hand. She climbed on top of him and rode him like the African days. She was hoping he wouldn't come. She tried to hold him but he came and she felt it in her stomach.

She laid on his chest and talked about school and her family. He walked to the bathroom and took a leak, when he came back he was ready for round two. They went at it until they fell asleep.

She woke him up with a lot of questions like, "Will I see you again? Do you love me? How can I contact you?"

With tears in her eyes he told her, "The answer to your question is yes! You'll see me again and you'll always be in my heart. I love you enough to protect you but you won't make it in my life. People are taking shots at me every day. I just had to save my baby's mama life by leaving her. There ain't no life for me right now. You know how your people say our destiny is placed before us? My life is already lonely not by choice but by force. The only way to protect what I love is to stay away. I need you to stay focused for your family and for me! Okay?"

"Okay, but I need money, I have a job working at a Radio Shack but I'm barely getting by. I've tried to get a job as a nanny so maybe I could stay with the family who I work for."

He picked the phone up and called Nina. He told her to put a million dollars in Kau's name. He turned to her and told her he would be looking out for her. He wanted her in Cuba but Mary would go crazy. He kissed her and showered together then he left. He got to the Hilton before everyone else did. When he went into the Penthouse he saw Mary and the twins sitting on the sofa. She still had on her purple nightgown.

"The door man told us you were coming."

He kissed her and asked why she was there? She said she had a message from Nikko to come. Now that puzzled him! This shit had Sonya all over it.

The phone rang and it was the door man telling him that Nikko was coming up alone.

"Nikko if you knew a war was jumping off between us and Sonya why would you call for them?"

"Rav, I didn't call for them! I called to check up on them, that's all. Sonya! Let's get them out of here! Where are your men?"

"They were partying last night, we can move them. Ain't your Limo out there?"

"Yes! We can put the twins in separate Limo's. Rav I'll feel better if you call them because I didn't send for anyone."

"Y'all know Relena is upstairs too?"

"My sister is here too?"

He called for Relena to come downstairs. He looked at the penthouse and laughed, "Rav you're so TV, your penthouse looks like the Drummonds from Different Strokes." They all laughed as Relena came down the steps in a white, Jumpman jogging suit.

"Mary why ain't you dressed?"

"If you planned on going to Six Flags why did you bring the twins?"

"Poco agreed to keep them. Mary, go on and get dressed."

As Mary walked away everyone saw how Relena looked at her ass and said, "Hell Naw!"

The girls just laughed and said, "You said we had to get along with each other."

Mary went on upstairs and they sat on the sofa. Relena sat in Rav's lap and told him he still had the scent of who he was with last night on him. So, there would be no kisses for him. He laughed and told her that was impossible, and then she kissed him goodbye. Nikko looked amazed and Rav told her, "If you wanted to know if I was with someone last night all you had to do was ask. So, don't give this silent shit, if your that good you'll know who I was with."

She laughed and said, "You're right, I was just trying to pick you."

He picked up his phone and called Alex, but his phone just rang. It was unusual for him not answer his phone. So, he called Gino and Gino told him Alex had left for New York to take care of some business for Nikko. He looked at Nikko and asked, "Why all the secrecy?"

Nikko looked at him puzzled and said, "Rav for the last month or so you've been on high guard and tell me why you didn't you tell Gino and them to come?"

"Nikko why are you so over protected? You act like you know something is fixin to happen. I feel you're out to get me. You nearly got Tasha killed yesterday, you pointed where she was. Then the secret trip to be with Sonya, shit just ain't adding up. Maybe I'm trippin but I know you're in love with Sonya and you'll do anything to protect her. You're to blind to realize that Sonya don't care about you. She got three loves in her life. Me and the twins. We'll always find a way to each other. Why and how? I don't know, it's just something about the bitch. But I can tell you this right now and this is a promise, I'm a loyal nigga and I've never betrayed anyone before in my life. If something happens today I will hold you responsible, because you got all of us here." Nikko looked at Rav and smiled because he was now thinking like a boss. His heart was hidden and he liked that.

"Rav, I'll take full responsibility if anything goes wrong because I'm sure nothing is gonna happen cause no one knows we're here."

Rav looked and smiled and said, "Let's go!"

They walked out and got on the elevator, the girls and the twins were in the back and they stood in front to protect them. Rav pulled the chrome 45's from behind his back and hung them down by his sides. He had them pointed at the doors as they opened. He stepped out with them tucked under his jacket. Nothing looked odd to him so he motioned them out.

They walked through the lobby in silence. Mary carried Nodiya and Relena carried Nidiya. Nikko opened the door as the Limo pulled up. All of a sudden, he heard some motor cycles coming fast.

"Get in the Limo, Hurry!" Rav yelled.

The doorman tried to open the door but it was locked, Rav looked at Nikko as they ran back towards the double doors but when they got there they were locked.

"Hit the ground and crawl to the front of the Limo!" Rav yelled.

Before he could say anything else a swarm of bikes came into the lot shooting automatics. They all saw Mary with Nidiya covered with her body trying to protect her. Nidiya and Relena were hidden behind two large flower pots on the right side of the door.

Bullets were flying everywhere. Rav laid on his side and took out two of the riders at one time. He yelled to Mary to try and get to the flower pots. As she begins to move the Limo door opened and Sonya stepped her right leg out. Rav looked up at Sonya and yelled, "No! No!"

Rav took a shot at Sonya but Sonya pulled out a 45 and shot Mary in the back of the head. Mary slammed face first to the ground still cuddling Nidiya.

Sonya stepped out wearing all black leather and grabbed Nidiya and put her in front of her face, using her as a shield from her daddy. Once she was in the Limo all the shooting stopped and her and her men drove off.

He rushed to Mary and turned her over and put her head in his lap. He kissed her lips, they were still warm and for the first time in his life he spoke Spanish.

"Y-hue puta yo soy el!" he spoke the same words again and they meant "I'll be a Mutha Fucka!" For the first time in his life, he couldn't keep his word. It never failed everyone in his life had to leave or die.

He looked at Relena and Nikko and yelled out, "I'm gonna kill that Bitch!" Relena grabbed Nidiya and went by his side she told him they had to go the police were coming.

Then he yelled out, "Yo mataese puto! Meaning, "I'll be a Mutha Fucka!"

He kissed Mary for the last time as the Limo pulled up. Nikko knelt down and grabbed him by the shoulder and told him they had to go. He wasn't hearing nothing anyone was saying. A crowd started to gather round them.

He reached for Nidiya and she handed her to him then he looked at Nikko and told him, "Eres un trai cionero vele antes de que te mate!" which meant "You're a traitor, go before I kill you!"

"Rav I'm not a traitor and I'm not getting outta your face. We gotta get outta here, leave her!"

Rav looked up and saw Arod pulling up. He wondered why his Limo never came out. Then he saw the white Limo pulling up behind Arod, Niger and Gino. They jumped out of the green hummer and grabbed the baby outta his arms and helped him up.

He picked up Mary's bloody body and carried her to the hummer. Neither man cared about the blood that was getting on them. They helped him put her in his lap and pulled off. When they pulled out of the parking lot behind Nikko the driver got out of his Limo and it blew up as he walked towards the double doors, they looked back and kept walking.

They followed Nikko to the Charlie Brown Airport and got on the jet to Cuba. He told the pilot to stop in Vero Beach, Florida so they could let Mary's family bury her. Nikko understood that and didn't say a word because he knew he was the blame for this. If he would've stayed on the yacht none of this would have happened.

He looked at Rav and told him there was no more talk, just action from here on out. Rav looked at him and nodded. Nikko knew his life was in danger, so if he was gonna die he was gonna die in the streets.

He thought about Ravenion's young life. How easy it was for him to was for him to love and how easy it was for him not to care. He looked at Relena holding Nidiya, playing with her. He hated Mary had to die for nothing, he hated he had to set her up because Sonya would kill her just like she tried to kill Tasha. Why didn't he see this coming? He looked at Rav cuddling Mary and closed his eyes. He looked at Rav and thought about the day that Sonya told them about him. How he'll be foolish to take the rap for the drug trade. Looks like he tricked everybody including his brother.

He got up and walked to the front of the jet and called Raul. He told him what had happened and how Rav threatened to kill him. Raul told him Rav was out of control and so was Sonya. He told him to kill both of them. He said as soon as they landed he would have a hit man kill Rav and Sonya.

He told him he missed him and he was ready for him to come back. Raul wasn't hearing that because if he came back the U.S. would send troops into Cuba to kill him or capture him. He wasn't trying to spend one day in prison. He told Nikko to kill Sonya because she's the only one who got him caught up and he had to kill Rav for his own safety.

Raul hung up and Nikko went back to his seat thinking on a way to carry out this hit. Relena never played with a baby before, she looked so happy.

Rav was asleep with Mary laying in his lap, out of the blue Relena looked at Nikko and said, "You know what? I want a baby of my own."

Nikko being sarcastic said, "Why don't you ask them tarot cards? You ask them for everything else. They told you Mary was gonna die, who else is gonna die?"

"Stop it Nikko! Stop it Now! And no Rav not gonna die as long as I got breath in my body. You'll die before any of us if you carry out your plans. Just leave well enough alone, I told you, you was making a mistake trying to live up to Raul's expectations. You should have come with me when poppa told you to. Now your life may be in danger. You ain't messing with people who fear us or our family. These are two heartless people. Rav don't care about no one at this moment. Sonya used you just like she used Raul and Rav. The only difference between Raul and Rav is the twins. She tried to get Raul locked up but tricked y'all with this plan of hers. In the end she's who she is. A Federal Agent that will take all of you down."

"Your tarot cards told you all of that Shit?"

"Go to Hell Nikko! Just go to Hell!" She tried to tell him in so many ways that Rav was gonna kill him, she really wasn't sure, she didn't want him to die.

She looked at Rav as he held Mary as if she was still living. A 23-year-old man, held so much responsibility and very little love. Here she was the same age and held no responsibility and very little love. The gods had promised her he would love her and he was showing no signs of that love.

The jet landed in Vero Beach and Mary's family was there waiting. It was funny because no one had used the phone to contact them. Her mother was just a little shorter than Mary, he hugged and kissed her. He looked at the short stout lady and told her how much he loved her daughter. She smiled and thanked him for bringing her home then turned and walked away. He watched her climb in the ambulance and break down in tears. The rest of the family loaded up in their cars. All of them were Fords and Hondas. Rav asked Nikko where the Limo was at and he said he didn't know who had called the family. Finally, the pilot told them when he had called the hospital for the ambulance they had contacted the family. Rav asked if they were ready to go back and they said they were. He knew the dope was ready in New York and told Nikko to make sure Hassan added the Sodium Pentothal in the drug.

"I know if the Sodium Pentothal scan put you to sleep imagine what it will do to the heroin and other drugs, they all combined will make your heart jump out of your chest. Hassan tested it on a rat and it lasted two weeks. So, he put some Lasix the superman and guess what? The rat stayed mellow for two weeks and went right back for more. Each time he shot him up he slept for an hour and was still mellow and even was able to eat. The double Lasix gives your body the water it needs to carry the drug and stops the drug from going straight to the heart. I'll be back in Cuba after Mary is buried."

He hugged all of them and kissed Relena on the cheek, grabbed the baby and hailed a cab. Just as he was closing the door Relena grabbed it and smiled and got in.

"Where to?" the White driver asked.

Before he could give him the address Relena told him the Rizma Palace. After they arrived they went in through the backdoor. They went up to her room in the elevator. He just looked at her and smiled. Her suite was beautiful, the door was gold and the living room was all ivory with marble floors. It was furnished with expensive furniture.

She walked him to her room, once again he smiled because of its originality. There were pillows covering the whole floor and there wasn't a piece of furniture in sight. In the middle of the room was a huge water bed. She told him there was a workout room and a Jacuzzi with an extra guestroom.

She looked at Nidiya and said, "I know y'all are hungry so let me feed you."

She ordered Gerber food for the baby and steak and potatoes for her. He told her he preferred a burger and fries with grape Kool-Aid. She smiled and ordered the food. She was watching him and knew his pain wasn't emotional, it was the pain of not keeping his word. She made him step out of his clothes and put on a towel. When the food came they ate in silence. He saw that she was very good with the baby. He began to wonder why she was really here but before he could ask the bell rang signaling his clothes had arrived. He wanted to shower but she wanted to bath him. He soaked and waited for her. She came in tying her hair up. When she stepped out of her robe he nearly fainted. She was so fine, so pretty and so right. She turned and gave him a back shot a smile and stepped into the tub. She laid herself on him and started kissing him.

She whispered in his ear, "No man has ever been here before so handle it with care."

He began to kiss her harder then turned her around and massaged her temple then her shoulders. They took turns bathing each other then stepped out of the tub. He picked her up and laid her on the pillow. They had no cover just the warmth from their bodies. He kissed her from head to toe and began to lick her warm slippery cunt. He stuck two fingers in her and she raised right up. He pushed his tongue inside her and she screamed as he penetrated the only promise on her body, a promise to love him and only for the rest of her life. He sucked her spur tongue and she came repeatedly and she felt a sharp pain erupting in her promise. He was inside of her stroking so soft and gentle and she finally screamed out, "Juan I love you!"

Her eyes rolled back in her head and her body shook so he started grinding harder and faster. She begins to speak in Spanish and she threw her legs up on his shoulders. As she was at the point of no return she asked him to marry her, she begged and pleaded and started screaming, "OH GOD! OH GOD! RAV! I'm. . .I'm. . .I'm. . .CUMING!" She shook and her whole body dropped, her eyes closed and she was asleep. He fell on top of her and soon he was asleep with her.

CHAPTER 13

Assigned to Protect Rav

Gloria got up at 6:45 a.m. and ate three Granola Bars and juice with an energy drink, and ran three miles. On her route she ran through Hell's Kitchen and saw Alex talking to a Chinese man. She watched them get into a black Benz and pull off. She hailed a cab and told the driver to follow them. They rode all the way to the Bronx and Prospect Ave. and went into a warehouse. She hopped out and looked through the double doors. She saw a nice way to slip in through the roof. The only way to find out anything, was to do her own investigation, she never trusted Alex anyway.

She went back to her cab and went home. Before the cab left she decided to go to an electronics store to get some small mics and cameras.

After going home to shower and then had the driver take her to a car dealership. She bought a black 2002 Mazda and then drove to the studio.

Everyone was glad to see her because her single was just released. It was getting a lot of air time too. When they gave her the news she almost fainted. Her dream was finally coming true.

As she thought about what she had seen confusion crossed her face and they noticed it. They all told her they were gonna stand beside her no matter what. Kelvin was deeply concerned so he told her he knew about her past and it didn't matter no more. No matter what it was they were gonna get through it. That's what she was waiting to her so she told them all to gather around and listen.

"I haven't been completely honest with y'all. A slave, I truly am, I belong to Cuban Mafia, I'm a trained killer and I'm assigned to protect Rav;

the guy y'all seen on TV." She paused and a tear fell down her face.

"I fell in love because he was my first and the only one to show me compassion and freedom. He helped free us by paying 250 million dollars back to Nikko. I feel as I have betrayed him and he left. After he left I came here. He told me I could leave at will. Today I saw one of his bodyguards without him and he was with the Chinese man. Everybody knows the Cubans and the Chinese don't get along. I can't contact him, I don't know if he's dead or alive. I'm so confused and worried!"

She broke into tears and went into the conference room and began to write a song about being in love with a thug. As she tapped her pen to get a beat she closed her eyes and started humming and began to write;

"I seen your face on the news the other day and my heart dropped at the site of you being wheeled away.

I'm gonna miss your smile and your sleepy face, how you use to come and hold me and say you'll never leave me. You'll love me until judgment day and you'll beg the Lord to go the other way.

AH, thug love is the love you gave me, and I'll be thuggin and lovin you for eternity. There's no other man in this world I trust anymore and with these wings our love will soar. Until heaven opens our love will grow, and I'll be your t-h-u-g. Thuggin lovin you for eternity."

Everyone looked as she wrote. It was exciting to see a young woman with so much pain that knew how to express it. They were all waiting when she came out of the booth. She laughed and walked out of the booth. They knew she was gonna go to the board, they knew her well. She made some adjustments and went back inside.

Kelvin stood and watched the DJ listened to the beat and put his own style to it. After he counted it down the music filled the booth.

Shots rang out and a woman screamed saying, "No! No! No!" Then the beat dropped and she begins to sing, *"I Seen Your Face the Other Day."* The lyric took them to the understanding of the second song. Kelvin wanted to put the single out right then. He looked at everyone and told them to come on so the sounds could be out by next week. Jenny asked what song was gonna be dropped from the album? He laughed and said that no song was gonna be dropped because they knew the first album would sell the second one.

They all rushed in the room and gave her the news. She smiled and dropped her head because her mind was still on Rav and his unknowing situation. They knew it and wanted to do something special for her but couldn't figure out what.

She told them it was alright and she would be fine and to concentrate on the new song.

Finally, it was ready to be shipped and after putting together a nice arrangement Kevin sent it to the copyrights office.

The song was sent out to all the radio stations in New York and New Jersey. Kevin sent 500 dollars with each single to get it played. He knew it would make her happy to hear her knew song on the radio. She would be the first artist to have two new singles out in a week.

No matter she was still down and before anyone could stop her she had packed up her stuff and left.

She was gonna catch a cab and then remembered she had her own car.

When she got home she sat in the half empty apartment until 2:30 p.m. Then she dressed in black and drove to the warehouse.

She parked up the street and walked the rest of the way. There were winos and hookers on the street, selling pussy and begging for money. She paid them no mind, her focus was on her mission.

When she got to the corner she saw the two-big black Buick's parked out front so she knew someone was still there. She walked passed it and into an alley. There were three dumpsters lined up so she crouched behind the first one and pulled out a crossbow. She shot it up to the roof. When she heard the hook strike its mark she pulled it until it took hold. She grabbed her duffel and began to climb. Once she was on the roof pulled the rope up behind her. She looked down the vents into the building and she saw four guards standing at the corners and one watching the cameras. She knew all she needed was to tap into their system and she would have a live feed. She traced the wires to the box and got her drill and opened the box.

She hooked her line up to their video feed of their cameras and set up four cameras of her own. Then she climbed back down and left.

When she got home she plugged everything up to her laptop and watched the video while laying on her bed. She thought about her life, past and present and she knew if she called Rav he would tell her to kill Alex and then she would be right back where she started at. She turned up the volume to hear what the guards were saying. They were talking about a shipment coming in on the Hudson. She knew if Rav had anything to do with it, it would be a hundred million or more. A loss wasn't in his mind anymore. She smiled and picked the phone up to call Niger, "Niger, this is Gloria. I'm looking for Rav and it's very important I speak with him."

"Gloria, where are you?"

"I'm safe," she assured him.

"You know he's in distress cause Mary just got killed and we're fixin to go to war with the Chinese. Sonya is hooked up with them."

"The more you talk the more I need to talk to him."

"Hold on Gloria and let me call him first."

Niger checked with Rav and he told him to have her call A.S.A.P. He clicked back over and gave her the number and hung up.

When Rav answered she said, "This is Gloria please say something."

"Something," he replied.

She smiled because he was being a smart ass but he wasn't mad cause he wasn't cursing. She begins to cry and said, "Rav, I love you with all my heart. I miss you and I'm ready to come back to you."

"NO! You stay in New York. Angel told me where you were and what you were doing. You have a life now and I don't want you to give it up for me. This is the only way I can protect you. Every female I know is distanced from me. I heard your song on the radio and I remembered when you sang to me. I know your voice and I know your name. That's how I'm gonna find you. Until I come for you, push it to the limit. Goodbye Gloria and remember I love you and I'm not mad at you."

"No! No! No! Don't Hang Up! I saw Alex with some Chinese. I have them under surveillance, there in a warehouse in the Bronx. I know a big shipment is coming in and I need to know what to do."

"I'll be up there in four days, just stay away from the warehouse. One love Gloria and I'm proud of you." She hugged her pillow and went to sleep.

She woke around 9:45 a.m. and looked right at the monitor. She saw

Alex talking to another Cuban, when he turned around she saw it was Nikko. They moved to the crates and removed the tops.

She turned up the volume and listened to them talk. This was all very odd because Nikko never handled business face to face, that was Rav's job.

"Mr. Chin, I'm very glad you decided to do business with us. I know you have already met Alex."

"Where is Ravenion?"

"He has a matter of his own right now so don't worry about him, he won't be with us long anyway."

"Over my dead body!" Gloria said.

"What we have here is better than meth. Everyone knows meth has become the most popular drug in the world. We have the drug to make meth number five and make heroin and crack number two and three. It is made the same way but has a downer effect. It's been around for ages but no one ever used a pharmaceutical with a street drug before. You'll be relaxed for hours. I give you superman."

He pointed and Alex brought some over from the crate. The drug was packaged in small medicine bottles the color of blood. It was in crystal and rock form. The lady nodded her head and smiled.

They brought three users from the back room. All three were female One Black, one White and one Asian. They all grabbed some of the drug and ingested it in their preferred manner All of them felt the same calming effect combined with a rush. All three of them walked back to the room with the rest of the drug and finished them. They all settled on the carpet and began touching themselves.

Alex took three more containers and three men came out of the same race of females. They took the same drugs and went to their rooms and got naked.

"Nikko said the drug would be popular because it was a sex drug."

They put the males and females together and watched them perform an orgy. Mr. Chin clapped his hand and told Nikko, "This would put the dragon on the map around the world." Then he asked about Rav again.

Nikko, not wanting to alert Alex to his plan of killing Rav told him he was dealing with a death. That surprised Alex because no one told him about any death.

They shook on it and Nikko told him that it was a hundred million dollars' worth drugs He told them to sell the crystal like they would sell meth and shipment of, dro, and ex would be in in a few days.

He told Alex to meet him at the Sun-Sun Massage Parlor. Alex told him he was calling Rav to let him know everything went well. Nikko whispered in his ear and as he spoke she read his lips. He told Alex that pretty soon he would be taking Rav's place. So, don't involve Rav because this was his deal He didn't even know why he was sent here, he told him it was what Raul wants.

Gloria jumped up and went in her bag and got the dart that was for Nikko She dressed like one of the Chinese messengers and rode down to Madison Ave. She slipped in and went straight to work. She checked every room and didn't see Nikko. So, she gave a fat guy a massage. He asked for the works and she asked what all he wanted. He gave her a hundred dollars for a dance while he jacked off. . .Nikko walked in and asked could she be his date for the evening? Yes.

Once in the room, Nikko stripped and a laid on the table. She massaged him and rubbed her nipple on his face. He asked for the needles meditation and she went to get the incense and rubbed his body down with alcohol.

Nikko asked her to come to the Hilton, Room 426, she agreed and started laying the needles in his back. She took the dart and slightly broke his skin along his spine. She held it there for three minutes took it out and did it again on his left side. The whole process lasted for an hour. She removed them and watched him dress. She promised to show up at 6:30 p.m., he paid her and told her to leave and get ready. She went to the counter and gave the clerk all five hundred she had made and told her she would be right back. She left walking. Nikko followed her. She went into an apartment on 9th and waited for him to pass. She went up the street and got into her car and went home.

After she cleaned up real good she took the dart and her clothes into the backyard and threw them into the fire. When she got back inside Alex was in the living room and Nikko was pulling up outside.

"Hey! Alex," yelled Nikko.

"Hey Gloria, why did you take the back streets home? I've been waiting across the street. I just happened to look in the cut and saw you standing by the barrels laughing at the winos." Nikko came in and hugged her; she went to light some incense to hide the smell of her body.

"So, Gloria, you have an album out?" he asked.

"How did you know that?"

"Because the radio says straight from Cuba Gloria Nalls and then "How Could You Leave Me" came on. That Rav is very smart he let you go out on your own so we could launder money through your album." She knew that was a lie, but a nice idea and she had to run it through to Rav.

"Your right, that was the whole plan, by me being Cuban they can't tax me so all the money will go straight to my account."

She knew she had to talk fast so she could go to her room and hide the monitor. She walked in the kitchen and got three cups and three root beers.

"I know this ain't up to par but I'm trying to live normal."

"I'm gonna put you in a big apartment in New York. You'll live like the rest of the stars live. You will be a great leader for our people. Damn Gloria! You did it! I never knew you could sing. I'm so proud of you!"

"Nikko, I produced my own album so I get like 60%, will that help?"

"Yes! You can do all kinds of fund raisers."

Nikko was happy he toasted to her and they drank the soda. She ran to her room, hid the monitor, and got the album cover. On one side of it was her face and the other was her walking in the park. It was self-titled Gloria. She signed it and gave it to him.

Alex looked at her and said, "You know Gloria, I slipped up and let go."

"That's right Alex, you can never tell a flower until it blooms." They all laughed.

Nikko felt special because he had a copy of the album before Rav did. He wanted to take her out but remembered his date, so he told them he had to run.

"Gloria, do you have any hard liquor? Because if you do I need the whole bottle."

"What's up Alex?"

"I got some MD 20\20 I give the winos for cleaning up."

"Good, give it to me."

She went to the fridge and got three bottles and gave them to him. He took the first bottle to the head and told her to fix him a ham sandwich. She got all the stuff and before she could use the butter-knife it was too late, he had already used his finger. He ate the sandwich and began to pour his heart out to her.

"Gloria, Nikko just made me his right-hand man. Raul wants Rav dead and I think Nikko wants me to kill him. I don't want to kill him. But I'll do it if I have to, what do you think?"

Not wanting to sound crazy because she thought it was a test, she replied, "We all must do what Raul say's. So, if Raul said it, it has to be done, so are you gonna do it?"

"I really want that position, I've been waiting on it for a long time. But this is the man who freed our people, the man who stood for us and believed in us."

"Then don't do it, we can live free Alex. Look at me, I'm doing my dream."

He took another swallow of the liquor and thought about Rav's words in the hospital.

"It's like he don't trust you, he don't trust me. Yes! I'll do it if I'm asked to."

That was all she wanted to hear, she could've killed him right then. But Nikko knew he was there, so she decided to get with Rav on this. She called the studio and told them she had guests and she would catch up with them in a couple of days. She hung up and went to her room and called Rav. He was the last person to call her.

When someone picked up she was surprised cause it was Relena. When she asked to speak to him she handed Rav the phone.

"Yeah!"

"It's me Gloria. I see you have Relena with you. What's going on?"

"Gloria, trust me, you wouldn't understand if I told you. But what's up with you?"

"What's going on Rav? I want to know now!"

"Remember this you'll always be number one. Your my protector. Just trust me, it might not seem good right now but in the end, you'll understand. It's all for us, please believe that. Remember, I'm protecting you. Now, what's up?"

"I believe you! Alex is here and Nikko just left. They're planning to kill you, Raul gave the order. Alex spilled his guts over ham sandwiches and MD 20\20. He's asleep right now. I told him your plan was for me to make it big in music so you can launder money through me. I can kill Alex now."

"No that will look too much like me, plus, Nikko knows he's with you. It will have to be a robbery or something. It can't come back to us. I'll be up there in four days. Just go about your normal routine. I love you Baby girl!"

That's all she wanted to hear and it was on. She had four days to come up with a way to kill him. Before it was over she would kill him, she promised herself that.

CHAPTER 14

The Funeral

Relena carried Nidiya down the aisle to the casket, Mary wore an all-white dress, her hair was in ponytail. She wore a silver necklace with a cross on it. Relena sat in the 3rd row and watched for Rav. Rav walked in with an all-white Sean John suit on with Mary's mother on his arm.

When they got to the casket she leaned on it and cried. Rav pulled his Sean John shade out with 14kt gold trimming and put them on.

Her funeral was small. Just family and friends and her ex-husband. Rav and her five brothers were pallbearers. They buried her at Brown and Steven.

After the funeral, on their way to the airport Relena broke and told him Nikko planned to kill him. He only laughed and told her he already knew. She told him to stop running woman to woman and marry her. She promised to protect Nodiya and Nidiya.

He took in a deep breath and told her she was right and she told him no one had to know they were married. She kissed him and they took a plane to Las Vegas. After they were married they spent one night making love at the Vegas Inn as husband and wife.

The next morning, Nidiya woke her by crying. She got up and fed her and changed her and rocked her back to sleep. She loved the fact she had a child and thanked him for her life. As she laid in his arms she kept saying her name, Relena Ellis.

He knew Mary would want him to marry cause that's all she ever stressed to him. He smiled cause at the end of the day he had a family. He rubbed her stomach and thought to himself, *"Yeah, we got to put one in there."*

He kissed her and told her to go home to Cuba, her and the baby. He had a lot to do! She told him she didn't want to live in Cuba, her and the baby were going to Atlanta. They'll keep in touch but she assured him she knew to stay out of sight. She also told him Sonya stayed in Buckhead and she was going to Stone Mountain. She would get her I.D. while they were in Vegas and would enter Atlanta as Relena Ellis. He smiled and told her to go to Cuba and get some men and a maid then go to Atlanta. She didn't want anyone in Cuba to know where they lived because of Raul. She stressed that to him and he said for her to come to New York with him. She told him he needed to trust her. They showered and left.

He called Gloria and told her he was boarding the plane from Vegas to New York and to meet him at the airport and to have him two Glocks ready. He looked at himself in the mirror. He looked like a made man, a boss to be. He was dressed in a blue pinstripe suit, blue Stacy Adams gators with a white and blue brim hat that cost Relena 10g's. He was truly a made man and he was only 23-years-old. He figured he would run the underworld for a long time cause he wasn't trying to die.

The plane landed and Gloria and Jenny were waiting on him as soon as he came out of the turnstiles. She looked like a million dollars, long wavy black hair and a long white dress that looked to be tailor made. It accented her body perfectly. Her shoes were perfect he noticed.

"Jenny, this is Rav."

They spoke and he looked her body over. He hugged her and walked to the Limo. Once they got inside she took off his jacket and put on his shoulder holster. She told him she knew he had rapped in prison and she wanted him to be on her next song.

He laughed and kissed her cheek, "Young Gloria we have a lot to talk about. Believe me when I say we do, let's just go to your apartment."

On their way home, the ride was in silence. Jenny was amazed by him because the only mafia she had ever seen was on TV. She knew he didn't like to talk that much and she could tell his heart was heavy. When they got to her apartment he noticed all the winos hanging out front. He asked her why they were there? She explained to him that they watched the place for her. He explained to her that she was making a place for the Feds if one wasn't already there. He said that she wouldn't know until it was too late and she had 24 hours to move some place safer. She agreed and told the driver to take them to the Ritz Carlton.

She called and reserved another apartment and was told it would be ready by noon the next day. Rav looked at his Rolex and smiled cause that gave her a whole day. Jenny went into the hotel and checked them in, they walked in arm in arm. People began to realize who she was and Jenny told her to run to the elevator. They didn't need to have any pictures of them together.

Once they were on the elevator she pushed the buttons for four different floors. They got off on the 5th Floor and then walked up to the 6th Floor. The room was a lot bigger than the one in Atlanta. The furnishings were extravagant and the bedroom had two large beds and the robes were monogrammed in the bathroom.

They went into the first room and she kissed him and then asked him to make love to her. He told her to sit down and let him explain something to her. Deep down inside he knew he was gonna have to sleep with her to prove his loyalty, because she had proved hers so many times before.

"Gloria, what I'm gonna tell you is gonna tear you down. What's done is done though. I'm married."

"Your what? I'm not hearing you Ravenion!" She jumped up and started pacing the floor, she balled her fist up and looked him in the eye.

"You betrayed me! I'll kill you!" she yelled.

She swung at him, he laid back on the bed and rolled off to his feet. She tried a round house kick and he grabbed her when she turned and slammed her to the bed. He climbed on top of her and pinned her arms to the bed.

"Listen to me, I don't love Relena. Raul has a hit on my head, Nikko is gonna try to kill me! You already know this! Relena is the last of their family members besides Raul. I had to do this to play my position. I'm not fixin to let Alex or Nikko kill me! If your love for me is as strong as you say it is you'll understand."

"Rav, I'm tired of being number two in your life!"

"Baby girl, you've never been number two in my life. My life is in your hands, how can you be number two in my life. You're trained to protect me and you even trained me back in Cuba. If something goes down I trust you with my life!" She broke her right arm loose and slapped him.

"I'm good enough to bodyguard you but not love you! This ain't no damn movie! This is real life! Real emotion! You don't play with people, people hurt! Every song I wrote was a message to you, I don't care about no power move! Me and you against the world, Bonnie and Clyde!"

"You got money and power and followers, nothin you can say will win me over because your only thinking about yourself. I hate your fucking guts!

I know you thought you could fuck me and I would be straight, I'll be damned!"

"What's the difference between now and then? I was a different man then! Now that I'm married you nut up, you just shot a dagger to my heart! I can't believe you think you're a sex toy to me."

"Don't play mind games with me and don't try to change the subject! Here you want to fuck me? My legs are already up, pull my panties to the side and fuck me!" He laid on top of her while she cried and then just held her.

"Gloria I'll forever love you whether you believe me or not. It will be you and me in the end. Husband and wife remember these words."

"I already killed Nikko, I used the dart I was saving for Sonya. I heard him tell Alex he was gonna kill you so I pretended to be a Chinese messenger at Sun Son, so he will be dead soon. That new disease is the new aids. I really wish you would just stay out of my life Rav."

"Gloria, are you sure this is what you want?"

"Didn't you say one time before you know your feelings are real is when your tears feel like acid? Well, my tears are burning my face."

He leaned over and kissed her face. He then told her to call the driver and go to the warehouse on Prospect. She used the phone and he got up and walked out without looking back. When he walked into the living room Jenny was watching TV. He gave her a number and told her to call him daily with a report on how she was doing. He told her to let him know when her sales drop.

He got on the elevator and went to the lobby. When he got to the Limo he was so mad a tear dropped cause this was the third time he didn't keep his word. Sandy, Mary, and now Gloria. He opened the door and told the driver to go to Prospect.

On the way, he called her. She was still crying, she yelled into the receiver, "Didn't I tell you to stay out of my life, I know it's you now stay out of my life!"

Neither one of them hung up, they just listened to each other breath. The driver parked in front of the warehouse, he rang the bell on the outside of the door. The camera looked down at him and someone popped the door. When he came through the door Nikko, Alex and Chin ran up to him, Nikko coughed twice so he didn't hug him. He told Nikko he was coming down with a cold.

They showed him all of the dope, the weed, pills, all of the first shipment. They asked what his plans were and he said not to rush because they had about 25 million to send over. He told Chins guard, a tall female to go get a roster of all the New York police.

But all she did was disrespect him when she said, "I don't take orders from you and my name is Amali." He looked at her and told Chin he needed to learn how to tame his animals before he ended up short one soldier.

"As a matter of fact, no deal! I don't train my people to respect no suit!"

Chin spoke to her in Chinese and pointed at the ground. Amali knelt down to his feet and kissed them and said she was sorry. She didn't know he was the Young Don and it would never happen again. She jumped up and told him it would take her a day or two to get all the info he requested. He told her he wanted their next of kin also, then she left.

They got into the Limo and Nikko started coughing up blood, so they rushed him to County General. Mr. Chin signed him in and Alex and Rav waited in the car. After two hours he finally came back and told them the doctor said there's no hope for Nikko. Alex told them to take him to Cuba because they had the best doctors in the world.

When Chin came out with him they had an IV going in his arm. Alex called and got the jet fueled and a doctor on standby. Rav called Relena and told her to come to Cuba because Nikko was very ill. She told him she had found a house and she was on her way.

They drove to the airport in silence, boarded the jet and Rav looked at Alex and saw the look on his face. Rav wanted to kill him right then. Instead he called Arod and told him to have everyone at the hospital. Three hours later Smokey was standing at the airport with the doc. He was happy to see his own men on point. As they were putting Nikko on the stretcher Relena landed so they all rode to the hospital together.

He called Gloria and told her to come to Cuba, he needed everyone for support. When they arrived at the hospital Nikko was attended to right away. Helen cried on Rav's shoulder, Alex paced the floor and Relena tried to keep everyone calm. They all watched Nikko through the door. They could see his heart rate was dropping.

Relena had the baby and went to comfort Helen. Relena was used to death. The tarot cards had told her he was gonna die anyway. But they told her Rav was gonna do it. The more she thought the more she realized that maybe Rav was gonna die too. She cried, confused because she didn't want to lose her husband.

Everyone was breaking down except Smokey, Leo, and Rav. He told Smokey to tend to Helen while he tended to his family. He walked her out of the view of everyone, she told him what the tarot cards had told her. But

Nikko is dying of natural causes. She told him she didn't want to be a widow. She had enough money to take care of them forever. He didn't have the heart to tell her he was the cause of the death because he too wanted to chop his head off. He rocked them both to sleep.

Later, Alex came and told them Nikko had died at 3:45 a.m., Friday, March 10th. He woke her and told her the news, she handed him the baby and ran to Nikko's bedside. She just lost her brother who could she go to for help? Raul was considered dead and wasn't coming back or out of hiding.

She looked at Rav and said, "You're all I got, I can't lose you. I'm ready to be a mom and a wife."

Everybody looked at her crazy, by that time Gloria had walked up and heard her statement to him. She felt crazy, she just pushed him into marrying Relena.

Everybody had crazy thoughts as the nurse came to wheel him away. A couple of bosses came to her and told her that her brother was a wonder boss and she was next of kin so she was the new boss. She had to appoint someone to run the underworld for her.

She looked at them and told them, "My brother hasn't been dead an hour yet and y'all are already looking for his replacement."

She looked at the Dutchman and the Italian and asked their names. The Italian answered Frank Mercado and the Dutchman was named John McAdoo. She told them the day after her brother was cremated a meeting was going to be held in the dining hall. Rav told them to get word to everyone and bring their right-hand men also.

Frank looked at John and said, "He just don't know he's through."

Rav looked at him and said just bring your men and let the people decide. He didn't want to show any violence, so he let them talk, Relena told him he was right it wasn't gonna go as they thought.

She said, "They have no respect for the dead or my family. Before noon that day I want them both dead."

He smiled at her and said, "Whatever you want Boss."

Gloria told her everything was gonna be alright and she had her back no matter what. She told her she wanted her to stay doing her music.

The truth is, she didn't want her around Rav, because he was her only family and she wasn't gonna let no one take him away.

They left and went back to the palace, Smokey and Leo were living like kings in Cuba. They had servant houses two rows down from Nikko. It was the highest rank one could get besides Rav. He called them to the gate and told them to enjoy themselves because it was about to be on. He told the guards not to let anyone in or out. He sent extra guards to protect Relena. He called Hassan and asked him to come. He sat at the kitchen table with a note pad and a pen writing down his different states and what he was looking for out of each one. Hassan opened the door and walked into the kitchen. He saw Rav was writing up the plan and walked around and began to massage his shoulders.

"My friend, everything you've done, you've done from impulse, am I right?"

"Yes!"

"So, you don't need no blue print you are the blue print. You don't need no evidence left behind. That's how you go to prison. Sonya called and asked me for some help, she wants me to show her chemist how to make the Superman. I told her I couldn't betray you. She wanted me to give her ingredients and walked her through everything. How about I make a way for you and your family to come and live in the U.S.? I told her I'm gonna raise my kids in Cuba. To be honest Rav I really want my kids outta Cuba."

"So, you telling me you plan on taking her up on her offer?"

"No! I'm asking you to do it!"

"I can't protect you in the U.S."

"I'm willing to take that risk. I hear Raul has a hit on your head and anybody will take the hit."

"Hassan, don't worry I'm gonna make a call right now and have your family housed. Once in the U.S. all you'll set up the labs and check them every week. I'm gonna give you three stores and get your wife on as a teacher over in the U.S. Do you have a place you wish to stay?"

"I want to stay in Alabama, York Alabama. It's small and I can settle down good cause I've got a hundred-grand saved up."

"That's all the money you've earned since you've been home?"

"Yes! That's all Nikko has paid me. He told me he moved me out of your house because you wanted to sleep with my wife."

"I never wanted her, I could have had her the same day I got you out. I told you about the oranges, so why would I sleep with her while you were in my house? I wanted you to feel comfortable. But enough of that! I want you to have me enough work to take over all of New York and New Jersey."

"I already got that. I have two shipments of each drug already."

Rav picked up his phone and called John and told him to set up a home and three stores in York, Alabama for Mr. Raymand Hassan. Also, to get with the Mayor and set up his wife with a teaching job and get his kids in school.

Hassan smiled because him and his family were out of Cuba. John told Rav to check out Cali and China Town. Rav told him he wasn't trying to take over the whole world. John laughed and told him the only difference between him and Scarface was that Scarface was on TV and he was for real. He said the world wasn't ready to meet the real Tony Montanna. They both laughed and he promised to check things out.

He hung up and thought to himself, *"Now that would be a nice job for Leo and Smokey. He called them and told them they were going to Chinatown after the service, one take the south side and the other the west side."*

He wanted them separated so they couldn't be taken out together. Rav told them to get some of the men from Atlanta and he said no because he didn't know who the Feds had flipped.

Smokey hit him with a real low blow when he asked about Cindy. Rav told him he hadn't had any contact with her but he was gonna check on her. Smokey told him he believed she was the one who gave them up because he found out she was working with Sonya. Rav told him he was wrong because Sonya and her sister was tricking her for the money so he told her to leave with everything. He told him that's why he gave them so much money in Cali. Smokey laughed and told him he was something.

Just before he hung up, he heard Relena beating on the door. He told Smokey to open the door as soon as he did she went to yelling.

"Where is Rav? I know he's with Gloria! Ain't Poco here? The guards said he left but the car is still here!"

"Relena, he might have taken the Benz or the Bentley."

"Smokey, where is my husband?" Rav knew she was scared, so he told Smokey to hand her the phone.

"Wifey! Wifey! Where is your trust?"

"Where are you? I need you here with me and the baby. I walked house to house trying to find you. Then I went to Gloria's and all the lights were out. She's not on this compound and neither is Poco. What's going on? I need you here to protect us. You don't know what's on these people's mind. Everybody will be here in the morning. These guards won't let us leave! Come and get us now!"

"I'm on my way, be at the front gate waiting on me."

Hassan looked at him and told him marrying Relena was a good decision. They both smiled and walked out. Hassan drove a brown Bronco and was parked behind Rav so he took his to the palace.

She didn't want to ride in the Bronco cause it had no style or class but she did it anyway. Her and the baby was standing at the gate with two guards. After they climbed in the guards saw them off.

"Rav showed no respect. They just let her get in without checking the truck."

"That's why we're leaving Cuba, they can kill me quick here. It would be harder to kill me on the street. Once I build this Army I'm gonna go against them."

"See Boss, that's what I'm talking about, you too damn smart!"

Relena leaned over in his arms, Nidiya wasn't asleep but she wasn't crying either. He played with ear and she just giggled. He wondered about Nodiya and what she was up to?

Relena read into his thoughts and said, "Don't worry we'll get her back."

His phone rang and he answered it, "Hello."

There was no response, just breathing. He knew it was Sonya. He didn't bother to look at the number and her breathing got harder like she was crying.

"Sonya, why are you crying?"

"I'm not crying, I just wanted to hear your voice. I love you Juan!"

"What are you scared of?"

"I just got word Nikko died of that new aids, I'm in the hospital now getting tested. I want this beef to end today. I want to spend my last days with my family. Just you, me and the twins. How is my baby doing?" He put her on the phone and she giggled into it.

"That's right everything's gonna be alright. I'm writing a book Rav so they'll know us. Know what we stand for and know through this war we loved each other. I've been thinking about this all day since I got the news. You remember how Forest married Jenny and she died at home? That's what I want Juan. Me, you, and the girls at home here in Atlanta. The house I bought for us. I saved your life, you owe me that much. You owe me that one wish." The doctor called her into the office.

"Sonya don't hang up the phone, we'll face the news together."

"Mrs. Anderson, there's no trace of the virus in your blood. You're a very healthy young lady. I ran two tests since your partner died of the disease but no sign of anything, you're clean and healthy."

"Rav forget everything I just told you. I'll catch you in traffic. I want my baby!" She hung up and Relena smiled.

"That's just like a bitch, they think they're gonna die so they make things right. As soon as they find out there's hope again they get back bitchy. I'm gonna kill that bitch myself. I promise you that! She won't destroy my family!"

As they pulled in the driveway, Relena sat up and looked. She asked where was the guard and the cameras? He told her he didn't fear death then he asked why she was saying something about it now? She never said anything about it before.

She just kissed him and said, "I got to protect my family."

They got out and walked in the house, Hassan left and they put Nidiya in her bed, cut the monitor on and walked downstairs. He laid on the sofa and watched the wide screen TV. She went into the kitchen and got two wine glasses and a nice red wine. She saw his pad on the table and read it. She smiled cause she saw he was gonna take over the states. He even had them a home in every state. That's what she loved about him.

He always had things planned out. She brought the pad and handed it to him. She told him to memorize all the info in it cause she was gonna burn it. He tore 8 pages out and threw them in the fire. He then started writing out the plans for Nikko's funeral. She poured the wine and laid in his lap, she was happy and safe. He put the pad on her stomach while he wrote. She watched him and his ways while he wrote.

He looked up at the TV, it wasn't on and he asked her if she wanted it on and she said, "No, she was watching the Ravenion Nalls Show, Live!" and laughed.

"You know, when Nikko became a made man he watched Scarface, The Untouchables and The God Father for a month straight. So, are you gonna watch them?" she asked.

"Ain't nothing Hollywood about me," he answered, "I really don't want this position. There are times I want it and times I don't. I really just want to live my life with my family. I don't want to run or put y'all in danger. So, this is once again an ungodly act of God."

"Don't think like that, stop blaming God for everything. It's just your turn, your time to shine. I'll forever protect you and I mean forever, you've got to believe that."

He kissed her and she turned over and watched TV. He continued to write his service plan and when he finished he watched her. She was so beautiful, he ran his hands through her hair and kissed her.

"I love you wifey." She smiled and told him she was sleepy, no sex just embracing and enjoying one another.

He was with that cause he was drained and that was her way of saying she needed to be comforted. He kept the pad on her stomach, picked her up and took her upstairs. He put her on the bed and watched her undress and laid down beside her. She undressed him, he raised up so she could pull the covers down and then over them. She settled in his arms and started crying.

"I'm afraid Rav, I don't wanna lose you. I really do love you. Rav, why did Nikko have to die? We didn't really get along because no one had time for me because I was a girl. Now look at me, I got to run the business cause Raul is a coward. He's running and don't even know he's free." He knew she wanted answers, but he didn't want to over talk himself or make any promises to her.

He remembered something Sandy told him, "Most people just want to be heard."

So, he just listened and showered her with lots of hugs and kisses. She loved him more for that. She fell asleep awhile later and he fell asleep a little later.

Just before dawn, she heard someone messing with the front door. She got up and slid the 9mm out put on the black silk robe and went downstairs and got behind the door. She looked at the baby monitor and sighed. If it wasn't for that someone would have killed them.

She looked up and saw Rav coming down the stairs in his black nylon boxers with his gun in his hand pointed towards the door. He got on the other side and waited for it to open. It was Alex and the two men who asked Relena about leadership. There were three females with them and when they saw the guns pointed at them they threw their hands in the air.

He looked at the floor and saw beer running from the bottles. He put the tech up and asked Alex what he thought he was doing?

Alex answered, "Just trying to have some fun with these hookers. You know we can't bring them to the palace."

"How in the fuck you bring someone to our home Alex! This is pure disrespect to me, my husband, and my child! You've brought all of these people here and you don't even know if one of them wants to kill us or not! That's two strikes, one more and your gone! Now get these people out of our house and clean this beer up!"

She pulled the gun back out and marched him to the kitchen to get the broom and stuff. He handed all of it to the hookers and told them to clean up.

She was furious and yelled, "How in the Hell did they get off the compound?! Now you see why I don't want to be on the compound? You're the boss and you gave the order for no one to leave and they did it anyway right by all the guards!"

"Relena, the man apologized!"

"I don't care Rav! You can walk up the steps but you gonna hear me! I don't care if he apologized, you see why I want some damn guards? I don't trust no one. They came here to kill us and you know it! I like Alex but I don't trust him. I want his father Ralph to run Cuba while we're away. I just don't trust Alex!"

He liked what he was seeing, she didn't even wake him. She was gonna handle everything by herself. He told her he knew now he could sleep, in peace with her.

She got mad about that and told him to go to sleep. Then she called and had six guards sent and some cameras hooked up. When she got off the phone he pretended to be asleep.

"You ain't asleep! So, you can't trust me, huh? I bet you can trust that bitch Gloria, huh?"

He didn't say nothin, he just turned over on his stomach trying to hide his smile and laugh. He couldn't stop cause she was fussing.

"I've been pouring my heart out to you and this is what I get in return? Fuck you, Rav! I'm lying beside my enemy!"

She slapped him on the back and he just laughed and rolled over and said, "Girl, I said that to make you feel special. I've been laughing the whole time!"

"Fuck you! Fuck you, Rav!" she yelled as she tried to stay mad but couldn't, she couldn't hold it in and she laughed with him.

He snatched her down on the bed, opened her robe, and started blowing on her belly making farting sounds. They were laughing like kids and then the baby started crying. She jumped up and went to change her, then she warmed a bottle and fed her.

"Relena, cooked some grits, eggs, toast, and bacon!"

"What's wrong with you cooking? Let me eat your cooking!"

He laughed and got the pans and toaster out. She sat the baby on the table and buttered some bread.

"Girl, your cheap, you know, that right?"

"Naw, Benson you're a good butler!" she laughed.

He cooked and she set the table. He put the food on their plates. They said grace and began to eat. After they were finished she bathed the baby and then they showered together.

She told him every day sex ruined a relationship, to her surprise he agreed. They got dressed and they both put on blue and white with matching Jordans. Her hair was in a ponytail and she put on a blue and white Jumpman fitty cap and some no medicine clear frame glasses. She turned and looked at him, he laughed at her. She looked like Whitley from a Different World. She grabbed his platinum Gucci link with a 20-inch cross on it.

"Do I look American?"

"Yeah! You look like one of us, let's ride!"

"Where are we going?"

"We're going to prepare for Nikko's funeral. I'm going to hold the service myself since he will be cremated. The way I see it, we can cremate him in the morning, after that have a gathering, eat and stuff like that. I'm gonna set up candles around a big picture in his front room and we have to get someone to relight the candles daily."

"So, your gonna talk at his service?"

"Yeah, then we're goin to the funeral home and watch the cremation. After everything is set up I'm gonna give it to them raw and uncut. Relena, if I have to kill everyone like I did before, I will. Our family is gonna rule this whole world. I'm even in on Vegas so we'll be traveling a lot. I got someone to take care of Nidiya."

"No Hell you don't! I'm gonna keep her by my side, she's my responsibility!"

"So, you don't need no babysitter?" he asked.

"What I need is someone who will travel with us."

"I can't have her with us all the time. Trying to protect both of you will be hard. That's why I want y'all in Atlanta."

"Hell No! I won't sit home and wait for that phone call. Relena, Rav is dead or Rav got locked up. I'm side by side with you not because I'm jealous but because I love you! Ride or die!"

"That's why we need a keeper for the baby, listen to yourself. You're in the streets with me. If they come at me they'll know they got a war on their hands. I told you I'm fixin to build baby! I believe I can take this world by storm, I'm the unwanted don, that means what I say goes!"

"No, we're the unwanted don's what we say goes! We're a team Rav! Okay, let's get all the cards on the table. I knew Mary was fixin to die, I told her when all of us was in this house together. I also knew I had to catch you vulnerable, trapped in different emotions. I knew the only way to catch your emotions and keep you focused was to make love to you, because you think with your dick! I knew once I made passionate love to you and showed you the real me, open up the worlds to you, I'd have both of my dreams, which was you. I've prayed for you my whole life! I couldn't see you going back to Sonya but I knew you would cause y'all always find your way back to each other. When I turned that last tarot card I seen Nikko dyeing. I also saw you killing Nikko or him dying because of you. When Mary died I thought you would kill Nikko but he died on his own. Which is funny cause no one he deals with has AIDS. Ain't that funny? My second dream was to run my family business because they always put the business before me. By you being Nikko's right-hand man that makes you my right-hand man. I knew they would out vote me or take over by force. Meaning killing both of us. So, I married someone I knew they feared. They didn't fear Nikko. Look at how they tried him with the money. Nikko had informants around him. They fear you Rav. So, you become the new boss through me, so that makes it an us not a you! It's like pieces on a chess board. The little guys like you are real important. If you push your pawn right you get a bishop or a night or the most powerful piece on the board, the Bitch! I know you pushed your pieces but I pushed mine even better. You got a queen and I got a king. Side by side we rule the whole game. I know you thought you was the only one jamming, It's no longer a game between us. Rav, lets war against them, not against each other. You know us Cubans don't go out bad, so are we partners in this world or are we separate enemies?"

"Relena you're something else!"

Not wanting to show the surprise at being played in the game by a bitch, he just laughed and walked downstairs. She grabbed the baby and walked behind him.

"Ravenion. I'm still your wife. I'm just not as week as you thought I was. I'm not gonna let you play me weak. I'll always worship the ground you walk on."

She got mad with herself for killing his ego, but she didn't like that, "I" shit and she wanted them on the same page. She read his expressions, they stared at each other in front of the door. His expression called her a bitch.

"This Bitch! This slick Bitch!" were his thoughts.

He looked at her and thought to himself, *"The Bitch was playing me all along, I got to kill her!"*

He opened the door and saw the people and the guards hooking up the cameras, he didn't even close the door behind him, because he wasn't coming back to this house again.

She waited on him to open the door for them, he was so torn that he forgot. He just cranked the car and started to pull off.

She slapped the windshield and he stopped. She opened the back door and put the baby in the car seat and closed the door; she flipped him the bird and walked in the house.

He felt as if he had to show her it didn't matter who tricked who, she was a bitch and a bitch wasn't going to dis him. He parked the car and left it running while he walked in the house. He heard her upstairs going through the drawers, she didn't hear him come up the stairs.

She was speaking in Spanish saying, "Fuck it! I'll do it all myself, soft emotional ass American Nigga! Killed all those people and catch feelin like a bitch because he didn't get what he want. Dumb ass nigga got everything he wanted, stupid ass nigga!"

When she slammed the last drawer, stood up, turned around her eyes widened in surprise. Him being mad and understanding what she said, he slapped her down to the floor. She rolled off her stomach to her back and pulled a 9mm from under her shirt.

Shocked the shit out of him cause the bitch really was gangsta. She pointed the gun at him and told him, "Get back before I bust a cap in your ass!"

He took two steps back and lifted his shirt showing her he wasn't armed. He turned around walking toward her and reached under his arm and pulled the Kiltech out.

She started screaming, "You need to tighten up you tried me!"

Walking toward him with the gun pointed at his kidney, before she knew it he round housed her making her drop the gun. She looked up and saw the Kiltech she dropped to her knees begging for some understanding.

"Get up wifey!" trying to calm her before he killed her.

"Relena, I don't take no disrespect from no nigga so I damn sho ain't gonna take it from no bitch. You say you want to be on the same page, we'll never be on the same page. Just understand your position. Your position is that of a bitch an outright bitch. If you don't understand a bitches position you better learn one quick! I ain't got no problem putting this Kiltech to work in you. From this day forward its nothin but business between me and you. There's nothin feminine about you, you just a nigga to me, you got that?"

"You're full of shit, it just shows your insecure about your manhood. Most men would be happy to have someone like me on their side. If you wouldn't have married me you wouldn't be the boss. You still be a run and shoot Mutha Fucka! Taking orders, never being able to voice your own opinion, you'll be what you are an enforcer. That's all!"

He slapped her down again because he was gonna kill all the bosses anyway so she was just wasting her breath. She grabbed the 9 while laying on her back and pointed it up at him.

"If you put your hands on me one more time we'll die her together. I'm a Cuban and them guys out there will kill you and the baby out there. You're not the only ruthless human on earth."

He walked up on her, put the Kiltech between her eyes, grabbed the nine and put his foot in her throat and told her to stay out of his life.

"You are not Scarface, you don't own the world, that's Hollywood Ravenion. You need to wake up before you die an early death. They're gonna kill you Rav."

He walked out and she laid there crying cause she just destroyed her dream and most importantly her marriage. She jumped up and ran behind him but he was already gone, him and her baby. All she had to do was keep quiet and play the backseat. But no! She had to open her big mouth! She pulled out the tarot cards and asked the Gods if it was over. She turned over a running horse so she jumped up and looked for the keys in the bedroom. Then she remembered she saw them hanging on the kitchen wall. She ran downstairs and grabbed the keys to the black and white 68 Chevelle. She jumped in and cranked it up. She asked the guards at the gate which way he went? He told her left so she knew he was going to the morgue. So, she turned around and hauled ass.

He was only about 10 or 15 minutes ahead of her. The morgue was only 30 minutes away from the house so she could catch him before he got there. She seen him and turn left, he wasn't going to the morgue he was going to the farm. She rode behind him, he parked in front of the blue farm known as the ex-farm. The farms stood 400 feet from each other. He grabbed the baby and walked in and she followed him. He was talking to Hassan, she listened undetected.

He told Hassan to triple the shipment, Hassan told him it might be too much for the ship. Rav suggested using three ships, two for the drugs and one for a decoy.

Relena argued it wasn't safe and the tunnels from Cuba to Key West were best, under the water.

They could ship six times the amount. She told them to ride down the coast with her. She had some whales and dolphins that could travel nonstop. "These will be controlled by computers and can be monitored by their heart beat. They can move 50 times the dope and send the money back. Their equipped with blades in case they are caught by nets. If someone intercepts them our computer expert will protect the drugs. After Key West we can move them to Cali and have traffic from coast to coast.

Being nationwide is the goal and I have a lot of spots under my control that I've been shipping to on the down low.

Rav, please understand we will still be under your command. I just wanted to voice my opinion and give you new ideas to go nationwide. I have everything mapped out. This has been a six-year process. It has cost over 30 million dollars. He looked at Hassan and smiled, they walked out and got in the Chevelle and drove down the coastline. When they stopped they didn't see anything but trees and sand. She walked them through some trees and right to a camouflage house.

Inside they saw maps on all the walls with red point makers all over them. There were three rooms in the house and one had computers and two beautiful females. She showed them the rundown and showed them how they would keep up with all the shipments.

Rav couldn't believe it, he was fucking with a drug wizard. He knew he had struck gold with her. He didn't want her to know his pleasure so it would be guaranteed success.

"Great job Relena now let's go and check on Nikko's service. You'll have to stay behind and make sure everything is packed, Then I want you to get on a jet to meet the shipments and that means you'll need lots of boats."

"I already got them! Have you ever heard of Fresh Catch Seafood? My grandfather started it years ago. That's how my family got into the drug game without Fordel knowing."

"So, are these boats everywhere?" he asked.

"All over and Cubans run them so they know what time it is."

"Handle your business then. Now take us back to the farm."

She could tell he was pleased but she knew it wouldn't last long so she just went along with it. When they got back to the car he sat in the back holding the baby.

Hassan noticed the tension between them so he said, "A house divided against itself will fall." Neither of them answered so he drove the rest of the way in silence.

As soon as they arrived, Rav put the baby in her seat and left in the Benz. She looked at Hassan and said she thought she had destroyed her marriage by being straight with him. He told her to just be cool cause as soon as the money started rolling in he would come around. She kissed his cheek and left for the service.

When she arrived and saw Rav watching the mortician embalm Nikko. The body would be ready for cremation the next morning. He called the palace and told Jody, the housekeeper to set up a thousand seats on the beach. He also wanted someone to sing, *"Born By The River."* He told her to put the big picture of Nikko in the main hall with candles encircling it. She told him it would all be ready.

He hung up and called Alex and let him know he was now the overseer of South Cuba. Rav told him he was still over all the shipments and his pay was a hundred thousand a year. Before he hung up he told him he would see him at the funeral. He looked at Relena and didn't say a word. When he got into the Benz he called and got the jet fueled, he was flying to Simi Valley California. He just pulled off cause he knew she would follow him. He looked and she was right behind him.

When he arrived at the airport he boarded the jet. When she approached the jet, he closed the hatch and told the pilot to take off. He saw her pick up the phone so he told the pilot if she called to tell her he was making a quick trip to Atlanta and would be back in 10 hours. She stood staring so he just laid his head on the glass.

He smiled to himself cause he really didn't have a reason to be mad at her. She's just trying to keep her family; he almost called her but he knew he couldn't break.

Nidiya was a great baby, she didn't wine or cry. It's like she knew what was going on. That's why he had to get her somewhere safe.

He needed to see his little man. He wondered what they were telling him about his dad. He hoped he understood all that was going on. All he remembered was Tasha's sleepy face and it is going from happy to sad cause she had to return to witness protection.

He called Nina and asked her where they were in Simi Valley. She told him they were at 1632 Walnut Grove. She had drawn out 2 million when she went in and had been spending wisely. She told him the house was under surveillance and to be careful.

When he hung up he looked at Nidiya and she was looking up at him smiling. He picked her up and talked to her as he walked her around. "Well baby I can only hope you'll understand this move one day. I'm gonna have to send you to your big brother and stepmom. She loves you just like Sonya.

"Your daddy might die in the next few days, so I just want you safe cause I love you," she said as she wrapped her hand around his finger. He saw both strength and hurt in her eyes.

He saw Relena cry for the first time that day. She really loved the baby, she loved both of them. She cried when Nodiya got taken, she will probably go crazy now that Nidiya is gone.

He checked with the pilot to make sure he had a car and driver waiting for him. The pilot said they would be landing in 5 minutes and the car would be waiting.

The plane landed on a private airstrip, the car was waiting. He asked the white driver where he was from, he showed his credentials and helped load the baby in. Rav sat in the back and told the driver where to go and sat back for the ride.

As they traveled, he kept a close eye out for tails and didn't see any. After about 30 minutes they were there. It was a big pretty white house. There were four steps leading up to a beautiful porch. There were two swings for the children and a big screen and glass door leading into the house.

As he approached the house he had some second thoughts about what he was doing but he needed to secure his daughter. He knew he was punishing Relena but he knew he was doing the right thing. He turned the knob and entered without knocking. Nancy was sitting on the couch.

She looked over her shoulder and said, "Oh My God, Juan! Tasha, Richard! Y'all hurry down here!" She had to pinch herself to make sure she wasn't dreaming.

Richard was the first one down the stairs. When he saw who it was he went to him and hugged him.

"Well Richard, I see your coming around. No suit or tie just black pants and a T-shirt. Old Gangsta ha!"

"Juan are you okay? How did you know where we were at? Tasha told us what you did and why she came back. You really surprised me."

"Where is Lil Juan?" Nancy stood up. She was wearing a nice white shirt and tight-fitting jeans.

She answered him and said, "He's right here on the floor asleep. What do you have there?" He handed her Nidiya and went to pick his son up off the floor.

"Wake up little man! You are going to be so tall, wake up!"

He looked at the clothes Tasha had him dressed in. Blue Air Force Ones, Polo shorts and matching Polo shirt.

The child woke up and looked around the room. Nancy said to him, "This is your daddy!"

He recognized his father but reached for Richard first. As Tasha came down the stairs she nearly broke her neck trying to get to him. She hugged him from behind and kissed his neck.

"Mama! Mama! Daddy! Daddy!"

"Yes Juan, He's your daddy."

Juan hugged and kissed his son. He couldn't hide the tears any longer, his little man was alive. As they sat on the sofa he asked Nancy if they had a camera? She ran upstairs and got it and all of them got real close on the couch for a picture.

"Tasha, this is my daughter Nidiya. Her mother is who tried to kill you. I have another daughter also; Nidiya's twin Nodiya. Sonya killed Mary and took Nodiya out of her arms. I just made "Don" over all the world bosses, I can't raise her Tasha. I need your help. I promise I will never reveal your location to anyone one or put you in danger. I have to find Sonya and get Nodiya back. She's the boss over the Teky Mafia and she answers to no one and she's dangerous."

"Juan you don't have to explain anything to me. I'm glad you trust me enough to raise Nidiya. Her last name is Ellis, right?"

"Yes, I'll have to get her birth certificate for you. I had to come without any guards. Your house is under surveillance. I'll drop by from time to time. Remember if you call me to call from a secure line."

He turned to leave and they hugged on the porch and as he walked away he said a small prayer, "Lord please protect my girls, especially Nodiya."

When he got to the airport he felt strange without his little girl. Then the pilot called and told him he needed to get to the plane cause the Feds were on their way to the airstrip.

He jumped out of the Limo and gave the driver a wad of bills and hauled ass to the jet. As they got in the air he could see the Feds swarming all over the air strip. He laughed and called Tasha and told her what just happened.

"They came and what did they say?"

"They wanted to know where you had gone. I told them you came and dropped the baby off. You know my father is a lawyer, so he drew up guardian papers. I showed those to them and they left. But just before they pulled away they received a call saying a jet was leaving from the airport and they tore out of here. Just try to call every couple of weeks and I'll give you a report, okay?"

Before she hung up she blew him a kiss. As the jet climbed he looked out over the horizon and saw a flash of Sonya's face so he called her.

"Sonya, lets end this beef between our families and bring them back together. I don't feel comfortable with Nodiya there without my protection. Let's bring them together to protect them both. I love you and I miss you!"

"Rav, Nodiya is okay, she's highly protected. On top of that, I got her a keeper that stays with her. The girl says she knows you and she doesn't know about any beef."

"If you try anything I'll kill her. Bring my child back and this beef will be over between us and you'll never see us again. I promise!"

He hung because she was talking stupid he already knew where she was keeping the baby so getting them would be very easy. He would send them to London cause that's where he was going when all of this was over anyway. He closed his eyes trying to block everything out. He knew after today this would never be over.

The ride and the day finally got the best of him and he fell asleep, He dreamed about Blue so he called her when he woke up.

"Hello, Baby girl I miss you! How are you and your child coming along?"

"We're both fine. I'm six months along and it's a little boy. I'm naming him DeJuan."

"Why you gonna do that?"

"Because I want a reminder of you!"

"Blue, is that my baby?" he asked her.

"What makes you think that?"

"Cause you're not six months your four months and that's why I called to check on you."

"You're lying, you don't know how many months I am. Do you want the baby to be yours? What will I tell people about his uncle being his daddy? Juan, I got someone who's willing to take care of us so please don't do this. Just send money from time to time and I promise he'll be okay."

"Okay Blue, I feel you but you call if and when you need help, alright?"

"As long as you promise to stop by and visit from time to time."

"So, is the ole boy making you happy?"

"Yes! He's Black and he's an engineer. We're leaving Seattle next week and going to Europe. We'll come back for a week and then we're leaving for good."

"So, how am I gonna send money?"

"I still got your number and as soon as you take a vacation you can come to see us. I can't wait to feel you. Promise you'll come?"

"I promise."

He hung up and he felt the jet starting to land. He looked down on the runway to the spot where Relena was standing when he left. She was still there! In the same spot!

He laughed cause he couldn't believe she was still there. He was gone for 10 hours! It was dark out and she was sitting on the hood of the car.

When the jet landed and the door opened she was standing there with a look of disappointment on her face and said, "Rav, where's my baby?

"I guess you have to have one before you can claim one."

She started crying, "You know that's a blow to me now where is she so I can go get her?"

He didn't answer her and he walked by her to the Benz When he opened the door he told her, "Niggas don't love nor can they have a child Nigga!"

He closed the door and crunked the car and drove off. She pulled out right behind him. He called Gloria and told her to meet him at his room at the Hilton. He didn't even care that she was following him.

He knew he couldn't fuck Gloria, he just wanted to talk to her. When he arrived at the hotel he got out and wave at everyone and Relena was right beside him, keeping pace with his step all the way.

He hoped Gloria had gotten there to make her jealous, the elevator door opened and he went up to the 13th Floor. She just stared at him and he used his key to open the door. When the elevator door opened Gloria was standing there.

"Oh Hell Naw, she got a key to your floor too?"

"I'm his protector, it's my job to get here and check things out."

"You ain't got to answer her."

They walked out and Gloria opened the door and let them in. All the lights were on, he sat on the sofa and told Gloria he needed her to sing at Nikko's service. He wanted her to sing, *"I Was Born By The River"* in Spanish and in English. She agreed before he could say anything else, she walked out and slammed the door. He jumped up and ran out the door and pinned her to the wall. Relena looked out the door.

"You need to get your act together. This is the last time you disrespect me! You understand?"

He let her go, she pushed her sweater down and said, "Yes Sir! She wanted to say more but she looked over and saw Relena. She truly thought they would be making love by now but the bitch was there. He looked in her eyes and saw the disappointment there.

He smiled and said that's all, she got on the elevator and left. He walked back to the room and closed the door.

Relena went to the bathroom and ran some water in the tub. He ordered food from room service. Steak and salad for himself, he didn't even bother to order for her When she came out of the bathroom she joined him in the living room. He was sitting on the sofa; the fire was burning in the fireplace.

She walked to the stereo and put on some Keith Sweat, *"Make It Last For Ever"* filled the room. She walked over and knelt down in front of him and kissed his right cheek. He watched her as she pulled off her top and bra. She wiggled her tits at him and leaned over and bit the stiffness of his erection. By the sight of his erection she smiled to herself cause she knew they would be making love soon. She stood up, kicked her shoes off, laid in the floor, and then rubbed her toes on his stomach. Then she put both feet on his dick rubbing back and forth smiling at him. He closed his eyes and he leaned back with a smile on his face. He looked at her with lust in his eyes. He wanted her and she knew it. She put her legs up in the air and slid off her pants and panties in one motion, showing him the hairless lips that were demanding his attention. She spread her legs like a stripper and blew him two kisses, turned around and moved her ass up and down. He didn't know she could dance but there were a lot of things about her he didn't know.

She lifted herself up and walked backwards to him on her hands. He was amazed at her strength and mobility. She spread her legs wide and sat down on his lap. She slid in a back and forth motion. She could feel him on her thigh. He relaxed his arms on both sides of the sofa and she noticed he reached and grabbed something. When he raised his arm, he moved her to the side and cut the TV on and the music off. He flipped through the channels and found Sanford and Son and began to watch the TV.

"Rav, what's wrong with you?" she asked.

"What part about I don't see anything feminine about you don't you understand? You need to go take a cold shower because I'll never make love to you again. Your tarot cards should have told you that, or maybe they did, you just don't want to believe it. Go talk to your gods because I don't want to see you or talk to you!"

She got up and grabbed her clothes off the floor and walked away. She couldn't let him see her cry. He wouldn't believe her tears anyway. She got in the water and cried. The phone rang and it was the elevator operator telling him his food was at the door. He asked if the server was searched and was the food checked? He assured him it was and came through the door. When the waitress came in he asked her if she would like to make a thousand dollars?

She asked, "How?"

He looked at her real good and told her to turn around. She was right and had an ass like a ghetto chic.

So he told her, "By having sex with me!"

"Mr. Rav, your wife Relena is here, right?"

"Yes."

"I'm afraid she'll have me killed!"

"Maybe she wants you too!"

He knew it would destroy her to get out of the tub and see him fucking another woman. He hoped she said yes but out of fear and respect she said no and left. He called the elevator operator and told him to tell her to get her ass back in there now! A timid knock at the door and she came back in.

He looked at her legs below the green skirt of her uniform and unbuttoned the vest over her top. He went in his pocket and counted out 10 hundred-dollar bills and stuck them in the left side of her bra. He led her to the bedroom. He could see Relena in the tub so he called for her to come out. He watched her get out and put her robe on and she came into the room.

The waitress had her back to her. He motioned for her to suck him off. She leaned back and took him in her mouth sucking him real slow. Relena's eyes widened as she watched. When she started stepping towards them he reached behind his back and pulled out his 45 and pointed it at her. Tears started to fall from her eyes, she couldn't watch anymore. She went back to the bathroom and closed the door. She knew the girl was only following orders.

Ten minutes later, she saw the girl in the bed riding him, she held her stomach and knelt forward.

"Relena, come and join us."

The girl looked at Relena and knew she had made a mistake. He turned her around and started hitting her from the back as he watched her lay on the floor and cry.

"You see, a boss don't have feelings or emotion. You got to lose everything to become a good boss. Do you hear me?"

She looked up and saw the gun on the table. She jumped up and grabbed it and pointed it at them. She told the screaming girl to get her shit and go. He was still inside of her so he started fucking her harder as she cried.

"I said get the fuck outta here, right now!"

"I can't he's got me!" She walked over pointing the gun at him and slapped him. He just laughed and fucked harder.

"Hold up Relena I'm Cumming!" he laughed and came then let her go.

She jumped up and grabbed her clothes and money and ran to the door

"Stop and get dressed first and go back to work," Relena told her.

He looked at her as she got dressed. He felt so good but it was so bad cause she was fixing to snap. Relena told her if she said a word to anyone she would have her killed. The only reason she was still alive was because she was following his orders.

After she left, Rav just laid in the bed naked and asked, "Relena, you still want to make love?"

"Get up Rav before I kill you!"

He turned over and she put the gun to his head and said, "I mean get your ass out of my bed!"

He just laughed and rolled out of bed facing her. They stood face to face and eye to eye. She didn't see any fear in his eyes. She wanted to be strong like him but she couldn't with rain drops in her eyes. Instead she put the gun to her temple.

"Is this what you want Rav? You want me to get out of your way? I put all of the cards on the table because I didn't want to lose you. I guess honesty don't mean shit to you! I want to be your soul mate, your partner, side by side. Every man needs a strong woman with him; you don't need a weak-minded bitch Rav! You don't need nobody that's gonna suck you, fuck you and kill you! I don't want to be like Nikko, Hell Smokey is fucking Helen! She ain't strong Rav but I am! I know you've had strong women in your life; Sonya, Tasha, Sandy, Gloria, and Mary but where are they now Rav? Huh? I'm stronger than them. I'm not even mad about this situation, I'm mad because you fucked her thinking of me! I made your dick hard not her! You only did it to get at me, you didn't enjoy it! What the fuck do you want from me?"

Tears were streaming down her face. He walked to her and touched her face and opened her robe. He ran his hand from her face to the side of her breast then he lifted her chin and kissed her.

She was so confused, she didn't know if he was testing her or really wanted her. All she knew was she wanted him but then she thought about what he said when he was fucking the waitress, "You had to lose everything to be a great boss." Had he lost everything to be the boss, she wondered?

She remembered the look on the waitress's face. She was enjoying it even though she was scared shitless. She even knew she had nutted because of the smirk on her face as she went out the door. Then she thought of Gloria. Did he call Gloria there to fuck her? The thought made her scream.

As he was kissing her nipples she slapped him with her left hand, and yelled, "Do you think I'm stupid or just a lost and confused bitch? I'm more than a wet pussy, Rav! I got respect for myself!" She pointed the gun in his face, it was her gun.

He laughed and asked, "Do you want to shoot me in the back of the head?"

He turned around and he heard the gun click. He turned back to face her and said, "Do you think I'm stupid enough to keep a loaded gun on my dresser after I just fucked another woman? In your bed?"

"What were you gonna do, kill me yourself?"

"A boss wouldn't have thought murder cause if you killed me you would kill yourself cause you know they would overrule you or take you out. You see who got the upper hand? I do. You think these people respect you? They don't, these people are tired of your family leadership. That's why I did what I did! You should have come to me in the first place and we wouldn't be going through this shit now. Now you see why I called you a bitch? A bitch thinks from her emotion and her pussy. Y'all think your pussy is the answer. You thought you had me pussy whooped but I married you because I wanted a life partner and a friend. Not a gangsta! A bitch can be either smart or she can be stupid and right now you're a stupid one! You thought I was weak for Mary but I wasn't."

"True indeed you are my wife but we can't be husband and wife. Because we're both targets by tomorrow. Don't get me wrong I want to make love to you but I can't get used to having a family and not having one. I'm not always gonna be there with them. That's why I took Nidiya away not to hurt you. At any time, you chose to be my wife they would all be here with you but I ain't got no wife I got a crime partner. I didn't tell you to lay your cards on the table, you chose to do that. I want to feel love!"

"How did I know Nikko was fixin to die? I didn't so you can't say I married you to be a boss. You say ride or die, I don't want that from you. I got Gloria for that!"

"I can't guarantee your safety, you got to do that yourself. I'll never let a sucka get up on you but at this moment you got to prove yourself the same way I did. I didn't fuck my way to the top and neither are you. Raul is in hiding and when he comes out neither of us will be boss unless one of us kills him. To be honest I hope he does come back because I want my family. Tasha couldn't handle it and split so now I'm still looking for that family."

"I want a family too!"

"No, you don't, you want leadership. I'm tired of giving you game when no one gave me shit or took me under their wing. Now get the fucking gun outta my face before I knock you out!"

"It's not loaded so why should you care?"

"You've shot at me before now get it outta my face!"

Before she could move her arm down he hit her other arm with a block and upper cut her with his other palm. She fell to the wall and slid down. He dressed and called the elevator then he got a call from the desk clerk told him there were some mobsters in the hotel bar talking loud about the meeting. He told them to call that same waitress and bring her back to his floor.

Ten minutes later, the elevator door opened. A heavy-set Cuban stood in the door in a hotel uniform. He motioned for him to get in the elevator. The door was closing, then he saw Relena running towards him pointing the gun saying, "Hold the door!"

The door closed and he asked the waitress what her name was, "Kelly Sir!"

"Kelly, are you alright?" he asked.

"I'm scared Sir!"

He hugged her and told her not to be afraid. He was kissing her as the door opened and he saw a lot of the bosses looking their way. Either they looked like they wanted to draw or they were just surprised not to see Relena on his arm.

The door closed and they walked out of the hotel and waited for his car to pull up. After it pulled up they drove off a little ways and he parked the car and told her go back to work. They went in through the kitchen and he went in the office keeping the light off. He wanted to see their reaction when Relena came off the elevator alone. She came out still holding the gun. She looked to the left to see if she could see him. All she saw were the mobsters looking at her and pointing toward the door. Signaling that he was gone.

She went out and got in the Chevy and they came out a couple of minutes behind her. He wondered if she had found the bullets. Then he called Alex and told him to get his people and drive towards the hotel and be looking for the Chevy, he told him a mobsters were behind Relena.

He hung up and ran through the kitchen and out the back to his car. He popped the trunk and took out the Keltech and 64 round clips. He jumped in the car and pulled off, he turned left towards the palace. He knew they were trying to hit her so he drove as fast as he could cause he didn't want nothin to happen to her.

When he caught up to them they were in a black Suburban. He called her but she didn't answer. He texted her a 911 message and she didn't respond to that either. So, he called Angel and had her try. She finally picked up.

"Relena, do exactly as I say. Drive past the palace and look out your mirror, you'll see two Suburban's following you. Why in the fuck did you turn off? Get back on the road so Alex and them can meet you head on. I'm behind the second suburban. Are you loaded?"

"Yes Rav, this ain't no drill! This is real right?"

She turned back on the main road and drove a quarter mile when she saw the Bentley. She slung the Chevy around and jumped out shooting. They ran past the car, the passenger in the first truck started shooting. Rav stopped the Benz and got out in the middle of the street and started shooting. The lights from the Benz lit up the dark street. The second truck slammed on the brakes but the first truck crashed into them. They surrounded the truck and Rav told them to get out. When no one moved they started firing. The driver started bowing the horn and the door opened. Rav got them out and had them lay in the road. Some of them were wounded and gasping for air.

Relena walked up to the driver of the first truck and put a bullet in his head, "Now I'm asking one at a time, who sent y'all?" No one answered so she started shooting and didn't stop until they were all dead except one.

He asked her, "What if I just point out who it was and maybe you give me a job?"

"For what? So, you can turn on us too?"

"Relena give him a chance."

"Rav, I feel everything you told me, I'm not giving no one a second chance to kill me! In the morning you show me who sent y'all and if you kill them then I'll give you a job. Do we have a deal?"

"Yes!"

"What's your name?" Arod asked.

"Marcel"

"Marcel, load them up in the first truck and take them to the palace entrance."

He got and gave his nine and started loading them up. When he was done he drove them to the palace. He parked and got out and went to the trunk. Arod popped it and put Marcel inside and drove around back. They put him in the first house and left one of the females with him until morning.

CHAPTER 15

Grady Hospital

Sonya walked out the doors of Grady Hospital with joy. It was like receiving a second chance at life. She enjoyed the air but most of all she enjoyed seeing her baby girl. Kau stood in front of the Limo wearing a purple body dress. Sonya was dressed in purple also with a white fur. Nodiya finished the set with her purple dress, hat and shoes.

"I hope everything is alright Ms. Sonya."

"Kau, I'm fine, no HIV or AIDS and I got a chance to speak with Rav."

Kau was so surprised, her whole face lit up. She said to Sonya, "I didn't know you knew Ravenion Nalls."

"Didn't you say you were from Africa?"

"Yes, that's where we met. He's the one who funded my education."

Sonya smiled because she knew she had two valuable people that belonged to him now. They got into the Limo and Sonya smiled at her.

"Kau, do you know whose daughter your holding?"

"Is this Ravenion's baby?"

"Yes, she is a twin."

"You must spend time with them on a separate basis?"

"No, he has a child with him and I have one with me, we got into it so I took one and he took one. Childish but it happened."

She didn't want to tell her how she got Nodiya because she might be a loyal bitch of his. She closed her eyes; her mind went back to their conversation. Even though they were at each other's throat he was still willing to be on her side in tough times. He was wrong though, he blamed her for killing a bitch that wasn't even dead. She thought about it and picked up the phone and called him.

"Rav, do you know a girl named Kau?"

"Yes, why you askin?"

"I have her here with me taking care of your child. So now you know I have two of your people with me. Bring me Nidiya so I can mother her."

"Sonya why did you really call me? The doctor said your straight so what's up?"

"Rav, you know Tasha and your son are alive, so why are we still beefing? This makes no sense! We supposed to take this shit over together."

"Sonya, you betrayed me when you slept with Nikko without my permission. Plus, you tried to kill Tasha, then on top of that you killed Mary for no reason. She didn't have nothin to do with any of this. She was only keeping the twins. Then you put a three million dollar hit on my head. You know I can have you knocked off at any given time. If you let one hair on their heads get harmed you are one dead bitch, so you make sure their hair grows long and shiny. Now drop your clique and get your ass home!"

"So, you'll leave Relena?" she asked.

"You know why that happened?"

"Get rid of her and we can run this shit like we planned it."

"I'm not made yet and this bitch has done flipped the script, but any way Sonya, drop the hit before I come back to Atlanta. Any time I feel in danger I'm coming after you, nice speaking with you."

"Sonya your gonna let me speak with him?"

"He hung up, he's in Cuba."

She just dropped her head because her plan went backward. She only slept with Nikko to get information and to help her find Juan Jr., she forgot about the hit. She couldn't let up because Kim asked her was she sure about the hit? She was so angry about him getting married she said yes.

They arrived at her Buckhead home, Kau looked at her when the Chinese female guard wearing a purple suit and tie with a black Glock in her hand, opened the door. Her smile turned to confusion and her skin turned pale. Something about their conversation must have went wrong, she wasn't gonna probe or nothing because she knew she worked for a serious woman and the child she was keeping belonged to a dangerous man. Who she loved.

She got out of the Limo and went into the house, Sonya watched her as she went into the house. She told the guard she wasn't to leave and told her driver to take her to Kim's house in Alpharetta.

She closed her eyes remembering everything the Feds had taught her. She remembered all Rav had taught her about one emotion. No other man in the world could hold her heart. She was gonna tell Kim to take the hit off of his head and it was over.

She wanted her family and she wanted Nidiya. Then she thought about it, there would never be a them as long as money drugs and the streets were in the world.

Kim stayed in the 1200 block with security at the front of the street. The driver showed Sonya ID and a guard came on a motorcycle and escorted Sonya to the big brown mansion sitting in the middle of the circle. The gate opened and they drove up the moon shaped driveway. The grass was even on both sides of the driveway. The Limo stopped at the front door. The guard got off the bike and opened the door. She got out and he led her into the house.

When she was inside she saw all the Chinese culture hanging on the walls. Kim was standing at the top of the staircase wearing a brown suit of fine material. He came down and knelt down at her feet and asked what was bothering her.

He escorted her up the stairs to a big room that was fully equipped with four masseuses. He took off her fur and watched her undress. One of the other females gave her a towel to cover up with and laid her on the table. He laid next to her and they began their massages.

Before she could say a word, he said, "Sandra, one must let go of a lost love, your love is trapped between the worlds. You have become enemies because you had no foundation. Sonya, since I've known you and studied Ravenion, I know he taught you not to act off of emotion and fear. So please help me understand why he have complete control over you? You are a danger to yourself and others when your mind is trapped by thoughts of him. How could you kill so freely and submit to him so easily?"

"I don't know! At times I feel as I need him and I can't breathe without him. I've never loved before him. Have you ever dreamed of the perfect right person? Rav is that person for me. No matter what we go through we always find our way back to each other. He's married but it ain't real. When I went to the hospital this morning I called him. He was willing to come and aide me, he stayed on the phone and we faced the news together. I saved his life and he gave me my life. I don't want to war with him, we had a plan to run this together, now we are solo. He's smart and he can help us. I watched him go from a nickel and dime hustler to a billionaire. He sold me for two billion dollars."

"That's it, you made him and you deserve your share. That should make you angry, that he's sharing you with another woman who means him no good. I just got word he's got a shipment coming in through Savannah in four days. Let's take what's yours, kill the whole boat and let him know we mean business. I know of three of his spots on Bufford Hwy. Let's go and take them over. I have people that will help us kill them off. No Cuban should run Atlanta, you should. This is your place! Let's do this Sandra! Let's take over his dope spots and take what you built! He'll have no choice but to relocate and we'll take that over too!"

"Now you're getting it Sandra, on top of that he'll submit to you. You'll have the power and we use his own drug to beat him!"

Kim smiled because he finally got her thinking. They dressed and went back to the Limo. He called Sili, one of his captains, and told him to get everybody to the warehouse on Fulton Industrial. He looked at his watch, it was 9:43 a.m. He knew this was the right time to hit them, they should be resting.

He asked Sonya about silencers and she told him the only ones were for the Glock 17's and AK's. He looked at her and smiled and said, "That's all we need!"

When they arrived at the warehouse there were all kinds of cars; Benz's, vans and motorcycles. She walked in and saw over three hundred Chinese men and women. She stood at the step while Kim spoke in Chinese to them. He told them that they were on the rise, it was time for Ms. Sonya to get what she paid for. He told them that they were gonna take over Ravenion's spots. He instructed them to kill with no mercy. He told them the names of everyone they were gonna hit. Apple Tree, North Pointe, Leigh Heights, and he paused and said Shallowford Crossing. Everything in a line from Tucker to Duluth, GA.

He told them with all this crime the police wouldn't know where to start. "It's Tuesday morning and people are at work," he explained. Next, he went down a list from Duluth to North Pointe giving out addresses and apartment numbers.

Silence fell over the whole warehouse. Everyone was waiting on orders. Kim and Sonya walked to the rear of the warehouse into the storage room. The weapon was hidden on the shelves inside the entrance. She turned the light on and the shelf folded back out of the way.

Inside the guns were on a cart, she wheeled it out and he saw her walking backward toward him. It took twenty men to lift the box and distribute the guns. He put them in groups of 25 and instructed them to put silencers on.

Sonya got in the Benz with three women in tight body suits with matching jackets. Sonya told them they were just riding to see things through, but if anyone confronted them then they would shoot to kill, police included.

She looked at them and asked if they were family because they all looked alike and dressed alike. One was dressed in red with matching shades and another in blue with the shades and the third with green the same way.

Sonya looked at them all in lust and wondered to herself, "Damn! What the Hell has he turned me into?"

They pulled off behind the bikes and two Chevys, four deep. The ride was quiet, no music, just focus. She didn't realize the girls were looking at her through the mirror. She was surprised when she felt one of the girl's hands rub her thigh. She just smiled and didn't say a word. She patted her hand letting her know it was alright.

Out of the blue, the girl rubbing her thigh said, "My name is Len."

Sonya just laid her head back on the rest and enjoyed the sensation. With her eyes closed she saw bullets coming at her from every direction. She wanted to pull out but it was too late.

As they got off the Buford Hwy Exit they took a right at the end of the ramp onto the highway. She checked her Rolex it was 10:30 a.m. Kids were in school and people were all over, walking up and down the street and in and out of stores.

They turned into some apartments, them in the front and the bikes to the other side. There were three buildings per parking lot. She liked North Pointe, they were quiet and had a pool next to the playground, lots of shops and store nearby.

Sonya asked Len if she would like to live there and she said yes, she would. Sonya had the driver pull down to the last section, she pointed at the last apartment downstairs by the woods.

Sonya got out and walked to the sliding door, she looked and looked back. Len was right behind her and Yenny and Tara were there too. Neither one of them had their guns out.

Sonya knocked on the sliding door. A female opened the curtain and saw them and opened the door. She was a pretty blonde wearing a number 8 Lakers jersey. Yenny asked for Todd, she knew she bought dro from him whenever they were in that neck of the woods. The girl recognized Yenny and they went in and sat on the couch. The living room was flushed out with lots of expensive furnishings. Sonya grabbed the remote and turned the TV on. She put it on cartoon Network and watched Bugs Bunny until Todd or the girl came.

Todd was a big Cuban, about 6'2", 265 pounds. He came down the steps with a pair of sweatpants and no shirt, a Gucci chain hung from his thick neck. He looked at Yennifer and threw 7 fifties at her, she caught them, they were in a sandwich bag.

Sonya turned up the TV and pulled out her Glock 17 and yelled, "Listen, I'm Sonya, Rav's baby's mama. I know you've heard of me so I'm gonna make this brief. I know how Rav roll, I want all the money and all the dope. I know everything isn't in this house, but I want all that's here! Now!"

"I'm sorry Sonya, I don't think you know Rav, he came and got everything two days ago."

"Tara, go upstairs and get that pretty blonde, Yennifer I want you to go to the hardware store and get me a water hose."

After Yennifer left, Tara went upstairs to get her and bring her down. When she saw it was a robbery she dropped to her knees beside Todd. He was standing at the entrance of the living room and the steps. Len and Tara drew their guns and pointed it at Todd, Sonya tucked her Glock into her waistband and laid the fur on the sofa.

She walked over to them and said, "Move over Todd!" He moved over and she knelt down in front of the blonde, eye to eye.

"Listen, I'm gonna ask you a few questions and I just want simple answers. How long you been fucking Todd?"

"A year."

She didn't have any tremble in her voice, she knew she wasn't gonna break just cause some guns were in her face, she had been trained to take all information to the grave with her. She stood up as the girl looked into her pretty green eyes and back handed her.

She screamed out, "Ah Shit!"

Sonya unbuttoned her shirt and took it off, her purple bra stood firm. She walked in the kitchen and grabbed a frying pan from the top of the stove and hit her with the hot bottom of the pan.

Todd screamed out in Cuban, "Stand strong!" She took the nine from Len and shot him in both knees and he fell to the ground screaming.

"Shut up Bitch, now you stand strong. Stand up before I shoot you in that big fat ass of yours." Len smiled as Todd tried to stand. She turned to the blonde, her nose and mouth were bleeding.

"You see, this Son of a Bitch can't even protect himself! I know you know where the work is, now tell me!"

The girl looked up at her and said with a crying voice, "I'm just a whore, I don't know where nothin's at!"

She beat her all over the head and face with the frying pan. Len and Tara couldn't say anything cause they knew it showed power. The blonde fell face first to the floor, blood spotted everything. Len looked at Todd on his hands and knees and kicked him in the face.

She said, "Stand up Mutha Fucka! We ain't playin with you Todd, where's the money?"

Before Sonya could say a word, Len shot him in both shoulders. Tara walked behind him and shot him in both of his ass cheeks.

"Todd, we mean business! Don't die for a Mutha Fucka that don't even know your name!"

He looked up at Sonya, he couldn't give in to a bitch, he couldn't cross Nikko out so he just laid down face first and told her to kill him.

Yennifer walked up through the door with the water hose, Sonya hooked it to the sink and unwound it. Then she turned it on and stuck it in the blondes' pussy. Yennifer held it there and kept pushing it upward.

"The human body can only take about 5½ gallons of water before it explodes so don't blow yourself up!"

She hit her again in the back of the head with the frying pan, Len shot the blonde in the back twice. The girl hollered, "Upstairs in the mattress in both rooms. Look in the kitchen, the dro and the pills are in the freezer. The pills are in the cereal boxes on top of the refrigerator. I know there's a shipment coming in to Savannah from Miami, 100 kilos of pure heroin and coke and a million pills. I've told you what you want, please get this hose out of me! Please! I've told you everything!"

Len shot Todd four times in the back of the head, Yennifer went upstairs with a trash bag and got the money. Tara got another bag and loaded all the pills and dro. After they loaded everything they shot the blonde in the head twice. Sonya walked over to the sink and cleaned her hands with the dish soap, dried her hands and put on her fur and left.

On the way out she told them, "Good job!"

They drove back down Bufford Hwy to the light, Kim pulled up beside them and told them they got everything and were heading to the warehouse. She told him to get a team ready to go to Savannah but she didn't tell him the name of the boat.

On the way to the warehouse, they listened to V-103. When they arrived, Sonya stayed in the Benz and the girls went in, Kim waited for her at the door. He walked to the Benz and saw her with her eyes closed and head on the rest. He tapped on the window, she leaned over and let him in.

He slid in and whispered very softly in her ear, "When we take from someone we love, it hurts. But when we accomplish our intention it feels great because we've captured the attention of our mate. Just think if he never crossed you we would be building together. He betrayed you when he didn't trust you, when you cried out to him about not killing Tasha and taking baby Juan. Just relax my Sandra, if only he had taken your word. He never really loved you Sandra. He never really knew you. He knew the Federal Agent Sonya but she really never existed. But he did know Mary, Gloria, Tasha, and Relena. You Sandra are just one of his many kept women. One he just takes care of for when he was down bad and needed someone. The twins were a mistake to him, not to you, you wanted them so y'all could run away together. He wanted them to keep the Feds off of his back. We got to get the baby back, my Sandra."

Tears streamed down her face because he was so right, she was his whore, his fo sho woman for a piece of ass whenever he needed it. She looked back on their relationship and how many women were in front of her. She still wasn't number one. Now he married a bitch he didn't even know.

All of a sudden, she raised her head up and said, "I'll kill him!"

It was like Kim had put her in a deep trance. She wiped her face and opened the door. Kim got out and extended his right arm. Hand in hand they walked in the warehouse.

Everyone was waiting on her to come in. Len and Yen bowed at her feet when she walked in. Tara came up with a white sheet of paper that read, "1.7 million dollars in cash, 700 Mustang ex-pills and three pounds of dro. Tara went in her pocket to get the Herring Bone necklace with *"The World Is Yours Pendant"* it was a globe with the words circling around it. She bowed her head and Tara put it around her neck.

"Listen up! I need a hundred bodies to come on this mission to Savannah with me. The dro y'all can smoke and Kim put the money with the rest of the millions we've collected in the last couple of months. We are increasing! We are going to get this heroin and pills and we should be in Sapelo, Ga in about three hours. We are looking for a Fresh Katch boat with the three K's. If the boat is on the water we are gonna need some speed boats, if it's in port we'll just walk right in. When we get what we're looking for we have to kill everyone on the boat," she yelled.

They all cheered, she didn't pick no body but her three girls and they walked out together. They got in the Benz and waited for the men to come out before they left. Kim called her and said he was staying to off load the pills and make more work.

She watched the men load into their cars and pull out. Yen pulled out behind the last car. Len was sleepy so she laid her head in Sonya's lap. Sonya ran her hands through her hair until she closed her eyes and went to sleep.

She looked down at Len and said, "If you're gonna be with me your gonna be tested for AIDS cause I'm not fuckin' with men anymore."

She had to admit it to herself that Rav had taken her down through the mud. She closed her eyes and saw herself dyeing again and this time saw her killer and it was Rav.

She looked out the window at the cars as they passed, she knew she was crossing a line and she knew it was wrong. Too many innocent people were dyeing behind their own personal war. She heard Kim in her dreams telling her she was gonna die.

She smiled and told herself, "Once again Sandra you've lost! No matter what you do your family will never be one."

She wanted to break down and cry, just like him she only wanted a family. She looked down at Len, she knew she couldn't take Rav's place. No man or woman ever could. She picked up the phone and called him.

"Rav, why did you destroy our family? You married Relana and destroyed what we had, every hope and every dream! The twins mean nothing to you and since you destroyed our family I will destroy you! I will take over everything in the South and you can kiss it goodbye! We built this shit, not Tasha, Mary or Relena but us goddammit! You chose two Mutha Fuckas who raped me over me!" Tears rolled down her face and onto her fur.

"I was just a fucking whore to you! I'll kill you! I will destroy everything about you! These twins will grow up without a mom or a pop and when this is over we will lay side by side! I made you Mutha Fucka and I'm gonna destroy you! I'll kill you! I swear to God I'm gonna kill you!"

She hung up close her eyes and went to sleep. Yennifer had been watching her as she talked, she saw the tears. She wondered who her babies' daddy was? She asked Tara in Chinese if she heard the conversation? When she said yes, she asked her who was her baby's daddy.

She replied, "The Young Don." Yennifer's eyes widened in surprise.

"So, you're telling me were going up against the Young Don Ravenion?"

"I'm afraid so Yennifer."

She just looked at Yennifer and said in Chinese: This bitch fixin to get us all killed! She's too emotional and will end up turning on us."

"No Yen! She'll help us, if we stay true to her, then we can join the

Yellow Dragon with my brothers, Twon and Damon. I spoke with them last night and they told me to keep an eye on her. Kim don't really trust her either. So, I think Kim will kill her and join us with them. Kim and Chin was the two top leaders in the Thailand Mafia. Why? Because they were helping each other. They left Thailand together and made a vow to take care of each other. I believe they are planning to take over completely."

"Tara, whatever happen we got to make sure we're covered!"

"We'll be okay Yen, I promise." They turned off of 20 to 95 South.

"Yen, doesn't the coastline run through Sapelo?"

"Yeah, that's where we're going to Sapelo. I don't know why she said Sanannah because Tybee Island isn't for shrimp boats. I'll call Craig and tell him to go to Sapelo."

When she called Craig, he told her Kim had called and gave the direction and confirmed that the boat would be there 10 minutes before them. A white boat at the south dock. She hung up and said he was on point.

Len woke up and discussed the mission with them and tried to figure out what was going on. They told her who Sonya's baby daddy was and who they were robbing. Len didn't show any fear. She told them to stop at the hardware store and buy some spray paint. She wanted the Young Don to know who he was up against. She was gonna tag the boat with Sonya's name and the Teky Mafia.

They turned off on Exit 136 and followed behind the six cars of men. They rode the speed limit the whole way and stopped at Bar rental agency and rented a van. ACE hardware was across the street, that's where Yen bought the spray paint.

Sonya was still asleep, Len started to wake her and tell her they were there but Tara said not to because she wanted to surprise her and they would handle the whole thing on their own.

The men loaded up in the van and drove off. Tara and Yennifer followed and went to the boat also, they couldn't let the men out do them. They passed the van and made it to the dock 10minutes before the men did. They saw the boat coming towards the dock, they looked at Len and asked her what was next?

Len looked around and saw the dock was filled with shrimp boats and one speed boat and said, "That's it!"

They went to the trunk and grabbed their weapons and a blanket. She put the blanket over Sonya as they laid her down so no one would see her. They didn't close the trunk for fear it would wake her up.

They walked down the dock looking for the owner of the speed boat. A white slim man was standing next to the boat and he asked, "How y'all ladies doing? Are y'all up for a quick ride?"

Yen answered, "Yes!" as they stepped onto the boat.

"My name is Len, this is Tara and Yennifer. You have a nice boat, is it fast?"

"My name is Mark and yes it's very fast!"

They pulled off going the opposite direction of the boat. When they got a little farther from the dock Len put her gun to the back of the Mark's head and told him to drive the boat towards the shrimp boat. She kept the gun out of sight as they approached. Tara and Yennifer took off their shirts, showing their tits to the five men on the deck.

Tara yelled up to them, "Ravenion sent us! There's more of us on the dock waiting, but we can start this party now if y'all want!"

As Tara knew they threw the steps down to them and they climbed aboard. Len told the driver to pull off and yelled to them she would be back. As they pulled off she shot the driver twice in the side. She cursed because he was too heavy for her to throw over the side by herself. So, she put him in the floor, covered him with the blanket, and then drove back to the boat.

When she pulled up no one was paying any attention because Yen and Tara was taking in the mouth and the ass. There were six men in all with their dicks out, she shot the first two and the other four threw their hands up in surrender.

"Damn Len, your just in time I sure didn't want this nasty Mutha Fucka inside of me!"

They got dressed and asked the other men how many more were in the bottom of the boat? Len made them call them to the top deck.

The men yelled to them, "Come on up here, Ravenion has sent us a treat!" When they came up they saw Tara and Yennifer with their tits out and proud.

"That Ravenion has good taste," the heaviest man said.

The men said, "Yes."

As they came up they didn't see Len with the Glock pointed at them. She told them to go to the Control Room.

As they walked in Yennifer said, "Men are so stupid! We know what's on this boat and when we pull up to the dock I want it all loaded on the van, do I make myself clear?"

They answered, "Yes!" as the heavy-set man pulled into the dock.

The men were ready to get into the boat when they saw the girls waving at them. Sonya smiled as they pulled up, the men jumped on and they jumped off. Len ran to Sonya and hugged her and kissed her on the mouth.

"We did it! We did it without them!"

Sonya looked around and asked, "Where's Yennifer?"

"She's still on the boat overseeing the men, let me tell you how we got them!"

She told Sonya everything even the part about them sucking and fucking. Sonya asked if she had participated?

She told her, "Hell No!" She kissed her and walked her to the car.

They sat and watched them load the van, when they were finished she saw Yennifer tag the boat and asked, "I wonder who's bright idea that was?"

Tara told her Len, she just smiled and called Yennifer in. When she got in the car and Tara pulled off Sonya told them to stay with her at all times. If they wanted to party it's alright, but they did everything together.

Yen laughed and said, "Hell No, me and Tara are strictly dickly." Sonya just smiled.

They rode back in silence. The girls didn't seem as excited as they were about the lick. Len didn't know what to feel, part of her wanted to be down with Sonya and the other part wanted the wild life. It was like Sonya knew what she was thinking. Sonya told Yennifer to pull over at the next rest stop.

Sonya thought about Gloria, she even thought about Evelyn. She thought back on her life when she was Lens age, how she wanted to party but Evelyn wouldn't let her. Yennifer pulled in at the rest stop and Sonya and Len got out.

"Len, I know you're not down with this lesbian shit but I'm not into this relationship shit. I just need to know if I decide to have a one-night stand, will it be a problem? I know you want to be wild but I want to be wild like the girl next door," she said.

"The answer is Yes! I want to taste that pussy anyway, I really want to suck on them nipples. I want to be wild too so let's all get wild together. Let's chill like girls are supposed too!"

"Cool, let me get y'all settled in."

"No! We already have a place to stay, we stay in a condo about six blocks from you. The girls are down with you at any cost. You don't need us to play bodyguard cause with us it's shoot first and ask questions later. So let's chill."

They smiled and hugged, got back in the car and Yen pulled off. When she didn't get on the expressway Sonya asked her where she was going? Yen said she wasn't sure but she had seen a McDonalds sign off the exit.

After five minutes the McDonalds was on the left, they pulled up to the drive through window. She didn't ask anyone what they wanted she ordered triple cheese burgers, fries and cokes and pies. After she paid and they got their food she pulled into a vacant slot in the parking lot. As they ate they joked about her and Len. They were all laughing and Tara went into the dash and pulled out three blunts and fired one up. Sonya noticed the smell.

"Ain't that a fifty-one?"

"What's a fifty-one?" Tara asked.

"A geek blunt, cocaine, and weed," she answered.

"Y'all are really out there, y'all really are!"

She looked at Len and asked her, "You, smoke fifty ones and remoes too?"

"You know it, pass me that fire and let me get high!"

Tara passed her the blunt and some fire, deep down inside Sonya hated that shit. It was like Jesus asking his disciples to watch for him and them falling asleep. How could they watch her back high?

Yennifer saw the dislike in her face so she didn't fire up. Instead she signaled for them all to check out her reaction and they saw she didn't agree. She put her head in her coat and got out mad as Hell. She went inside the restaurant and asked the cashier to call her a cab. She told the driver to take her to the nearest rental place. She knew she was in over her head because Rav had a point to prove and he would prove it one way or another. In reality she just wanted to marry him and have a family. She wasn't sure which one of them was responsible for tearing them apart, him or her?

Her phone rang pulling her from the bad visions of the grave and the little girls in black dresses.

It was him, she was afraid but she answered it, "What Juan?"

"Don't what me! What the Fuck have you done? Why are you doing this? You started this Shit wantin three to five million dollars. You have over 120 million dollars, what the Hell is wrong with you? Don't you know these mafia play for keeps! I can't save you! That favor I owed you. . .I just repaid it! I'm gonna kill you Bitch! This Shit is stupid! Why you want to war with me? Your kids will visit your grave once a year to bring fresh flowers."

"No! No! No! I'll give it back, I'll give you everything back. What is it about 7 million?""You can't give me back the lives I've lost. 50 men and women and then you tortured a woman by putting a water hose up her pussy, I want you to feel the same death!" He hung up and a childlike fear came upon her.

Her phone rang again, it was Kim, and a soft voice said, "It's alright, you've done nothing wrong, now he knows your about business. Your family is here waiting on you to came home. Baby Nodiya wants to speak with you." He put Nodiya's mouth up to the phone and she heard her breathe.

"What are you doing with my child?"

"Kau called me, she was worried you haven't called every hour on the hour like you promised. So, she was fixin to leave and go to your safe house and wait on your call. I told her to come to the warehouse, we're sitting in the Limo. Do you want me to send her back or have her stay here?"

"Send her home and tell her I said she did a good job. Kim, I see the grave."

"No! You see his grave, possibly the same siting he told you about, right?"

"Yes!"

"Go get back in the car with the girls, that's their way of dealing with the excitement, that's the only way they stay focused. Shoot first and ask no questions. My child everything is okay. I'll be waiting on you. Now, take in a deep breath and feel better."

Just like a woman in a deep trance, she took in a deep breath, stood up and walked out. The cab was pulling up. She pulled out a fifty and paid the driver for the fare then got in the car with the girls.

No one spoke, she closed her eyes and fell asleep. When she woke up they were pulling into the warehouse. She saw the red Benz so that told her Kau was still there with the baby. She walked in, the only ones there were Kim and Kau. They were in the office so she walked up the stairs and saw the chemist was still there working. She walked into the office and saw that

Kau and the baby were wearing matching red jogging suits. Kau sat in front of the desk and Kim sat behind the desk. Kau handed her the baby and she hugged and kissed her and told her mammy loved her.

She sat beside Kau and discussed the next shipment with Kim in front of Kau. Kim wanted to hit his tankers while they were still in the Atlantic. Sonya was cool with it, she just wanted to check all their traps. Kim told her the traps on Buford Hwy hadn't been tamed yet because of the cops. Sonya wanted to check out three new clubs. But really Sonya thought she just wanted a hot bath and to sleep for a few days. She told Kim to check everything and send her a fax cause she was going home. Kim walked over to her and kissed her left cheek as she stood. Kau looked at Kim and asked why she felt like he had the hots for her? He just laughed and told her not to be silly he was an old man who couldn't get it up.

Kau laughed and said, "That's why they got pills!" Everybody laughed and left.

CHAPTER 16

Want Marcel Killed

Rav stood at the entrance and waited on the Benz to come back. Relena wanted to be held, she wanted to tell him that she was scared. Her life had never been threatened with guns before, Nikko and Raul were her protectors. They were gone now and she was side by side with a cold-hearted husband who doesn't care about her fear and her needs.

The Benz pulled up to the entrance and Alex, Arod, Niger, and Gino got out. They told him Marcel was in the first house, he told them in the morning he wanted Marcel killed with the people who sent him. They nodded in agreement. Alex asked her if she was okay? She had been very quiet but she nodded and said yes, she was fine.

Rav kissed her on the left cheek and told her he would catch up with her in the morning. He needed time to think things out, he told Arod, Niger, and Gino to stay with her in Nikko's house. Alex looked at him puzzled, he didn't want to tell him Relena didn't trust him.

"Alex, you and Gloria sit with Marcel and make sure he calls no one! Relena is my wife, so don't let me get a call saying somethings happened to her."

Relena stepped from the door of the Chevy in front of him and said, "I don't know why you're telling them to guard me, because I'm going home, I'm sleeping in my bed beside my husband. Rav, I've had it up to here with this insecurity shit! Whether you like it or not we both had our own motives for this marriage, that's what brought us together. I'm sick of this shit! Alex, you and Gloria make sure he don't contact no body."

She jumped in the passenger seat of the Chevy, leaned forward and opened the door to the driver's side. Everyone looked at him waiting on his order. Then Alex broke the silence and said, "Rav, she's right. Her safety is with you."

He smiled and sat in the driver's seat, Arod closed the door. He started the car and pulled off. She wanted to say something but kept it to herself, she didn't want to argue, especially not now. He just saved her life, that shit he did in the hotel room, didn't exist anymore. Even though the male versus female shit was killing her.

She couldn't take it anymore so she spoke up and said, "Thank you for saving my life, why you did it I don't know. I never meant to hurt you Rav, but you keep putting this shit in my face. I just want to be side by side with you, I don't want to be out in a house in Atlanta, I don't want to worry about you. This was a prime example of what would happen if I was in a house in Atlanta, I would've been dead. I can't read the streets like you, now you should see why I need you as a husband instead of a right-hand man. Rav, look at me. What can I do to bring the passion back into our marriage? I'll do anything except stay sleepless in Atlanta. I can't protect myself cause anyone can be bought or moved to a higher position. Take Alex for instance, he thought he was gonna get your job, he was too stupid to realize he was gonna be your right-hand man. Ungrateful, even after you freed his people. That's why I'm gonna kill his ass in the morning!"

"Did you call his dad and tell him he would be running the show from here on out? We already got shit hooked up on the money tip."

"Rav I really think you should start using the whales and dolphins, something is moving in my Spirit about this shipment."

"Relena, that shipment is already on the water, if you feel that strong just send a backup. It's not like we got a supplier. We can take a loss but if we get through we're two shipments up."

"Rav, you never answered my question about our marriage, our passion. Rav, I need to be held and told everything is gonna be alright. Didn't you see the fear in my eyes?"

"Relena, I'm not gonna hold your hand through this life. Yes, I saw the fear but you chose this life. Passion never left our marriage, you left our marriage. What you want to fuck? You want me to say it's gonna be alright? I can't tell you that I don't know myself. I can't protect you Relena. I couldn't protect Tasha, Sonya, Gloria or Mary. The only way I can protect you is from a soldier's point of view. I'll make love to you the same way I made love to all of them, but now is not the time to be thinking like this, when we got a massacre tomorrow as well as your brothers funeral. And you better not cry!"

They pulled up to the gate and there were two armed guards with AR 15's. He rolled down the window and drove through. They pulled up to the house and there were two more guards. One opened his door and the other opened hers and stayed by her side. One walked through the house while they remained at the front door. He didn't like this at all. After the guard returned they continued into the house. Unaware of the baby monitors Relena ran upstairs and fell on the bed and started crying.

The guard looked at Rav and smiled. Rav told him to just wake them in the morning. He walked up, to the room, leaned over the bed and kissed her. Then he went into the bathroom and showered.

She remembered how he felt coming out of the shower, how soft his skin felt. The passion forced her to get up and she went into the bathroom. She undressed and got in the shower with him. He was sitting in the tub letting the water run over him. Then she noticed the water on his face wasn't from the shower they were tears. He reached up and grabbed her by the hips and guided her down onto him. She laid back and let the water beat down on her breasts.

He rubbed her thighs and whispered in her ear, "Ain't nothin wrong with crying. If anyone says they are that strong they are lying."

She turned over and sat on his dick, shifting back and forth with the water running off her breasts into his face. He knew he had to calm her in order to mold her, he wanted her strong and emotionless.

"Can you see my soul Relena? Can you feel my pain?" She put her hand on his chest and felt his heart beating, it wasn't racing like hers she didn't understand.

"Find my soul Relena like I've found yours."

Her eyes widened as she reached her climax, he took his right hand and put it between her breasts, as he leaned her back he pressed forward.

"Find my soul Relena."

She tilted her head forward searching for his soul. She looked into his eyes and saw a forest deep in them and she started moving faster.

"I found it! I found it! I found your pain! I found your opening! I found your heart Rav! Did you find my Heaven?"

"Yes, in the 9th firmament!" Her body shook, then the room started spinning, and God opened her heart to eternal happiness.

"Rav, I'll die for you!" She spoke of forever and her body fell into his and he comforted her.

He took his left foot and opened the drain, the water drained as he picked her up and stepped out of the shower. He carried her to the bed and laid her down. He covered her gently and let her sleep.

She was up making calls preparing for the service, he looked at her, she was wearing a white silk gown. One thing he always liked about her was she was plain like the rest of the girls.

"I see your awake, I've made sure the service is ready. I saw a piece of paper you sending Smokey and Leo to Chi Town even though they're on high alert."

"They can't stay around us?" He got up and brushed his teeth and washed his face, he walked over to her and kissed her on the shoulder.

"What's that for?"

"Relena, I can't be mad at you for protecting your family. Your right, that power hit me too! Just follow my lead and shoot first and ask questions later, no one is going to help us or guide us through this donship."

She kissed him and walked over to the closet and picked out a black Tux for him to wear. She didn't want any of her clothes or his to be anything but solid black.

He had made her happy with what he said, she thought she would have never heard the words come from him but they did.

"Rav, what do you mean we're gonna put a blunt and heroine and all that shit in Nikko's casket?"

"That's how we do it in the states, we bury real niggas the way they lived. All I know is my way of living. I'm 23-years-old, I'm hip hop now with this responsibility we are gonna need a mentor but who? All I know is we ain't gonna die like Nikko, we got one life to live and we're gonna live it to the fullest. You know we are two marked people so why die wondering."

"Once again Rav, this ain't Hollywood, we do things a certain way. We walk to the casket and pay our respects and the Father blesses him into heaven. After we gather its over we don't watch him go in the ground. Since he's being cremated we'll watch that and carry him to his room with the candles lit."

"So, I can't put nothin in his casket?"

"It don't make any sense with him being cremated."

"Your right! I believe Helen like Smokey!"

"Speaking of Smokey and Leo, I don't see any need of sending them to Chicago. They just come in here as hit men and leave right out, let them oversee shipments. Rav, let me ask you a question, How can someone go person to person if they was so in love with that person?"

"They never in love with that person, they loved the lifestyle. Would you go straight to another man after my death?"

"No, cause I'm the life style with you." She said that smiling, she kissed him and started to dress him.

After he was dressed he watched her get ready with a smile on his face. She was the finest girl he had ever had. She was truly a dime all the way. If she could become more dangerous than Sonya, more loving than Tasha and more protective than Gloria. She would be all of his girls rolled into one.

He took her by surprise once more with a poem, *"Relena, my every dream of a woman, I found them in you. The conversation that we share is like a fountain of youth, my first and last blessing, I give them to you."*

She dropped to his feet, kissed his shoes and worshiped him. He pulled her up and helped her with her black fur and they went downstairs.

Sammy the butler came out of the kitchen and said, "Mr. and Mrs. Nalls, I prepared a full breakfast for you just like you like."

He asked Relena if they had enough time to eat and she said they did. The table was already set and they said grace and ate. Sammy put warm Orange Juice beside their plates and told them it should warm them up cause it was chilly outside.

Arod knocked at the entrance of the kitchen, he was dressed in all black. "Are y'all ready? I have the Limo ready," he said.

They got up and walked out and were met by the guard. The disrespect came when Gloria got out of the backseat and opened the door for them.

"Gloria, I thought you and Alex was tending to Marcel?"

"No Relena, Niger, and Alex are tending to him, I had to practice the song for Nikko's funeral."

"I'm sorry Gloria I didn't know."

Relena got in first, Gloria looked at Rav with disgrace in her eyes. Relena saw it but kept her cool. He kissed her on the cheek and sat in the Limo.

She got in and sat in the front, Gino sat in the passenger seat. There was complete silence on the way.

The service was set up like he wanted, there were over seven hundred seats. There was a red rose colored back drop and matching carpet. There were pictures of Nikko and flowers surrounding his casket.

Relena looked at Rav as they walked arm in arm towards the casket. They heard crying as they reached the casket. Helen, Smokey, and Leo sat in the front row. Rav let her walk-in front in case she broke down and he could catch her. When she got to the casket she couldn't hold it in anymore and she laid across the casket crying and asking Nikko why he had left her. Leo and Smokey tried to pry her away and it was turning into a big scene. It was just what Rav didn't want, an hour-long service turning into a daylong service.

He knelt down beside her and looked at Gloria and nodded. She walked to the podium in her black dress and grabbed the microphone.

She went and knelt beside Relena and held her hand, she said, "Lord Bless this moment." The sound of music and a soft drum beat came through the air.

"I was born by the river, in a little tent and just like the river, my life has been like this ever since. It's been a hard living and I'm afraid to die. Not knowing what's on the other side of the sky. It's been a long time living, but I know a change gonna come."

Everybody stood and someone helped Relena to her feet, then Gloria hummed out a verse of her own.

"Life is worth the living and I swear we'll never die. As long as the earth keeps spinning and God keeps sending blessings out of the sky. Ooh let it rain…let the rain, rain down a change. Because it's been too hard living, and so many lives sacrificed. Lord, it's been a long, long time coming with but I know a change gonna come."

Everybody began to sing along and went through the verse four or five times. When she opened her eyes, she looked at Rav, then everybody else. They all had their hands in the air and singing, *"A Change is Gonna Come."*

After the song was over, Rav took his seat in the front row and the reverend began to speak. Gloria, Niger, Alex, Arod, Gino, and Rav walked to the six long poles tying down the material. Everyone was looking to see what they were doing. The wind took hold of the material and blew it away.

The reverend walked to the gold casket and opened the leg covering section. They all tapped their silver rods on the casket three times at the same time and white doves flew from the cage tapping on the poles, 21 doves flew from Nikko's casket and everyone was amazed!

The father spoke for the last time, "My son has been ascended to Heaven."

Alex, Arod, Niger, Gino, Smokey, and Rav picked up the casket and carried it to the hearse.

Once everyone had departed they followed the hearse to the *"Open Arms Cremation"* building. The building wasn't big enough for everyone so just Rav, Relena and Helen went inside. Everyone else watched from the parking lot. They had hooked up four cameras and widescreen TV's for everyone to watch. He was placed in a blue and white Cuban culture vase and returned to the palace. Everyone paid their last respects and he was placed in the center of his room.

Marcel walked close to Alex as they entered the eating area, the dining room was split but a screen was raised so everyone could see to each side.

All 33 bosses ate in the main dining room. They started the meeting. An older Black boss from New Jersey and an older White boss from New York kept looking at Rav and Relena. Relena stood and approached the two bosses and asked them to take a walk with her. They got up from their meal and followed her. Rav peeped what was going on and followed behind them. Relena showed them out onto the compound.

"Rav this is George Ammar from New Jersey, he oversees Atlantic City.

This is William Talley from New York, he oversees the export and import and the labor business. I noticed them looking at us and I also noticed they were the only two with weapons."

Before she could finish Rav cut her off, "What are the guns for gentlemen? This is supposed to be a day of peace not war."

"Yes, your right Ravenion, but Bill and I go by the code to protect our don. We are aware of the assassination attempts by the Dutch and the Italians and we are gonna deal with that after sunset. Ravenion we are with you and Relena. We know you both need mentors and we are willing to share all of our knowledge with you. We don't believe in bringing an old don in because we would be selecting a new one in four to five years. You understand?"

"Yes, don't worry cause all that is against us will raise their voices after sunset and then a new foundation will be laid," Rav replied.

He looked at George a tall light skinned man, he must have been well over 60. He had a head full of gray hair, clean shaven with a well-trimmed mustache. The holster and gun he carried was almost as big as his tall slim body.

Unlike George, Bill was bald with a thick beard and mustache but he too carried a 357 on his shoulder. He looked at how they dressed, old school slacks and jacket.

He looked at Relena and asked, "Will you still love me when I'm 60 something and looking as good as these gentlemen?"

She smiled and said, "If you look like them and dress like them we will still be don's, and we can still walk to the park, then yes! I will still love you even if we are in an old folks' home."

"Okay, here's a problem for you my mentors, Marcel was part of the hit but Relena didn't kill him. Instead she let him live to point who was responsible for the hit to begin with. It was a Dutchman, now he's promised to kill him if we let him live. Your call."

George looked at Bill and smiled, Bill nodded to George to answer the question, "It's simple, he was hired to do a job, it's not like he has hate for y'all, he was hired. I wouldn't kill him without knowing everything about the Dutchman and his life. I'll make him the Dutchman and with that he'll kill to stay a boss."

"Mr. Talley, do you agree?" Relena asked.

"One hundred percent," he replied.

"Then he shall see another day."

They walked back into the dining area, everybody spoke quietly as they entered the room. Two old bosses with two new bosses was unusual. Bill and George went to their seats and Ran and Relena stood at their sides.

All the sudden, Rav called for attention in the room and told everyone he wanted to call attention to the fact someone tried to kill him and whoever it was to not try it again. He told everyone to just relax and have a good time.

He wanted her to spare Alex since they were sparing Marcel. She grabbed him by the hand and led him over to Ralph Edward, Alex's dad. He was handling the new labor Rav and Nikko had set up. A lot of Cubans from the north were coming to the south for work so their plan was working good.

Edward smiled as Relena talked but it quickly turned to a frown. How could she become so cruel so fast? He looked at Alex from across the room. He walked over and knelt down at Rav's feet and begged for forgiveness for Alex's hate. He got up and asked them to please walk with him.

Rav remembered his face from when he first met him, Edward had hurt his back and still wanted to work for his family. He looked stronger now that he could stand straight up, him and Alex were nearly twins. He didn't change, he still dressed the same; slacks and suspenders with the wide brim hat.

Alex's mom, brothers and sisters ran up to him and hugged him calling him Alexander the Great. Relena saw tears of a friend in his eyes. They walked out and went to the front of the palace.

Edward stood in front of them, "Rav, I'm a Cuban and Cubans live and die for each other. What my son did was follow orders from someone in the same position as you. Alex loves you Rav, please don't kill my son. Just leave him here in Cuba with me, I'll deal with him myself, I promise."

"Edward Sir, it's not me I promise. Alex saved my life. He came and got me when the Feds had me locked up. It's Relena and its her call now."

He fell to his knees and Alex saw him from the window, he wanted to know what was going on so he walked out there. When he walked up he heard his father begging and asked what was going on. He jumped up and started slapping Alex wildly.

"How could you? How could you betray your family? Your friend? How can you disrespect yourself?"

Tears streamed down his face as he turned to Rav and Relena; "What have I done to be labeled a Traitor?"

"Alex, we know about your plan to kill Rav for Nikko. We know he promised you Rav's position. Then you brought two strangers who meant us harm into our home! The same stranger put a hit on me!" He wouldn't let her finish speaking.

"Relena, I must follow orders and that came from the top! I didn't mean no disrespect by bringing them to your home. They wanted to get away and have a good time. I thought no one would be there because Rav hardly ever uses the house. You even said you weren't gonna use it, remember it used to be a tour house?"

He stood in Rav's face with his hands in form of prayer, "Rav, let me ask you a question, if you had an order to kill me would you do it?" Everyone looked at Rav and waited for an answer.

When he finally said, "No! Alex hit his knees. The reason is because if the shoe was on the other foot, you were me and I was you, I would've been more loyal to you, because you helped free my people. When I first met you and you showed me that meth recipe, I let you go get everything you wanted. I even helped you rob pharmacies and cook the dope, when neither one of us knew what we were doing. Now that's trust. When you put your life in a friend's hand. Alex, I went up against Nikko and Poco for you, so why you couldn't at least tell me?"

"You're right, I betrayed you and I accept whatever y'all have in store for me."

"Mrs. Relena, Rav, I don't want my son to die! Please Relena I beg you to leave him here! I promise I will put him at the bottom of whatever business we start."

Relena looked at Rav, he smiled and said, "There's no greater gift than silence, I don't want him to die. I just can't trust him with my life anymore. Alex, my love for you will keep you alive, my blessing be upon you!"

"Alex, you're no longer a part of this family, form the respect of your family and my husband you'll live. Look not to earn one cent of our money, your no longer allowed on this compound or at none of the others. You're not to contact any of Rav's guards or Gloria."

She walked to him and kissed his left cheek, a kiss of betrayal to anyone who was watching. She reached out and he handed her his gun.

Rav turned his back on him. He dropped to his knees and said a prayer of forgiveness and left the compound. Rav felt a tightening in his chest like he just got shot.

"Why did Gloria show him that recording? Relena, Alex had plenty of opportunity to kill me. Why didn't he go through with it?"

"Maybe you should ask him Rav! I don't want to talk about this anymore, you should have let me kill him!"

They walked back into the eating area with the rest of the bosses and finished their meal. George saw the far off look in his eyes, like he just lost his best friend. He waited to see if his impression was right, so far, he was wrong. He thought he would call the meeting early, instead he just chilled and talked with Relena. It was like no one else was in the room but them. There was no sense mingling with the dead.

Gloria walked in and whispered something in his ear, he jumped up, pulling Relena, nearly dragging her out of her chair.

They walked out to the Limo and went to the old warehouse, Hassan was there waiting for them.

"Rav, it was Sonya!"

Relena lost, didn't know what was going on all she knew she was snatched out of her chair.

"How in the fuck did Sonya hit all three tankers? Somebody better give me some answers! Relena, you told me last night you didn't feel right about that shipment, talk to me!"

I don't know but I shipped the other shipment like you said."

They followed Hassan into the warehouse office, he showed them the recordings of the tankers. He replayed all three cameras.

The small tanker with the dummy in it got hit by the Feds. There wasn't much in that load, only a few kilo's, but they found that. The boat was going to South Beach to a small business down there. After that Ricky Brown stunt they laid low of that area. The tanker going to New York got hit in the channel going to the Hudson and the one going to Chicago got hit going through California. . .The shipment was supposed to go there first then Chicago.

He called Mr. Chin and told him the shipment would be a day off course because of the interception. Chin told him it wasn't an interception, it was a hit by the Teky Mafia. He asked how he knew? He told him one of the girls in the Teky Mafia's brother are in the Yellow Dragon and he told her they were hitting two tankers. She said she wasn't sure but she thought they belonged to the Young Don.

Rav asked why he didn't call when he got that information? He said he had called but everyone was at the funeral. He told them Tara was Sonya's driver but didn't know where she had hidden the drugs. Rav told him not to panic but just send his boys to Atlanta. They should go to Fulton Industrial, Bufford Hwy and Old National Hwy. He would be in Atlanta in approximately 22 hours.

Relena pointed out a tattoo on one of robbers left arm. A Teky saying in Chinese. Rav told him he knew it was them and Sonya. But he said he didn't know how she knew about all three shipments. She told him not to worry about that anymore because nobody knew the new way. She told him the best way to beat them is old but modern. He smiled and told Gloria to get everybody ready, he had a hundred men going to Atlanta. She said she would do it but reminded him she had to get back to her own life in New York. Relena couldn't believe the disrespect, Rav just shook his head.

Hassan told him everything was ready in Alabama so he would be right behind him. They got back in the Limo and Gloria didn't say anything she just stared at them.

"Gloria, what's this personal life shit you're talking about? I notice that ever since you found out about mine and Rav's marriage you've been very disrespectful. So please enlighten me on your personal life."

"Relana, I'm no longer a part of this life or family, they let me have my own life. I'm a singer in New York, I have an album out. Rav and Nikko let me go, I came back to show my respect and help fill in where he needed me."

Relena looked at Rav for an answer, he didn't say anything. Then Relena hit her with a low blow.

"Gloria, you're not going anywhere, I don't give a damn about no singing career. You're staying side by side with your family. You're a year or two older than me but you won't keep running off every time things don't go your way. You're not 16 anymore, this shit stops here!"

"But Relena, I've already recorded my album, Nikko got me an apartment off of 46th.. Relena reached over and slapped her and told her to stop it right now.

"Raul is your father and that is why you're treated so highly. Do you remember the night that Raul and Nikko got into it? Do you remember what Raul said? Tears rolled down her cheeks because she did remember.

Raul said, "She's mine, she came from me, you're sick and if you touch her again I'll kill you." She thought they were fighting over her not for her.

"Raul never denied you, your mother didn't want anybody to know because of Tony and all the stuff that was going on. My mother and father kept you in their house. In this life you just don't go out and pick a kid and show them love. Why do you think your mother stayed around Raul? This is your business as well as mine. I grew up under you and before my mother died she told us to take care of you and my mamma and brother didn't blow up in no ship. That shit was set up by Sonya!"

Gloria was crying because Raul got drunk one night and told her he was her father. Now it's been confirmed.

"Relena, I grew up a slave, I wasn't treated like you, I was before you yet under you. My father is not Raul, like I said I have a life to live. Driver take me to the airstrip, I can show you better than I can tell you. You've taken from me my whole life, it was always about you Relena. You've taken the only man I've ever loved and I'll be damned if you're gonna take my dream away too! I have Rav to thank for this dream, he made it all possible. If you're my aunt and you love me let me live my own fucking life! I've always been the one picking you up, not once has it been the other way around. I was your best friend, your sister, do you remember bitch? We made a promise to always be there for each other and never hurt each other. You knew I loved Rav, I told you! You've taken almost everything but you can't take my name! I'm the first and only Nalls. That's my name, Gloria Nalls!"

The Limo stopped at the airstrip, she opened the door and got out. She walked around to him and kissed him on the lips real hard, told him she would always love him, turned around and boarded the plane without looking back.

"Relena if Nikko knew she was his niece, why did he give her to me?"

"Gloria chose you but I was promised you. Damn, I didn't mean for her to run off, Nikko should have never agreed to letting her sing."

"Why get your niece killed? He probably let her go because he forced himself on her or Raul told him. That's a question we'll never know the answer to."

He called Arod and told him to get Smokey and the boy's ready and to meet him at the front gate. Arod told him all the guest had left. Some went home and others went to a movie in the theater. He told him he needed a hundred men cause they had business to take care of outside of Cuba.

Smokey, Arod, Leo, Niger, and Gino were waiting for him at the front gate. When the Limo pulled up they got in and he told them Alex's situation. He told them about the meeting that was going down. He called George and told him to get everybody together.

When they arrived at the corn field they got out and stood where the graves had been dug. He saw that there were 10 graves dug, all in a row. He told the men his plan and that he wanted them all buried right here. They all agreed and walked back to the palace.

Relena and Rav walked into the dining room where all the bosses ate. Arod and the men had went and gotten five AK's and followed them in with the weapons behind their backs. They were all smiling when they entered the dining room.

"George and Bill, can you both step forward please?" Relena asked.

They stood beside them at the entrance as Arod ushered Marcel into the room. He didn't know his 380 was empty. He walked over behind the Dutch and Italian bosses, pulled out the weapon and fired into the backs of their heads. Everyone's eyes widened in shock when the gun didn't go off. Marcel's heart dropped, he knew he had been tricked.

"Good job Marcel!" Bill told him.

"We were already aware of who you guys were we just wanted to see if Marcel here would live up to his word and he did, well done Marcel!"

George smiled and said, "Alright! Alright! Let's get down to business here. We are here to select a new Don. By law, Relena will always have leadership because of her family. Her family is why we are all joined here together. Through death Nikko took over for Raul and through death Relena took over from Nikko. By law Ravenion is her right-hand man. Now the selecting of a new Don is her choice and only her choice. By law, we'll respect her decision and honor it. If she decides she wants the responsibility, then it's hers. We will lead her and mentor her. Mrs. Relena, who do you select? We will if they will accept and live up to all the standards to be our new leader."

"I select you George." Everybody was amazed, including Rav. Everybody assumed she was gonna select Rav. They thought that was the reason for the marriage.

"Alright everybody, lets calm down! Relena we accept your decision and I give my greatest respect to you for making me your choice. Since I'm an elder I select who I think should be the don and I select the young one, Ravenion. Who do you select Bill?"

"I also select the young one."

"Now let us pick a third choice. Would any of you men like to stand for nomination yourself?" George asked.

The Italian stood boldly and went to George and shook his hand. George faced the room and told Relena he was stepping down from the nomination because of his age.

The others voiced their feelings and felt that if Rav was the new don then they would be picking a new one again in three to five years because he wouldn't listen and that he was all muscle. He's young with no knowledge, he won't accept the position of just sitting back and seeing the show, he wants to be part of the show.

The boss from Philly stood up, he was a slim White man with red hair and said, "No offense Rav, I love you as a leader. What are you 24 or 25-years-old? I feel like you will make it in some years, but not right now. It will take a lot of mentoring and it will be for you to decide. Look at Smokey and Leo, they're wanted across the world. Our people had to take the surveillance tapes from the courthouse because they clearly showed you and Nikko. Once you learn how to lead your people then you'll be a great Don but not right now. Let's vote George in and mentor you. You will still have the power to make decisions but George will oversee you."

Mikky walked over to him and George and bowed down and said, "No matter what happens today, I'm for you Rav, I know you'll need a lot of help from all of us."

George helped Mikky stand and thanked him. Everyone kept their focus on Rav, a lot of them would rather go to their graves than select him. No one said nothing about the Italian. Rav nodded to Billy and he nodded to

George.

While he was walking over to the Dutchman Bill spoke, "First of all we want everyone to know that no one will be allowed to muscle their way up the ladder. Ravenion made it possible for you all to be here today. If it hadn't been for his courage none of you would be here today. Most of all have forgotten that and the respect that goes with it. How could you turn against your leader? He's been your leader from day one and many of you failed to see that. From today forward no form of disrespect will be tolerated."

Bill pulled out his 357 and shot the Dutchman in the side of the head. Before anyone could react to that, he pulled his weapon and shot the Italian in the head also.

Marcel was a sweating Mutha Fucka as George walked over to him and said, "Marcel, go sit in his seat."

"Yes Sir, Mr. Talley," he said as he walked quickly to his seat.

Rav stepped up to speak, "A lot of y'all said you would rather go to your graves than let me and Relena lead you. I made y'all what you are right now. I killed your bosses and made you bosses. Before that you were just like me, a right-hand man and muscle. I know I'm young Black and ambitious. Most of you, that's what you're looking at: the fact that I'm not Cuban, Italian, Dutch, or White. It's because I'm Black, but here's the real reason why I was chosen, now show 'em!"

They all stepped back, Smokey, Leo, Niger, and Arod stepped forward and gunned them down, over 30 bodies laid out across the floor.

"I guess it is what it is!" George said.

"They all have right hand men so call them in here to carry the bodies to the cornfield. Call the groundskeeper and have him bring 30-wheel barrows. George listen to me; their man knows the status and what's going on in their cities and countries. Marcel I'm sure you will fit right in, whoever his right-hand man was, he's now yours."

The men came in and they were shocked to see their bosses laying slain on the floor. When the last man came in Ravenion closed the door. George and Bill's men walked in with a wheel barrow.

"Why do y'all have wheelbarrows, I thought we said 30? George asked.

"We were told to come with these," his nephew answered.

"Alright, everybody listen up! I'm Ravenion, the young one and this is my wife Relena, these are our mentors, George, Bill, and Mikky. Y'all bosses were color blind, we respect all people no matter what their color, do you understand me?"

"Yes Sir!" they all answered.

"Okay, y'all are now bosses, all of you need to select a right-hand man. We will meet again in 30 days. Now Marcel here is over the Dutch, find his right-hand man and fill him in on what he needs to know. If he's fucking up our shit, then kill his whole family. Do what you need to do just keep me informed. Your drug supply will double, that will show me how bad y'all want your jobs. No one knows what happened here today, they all went down in a plane crash in the Atlantic is the story. Now, if any of you are thinking about killing one of us, you better change your thoughts. If you even dream about betraying us, you better wake up asking for forgiveness. No one knows the young one is the new Don so keep it that way!" They all agreed, and he told them they all had to file reports to Mikky, George, or Relena.

"George I will see you in five days and in the meantime a family history is being put together on all of you and if anyone tries to hurt any of us its them that will pay."

"Ravenion, we know somethings wrong you're not just muscle any more you've got to trust us."

"Okay, y'all listen, we just combined business with the Yellow Dragons to cut down some of the heat. All we do is send our people out to oversee. I just got a call, my children's mom, Federal Agent Sandra Anderson better known as Sonya, has cliqued up with the Teky Mafia. The Feds tried to get me on some info that Erudo and Mandia gave them about murders and the drug trade. I was out on some strong medication because of my wounds. Alex took me and my twins out of the hospital with two armed guards at the door. Sonya swore revenge, she robbed all three of my tankers. The way she did it was she gave her captain the small bust and her and her crew hit the other two. My plans are to get to Atlanta to catch up that shipment. Don't worry, Relena just sent out another shipment, so we'll have double the amount, just give me five days and I'll be back with y'all."

"Rav, we're going with you."

"George, I can handle this, I don't need all of y'all, I don't need to be burying no elder, just please trust me."

"Do you have a plan?" Mikky asked.

"No, because I don't know what I'm facing. I can promise you this, once I get this shipment back I'll settle myself and Relena too! Just let me get this back."

"Rav, me, Bill and Mikky are coming along with you, just to keep your mind clear," George said.

He took in a deep breath and said come on, they walked out and got into the Limo. Rav thought about something, he didn't have a place to stay anymore. How could they house a hundred men? He was puzzled and then Mikky spoke as if reading his mind, "Young one, now you're thinking. Where can you house all your men? My suggestion is to find a cheap hotel and house them in groups."

Before he could answer Relena told him the Best Western on Bolton Rd. could house them all. Poco already made reservations for us at the Executive Inn on Fulton Ind. She also has all out transportation waiting for us at the airport.

"We got 222 through 224 and all the weapons are in the vehicles and she can give us all the info in the morning."

When they got to the airport all the planes were fueled and waiting. Rav, Relena, Bill, George and Mikky boarded the first jet and Niger, Arod, Smokey, and Leo boarded the second one.

Rav sat by the window with Relena beside him. He was seeing visions of death as usual and it was getting tense.

He whispered in her ear, "Every time I get on a plane I see myself dyeing in the clouds, help me understand my death."

"You're not gonna die so stop talking like that, I'm gonna protect you."

He put his head on her shoulder, she didn't want to tell him someone close to him was gonna kill him. That's why she was standing beside him, so no other female could get close to him. She touched his cheek with her left hand because he needed her comfort.

She looked around and thought about their life. As soon as Sonya was driven underground their life would return to normal. All they would have to do is call the shots. She got lost in her thoughts of killing Sonya, the many ways to make her suffer and how she would get a breast pump to feed the twins. She had everything planned out, two bitches to get out of her way and her marriage would be free. No bitches or niggas would be able to stop them, not even Raul. She made a mental note to call Raul and tell him they still ran everything thanks to Rav.

Her thoughts were broken as they landed at Charlie Brown Airport. Rav looked out the window and saw the Yukon's and Benz's they were promised. As they got off the plane they saw Mr. Chins white Limo. Relena, Bill, and George sat in the back and Mikky got in the front.

Smokey and Leo got into the second Benz cause they wanted to ride separate with their weapons in case they got pulled over. As they left they all spread out so Rav would be protected in case the Feds got a tip.

Amali got out of the Limo wearing an all-white body suit. She twirled around showing her pantieless figure. He smiled at her as he sat in the Limo.

Mr. Chin was sitting in front of him and Amali sat beside him. Chin wore a blue suit with blue Stacy Adams. The entourage left the airport. Rav watched as Relena and the others turned into the hotel, he kept going. He didn't ask any questions because he knew Relena would follow behind him once she saw he didn't turn in behind her. He looked back when Chin pointed, he smiled because both black Benz's were behind them.

"I see Relena is a good protector."

Before Chin could finish his sentence, the Benz drove in front of the Limo and slammed on the brakes. She jumped out with a Glock 40 pointed at them.

After the car had stopped, Relena climbed in the back and pointed the gun at Chin.

"What's going on? Where are you taking him?"

"Order your driver to pull over and get behind the Limo." Chin ordered.

She called the driver and ordered him to pull over. As soon as he pulled over they took a left and turned down into Sonya's warehouse. The driver stopped and popped the trunk and pulled out a rocket launcher, took aim and blew up the warehouse. She reloaded and walked to the left side of the building and fired again. The building was totally destroyed. They heard someone coughing from behind the building, walking, and dragging toward the top of the hill.

Arod jumped out of the Benz and chased the female down and brought her to them. She was young and Chinese around 18 or 19. She had a lab jacket on, when she saw Mr. Chin she spoke in Chinese to him. He asked where everybody was and she told him in Manhattan. She looked at him as he spoke to her, she was surprised to see he wasn't Mr. Kim he was Chin but they looked so much alike they were just dressed different. She kept her feelings to herself because if he recognized her he would kill her. She asked about going to the hospital and he told her there was no, need all she needed was water and rest.

He smiled at her and said, "I know you know who I am. Your life ain't in jeopardy because of the info you gave. I like you because you are young, you escaped death so that means you're not supposed to die. I'm gonna give you a chance to join my crew."

"Thank you, Mr. Chin, my name is Ameka and I'm gonna prove my loyalty to you!" Amali got into the Limo.

"Ameka, how are you doing and where did you come from?"

"Amali, I'm sure glad to see you," everybody looked at them puzzled.

"Mr. Chin, this is my cousin I told you about, the chemist who finished school at the age of 15."

"Is that right?" Relena asked.

"Then you'll do good in New York with the rest of the Dragons."

"Yes, I will, I'll give you the info you need once we get to Manhattan. I'll get y'all to the warehouse once I get a look at everything and I'll come out and get y'all. Deal?"

"Deal!" they all said at once.

Relena crunched her stomach in pain and tried to lift herself, she screamed out in pain.

Rav hugged her and asked, "Baby, are you alright?"

"I need to go to the hospital, I think it's my appendix."

Ameka reached over Rav to Relena and told her to let her feel her side. She put her hand on it and counted to six. Her stomach popped on the 6th beat.

"Get her to the hospital quick, she has an acute appendicitis! If she doesn't get to the hospital in the next 15 minutes she will die!"

"Where's the nearest hospital, Rav?" Chin asked.

"Southwest Medical just up the road!" Rav answered.

Rav held her as they sped towards he hospital Amali looked at Rav with a smile on her face as if she didn't want her to make it. She moaned in pain, Ameka told him to apply pressure to ease the pain. He held her as tight as he could but she screamed louder. He closed his eyes because it was happening again. God saw that he cared about her and was gonna take her from him.

His thoughts were broken when the Limo slid sideways into the hospital.

As they slid into the parking lot Rav opened his door and jumped across the rear of the Limo to Relena's side of the car. He snatched the door open and picked her up and ran with her towards the entrance of the Emergency Room.

When he approached the counter, he saw an old white nurse and he pulled out a wad of bills and counted out 50 thousand dollars and threw it down on the counter. The nurses' eyes widened at the sight of the money. She grabbed the PA Mic and page Dr. Cheney to the nursing station.

Two minutes later, a short White man with salt and pepper hair and wire framed glasses appeared and asked, "What seems to be the problem?"

Ameka told the doctor they had an appendicitis and they had already paid 50 thousand in cash for their services.

"Ms. Dixon have Room 311 prepped for surgery and 302 for recovery stat!"

She busied herself calling the assistants and getting the rooms ready, two assistants came from the left with a stretcher, they rushed her to the elevator. Rav had to stay with her til the end, but he sent the rest of the gang to New York under George and Bills guidance.

Amali wanted to stay behind with him but she didn't let him know her feelings. Then George spoke up and said someone needed to stay behind with Rav.

Bill said he had been taking care of himself for this long he could keep it up now. George knew Amali wanted to stay so he told her it was alright. He told her she needed to go anyway so she could oversee all the warehouses in New York and New Jersey. He showed them the Glock and ammo in Relena bags and then went and got on the elevator without looking back.

He called Poco and asked if she got the property on Panola Road. She told him she closed the deal two days ago. It was on 150 acres, six bedrooms and a four-car garage. Indoor swimming pool and she was getting the cameras hooked up for security this week. He thanked her and told her to find a home nurse for Relena and a doctor who would be ready around the clock and would make her feel better.

She asked him what was wrong with Relena? He told her about her appendix and that she was in surgery as they spoke. He hung up as the door opened to the 3rd Floor. It was a Black female nurse and he asked her to show him to where Relena was having surgery. She pointed him to Room 311.

He laid on her bed and turned on the TV. He found TV Land and watched old reruns of Sanford and Son. He didn't watch much TV but that old Fred had more game than your average pimp. He dated three women in one night. He realized he was hungry so he asked the nurse to order a pizza. She said she couldn't do that but they had pizza in the vending machine downstairs. He pulled out his money and didn't have any small bills. The nurse just smiled at him and said it was on the house this time. He had pulled out a hundred and it was still in his hand so he handed it to the nurse with a big smile. She smiled back and told him his meal would be delivered to his room.

He laid back on the bed and turned on the video channel. He listened to the songs and thought about all the females that had gone through his life. He thought about Sonya and when she was sick and thought she was gonna die. He couldn't figure out why she was doing this stupid shit. He wanted to call her and tell her to just give the shit back, take her money and he'd give Nidiya back and for them to leave. Because Relena and the Chinese are playing for keeps.

He called George and told him to tell everyone if they capture Sonya not to kill her, just bring her and Kau and the baby to him. He told Chin, he didn't want to say yes, but everyone agreed. Chin wasn't after Sonya he was after Kim for betraying him and leaving him to die.

As soon as they hung up, Poco called and said a Cuban was coming to the hospital named Carla. Relena knew her so she would fit right in. She also told him she had hired a female Doctor named Cheryl Batten and her charge was 30 thousand for the home service and 10 for the nurse because of who they were.

"Rav, Nina said you haven't called once to see what about everyone's balance, all your doing is sending. You do know that's your job, don't you? Do you need me to travel with you?"

"Tell her I know what the balances are; how are you talking to her?"

"By computer and she says you're three points off."

"That's because I wasn't adding this year's income."

"She said she was sorry."

"It's okay, have you got my baby?"

"Yes, we're on the way."

"It's 3:50 in the morning, Relena should have been out of surgery by now. She went in at 12 I think. Poco I need your breast sometimes and then I think about your relationship and turn to my own comfort."

"Rav, I'm not in a relationship now I'm married. I got married the day after you."

The doctor came in and he hung up the phone and said, "Hey doc, what's up?"

"There was septicemia but she is fine but it destroyed the ovaries."

"What's septicemia?" Rav asked.

"It's the poison that was released by her appendix, she lost your child. She was early in the pregnancy so we couldn't determine what it was. I know y'all have to spend a lot of time with her because she can't have another child. We've got her on penicillin and she will have to come in regular for the next three months."

The door opened and Carla and Cheryl walked into the room. They introduced themselves, Carla was the same height as Relena but chubby with fat jaws and black hair. Cheryl was tall and slim and high yellow with black hair. Very professional looking. She was wearing brown pinstripes and Carla was wearing green scrubs. He stood there and watched Cheryl point things out to Dr. Chaney. She told Rav that it would be best if he acted like he didn't know about the baby. Then she told him that she would never be able to carry child again. He was devastated. He looked at Relena, for the first time he saw her innocence and knew right then he really did care about her. He sat on the bed and stroked her hair. She was facing him and he saw all the IV's and breathing tubes. The doctor said they would be back to check on her in the morning and they were left alone.

He locked the door and laid behind her, he cuddled as close as he could get. He was never able to cope with this kind of pain, he just laid with her and she spoke softly.

"Thank you Rav, for being here with me, I wouldn't want to face this alone. I know we lost the baby, I've known about the baby for a few weeks now. I always was taking pregnancy tests to make sure I was still pregnant. With tears in her eyes she cried out.

"Rav, I want my baby back, please give my baby back! What have I done wrong? Now, I can never have a child, I love children!"

It was so sad he almost broke down. He just kissed her and calmed her and told her because tomorrow was gonna be great.

Cheryl and Carla came in there white nursing uniforms. Rav got up to use the bathroom, he had had to pee all night but he had been afraid to leave her side.

"Relena, I'm gonna try something that's really against medical code; I'm gonna drain the poison out of you. You see all these dark spots? I'm gonna get all that poison out. Then I'll give you some antibiotics and it will flush the rest out of your kidneys. I know you feel like everything's over in your life cause you lost the baby, but it's not. It's all up to you."

"I got to take pills anyway, I'll leave it up to the doctors. What do you think Rav?"

He didn't answer, he was asleep. She knew he was exhausted and needed the rest. She knew he would never admit to it because he was a typical male.

Cheryl looked at him, he looked so peaceful. She didn't judge him by all the awful things she heard. She knew he had stood by his wife, very few good men would still be here. Her thought was broken by Carla asking the doctor what he wanted her to give her. The Doc ordered some medicine and Carla put in her IV and told her to count backwards from 10, by the time she reached eight she was gone.

Carla ordered Rav a big breakfast and told him he had to eat it to keep his strength up. Then the phone rang and she handed it to Rav.

"Yeah!" he said into the phone.

"This is Amali, we're in Manhattan, the warehouse is on Broad Street, that's the next street behind the Apollo. It looks like we are gonna have to take them out with snipers. Ameka got in this morning. She saw armed guards at the entrance and I told her to tell them that we blew up their warehouse. She says there are snipers at every window. That's why I called y'all because I don't think we want a grand entrance because the cops will be here before we get in."

Carla woke her when the food arrived and fed her. He told Amali to stay clear that he would be there shortly. He looked at Relena and she grabbed his hand.

"Don't you leave me down here by myself!"

"I'm not leaving you by yourself, I'm taking you home. Poco and Helen are coming to look after you. I got a surprise for you anyway."

"I knew you was gonna leave me, we don't have a place to stay down here."

"Yes, we do! We have a nice six-bedroom house, 150 acres, it's getting guards and cameras right now."

"I don't want to go there alone."

"Helen, Poco and Carla will be there with you and y'all can do all that girl stuff until you get better. You can't do anything for three months and you know what it's gonna be like out here."

She just looked at him and she knew he was leaving. She wasn't showing any signs of weakness anymore. She picked up the phone and called Poco.

"Poco. Send two cars. One for me and one for him."

She hung up and pointed at the door. He laughed and tried to kiss her on the forehead but she moved.

"I'll catch up with you in 10 days, alright?"

"No, make it 30 days, I don't care if you ever come back!"

He laughed and walked out the door and then he remembered he had left his phone, he walked back to the room and heard her crying. He opened the door, walked in, grabbed his phone, and left. She should have known he couldn't stay because of who he was. He felt odd so he pressed the 1st Floor button, got off, looked out the window and saw the busy street. No one knew who they were except Carla and Cheryl. His heart told him to go back, but his gut told him to leave.

He called her and told her to get dressed cause he was coming to get her. She was puzzled but he told her to trust him. He got back on the elevator and went back to the 3rd Floor and walked into her room, she was putting her shoes on. Dr. Batten told her she was taking a great risk She was in the middle of dressing when the phone rang. He told her to lay down, he opened her shirt and looked at her stomach.

"She doesn't have stitches, where are her stitches?"

"They are dissolvable on the inside to prevent scaring. Rav, do you think I have a device in me. No one knows we're husband and wife in law enforcement."

"They were first to know."

"Do you think one of them is Feds?"

"No, I just wanted to see your wound. Now finish bandaging her."

Poco walked in with Nidiya, Relena eyes widened she wanted to jump up and grab her baby. She handed the baby to him and hugged him, he kissed her cheek and started throwing Nidiya in the air. She just laughed and put her hand on his face. When she saw Relena she started reaching for her and crying when he didn't give her to her.

Relena looked at Cheryl saying hurry up, she finished and Relena sat up and he handed her the baby. As soon as he grabbed her she stopped crying. Relena started laughing and thanking him, she was so happy.

I have the cars waiting, all the cameras are hooked up. I transferred everything to your phone, so instead of you having a weather update or sort update you'll have a home update. Just push the flash button and you'll get immediate updates and will be able to see everything that is going on at the house.

Once she finished bandaging her she called for a wheelchair and a few minutes later a nurse knocked on the door. Poco opened it and he rolled the chair in. Rav sat them in the chair, her and the baby. Poco rolled them out. As they stood in the parking lot he asked what car was his?

She told him the white jag. They got in the Benz and a slim Cuban opened the door of the Jag for him. The driver told him the jet was fueled and ready. They followed the Benz and went straight to the house. It was at the back of the street. The street only had three houses on it and theirs was the last one.

He smiled as they pulled up out front, it was a baby mansion. Theirs was the only one with perimeter security. She started crying when she saw what was inside. It was like a house from lifestyles of the rich and famous. One whole wall was a TV screen. It was like the Fresh Princes mansion in every way. He kept waiting for Jeffery to pop out but he never did.

"Rav, everything is set up just like her fantasy house and her favorite show is the fresh prince and everything is perfect. We know you won't always be here but your suite is set up at the Hilton in New York."

Helen walked in looking very beautiful, she looked just like the August weather. She wore a long black coat, when she took it off her black dress sang to him. She twirled around modeling for him, he smiled and said damn! To himself. He saw she was an older model of Relena. He looked back at Relena, playing with the baby in the bed. He told them he was gonna be there when they woke up and he would leave in the morning. He got in the bed with them and they played with the baby.

CHAPTER 17

In Manhattan

Sonya laid asleep with Nodiya in her arms. Kau watched her and wanted to wake her because things didn't feel right in her stomach. Being in Manhattan wasn't it either; because she slept on the ground back in Africa. She just couldn't put her hand on it, she looked out the door and seen Tara coming. They spoke as they walked in, Len walked over to check on Sonya. She jumped back and ran to the phone and called 911!

She looked at Kau, trying to talk to her and the operator at the same time. She held her finger up at Kau and told the operator she had a possible overdose or someone had poisoned her. She gave the room number and hung up.

"Kau, who all's been here?" Len asked.

"No one, we haven't been here too long ourselves. We haven't eaten or drank anything since our arrival. We were supposed to be in the Hilton. She got so sick we had to stop here and she went to sleep and I called y'all."

"What did y'all eat on that plane?" Tara asked.

For the first time, she showed concern for Sonya, something her brother told her was starting to make sense. All Kim wanted was the dope and the money. Once he got back up to the Chinese standards he would kill everyone who isn't Chinese and anyone who isn't helping.

"A Korean stewardess fed her some special fish and tea, I asked for the same order. I'll be damned, we had different fish. Mine was just broiled but hers had all sorts of spices and peppers."

The paramedics knocked on the door and entered the room. They saw

Sonya and she had started shaking, the two white paramedics rushed over to her and pulled the brown blanket back, she still had on her white fur coat. Kau got the baby out of her arms, she opened her eyes, they were creamy and rolling up into her head. She was soaked inn sweat. You could see her pink bra. He took her blood pressure while the other one took her temperature. Her blood pressure was 144 over 105. Her temp was 105.8. The rushed her to an ambulance, Kau and the baby rode in the back with her. The EMT told Tara to come to St. Mary's and not to follow behind them. Kau picked up the phone to call Rav.

"Rav, we're going to St. Mary's a Korean girl put poison in her food. Sonya is about to die! Come quickly I think we're in danger!"

The P.M.D. looked at her as if he knew who she was talking to. He looked at her and told her not to worry she'll be alright. He asked where was Sonya last night? She picked up the phone and called Rav.

He told her he was on his way and her name is Sandra Anderson. She hung up and told them her name, they radioed back and said she was a Federal Agent; Kau's heart dropped and she called him again.

"She's an agent, what should we do?"

He laughed and told her he already knew. And for her to chill and he was on his way and to call if them folks showed up. He thought about her captain and told her to call him. She hung up and called.

"This is Juan Sonya has been poisoned. She's going to St Mary's, what's her status? I need to know! I know about the money she gave you and I helped get your grandchild back. So, you owe me!"

"Juan, she's still active. She's in deep cover. We know about the hits and the murders, your all getting us good information. Right now, we're fixin to hit the warehouse, so call your men back. We understand Kim and Mr. Chin are back in business. You should know she's backing you on them courthouse murders. She took the tapes and transferred them to Nikko. The info that Mandi gave came back void. But INA is investigating you and Sonya. Juan, you have an informant with you or in your circle of trust, so do your homework. Don't go to the hospital cause INA will take you in."

"Look! Stand down, your fixin to raid the wrong warehouse, ain't nothin on Prospect, I know she told y'all that." He hung up from the captain, he stopped her from speaking.

"Kau, I'm not Federal. Sonya is keeping me safe. I'll be in New York in a few hours. I thought there was a beef between me and her. I really don't understand what she's doing. Keep me posted, alright?"

They rolled Sonya into the ER. Kau sat in the waiting room. Tara walked in and asked how she was. She said she didn't know. Kau told Tara the Feds were fixin to hit the warehouse. Yen asked was she sure and then she asked which one? She said the one on Prospect. Yen heard Kau and told her there wasn't anything there. Everything had been moved.

"Tara, I didn't know Sonya was Federal."

"Kau, she isn't Federal anymore, she's inactive. I did see someone on the roof taking pictures. I don't think she will harm us."

"I don't think so either." She didn't want to involve Rav because she didn't know who was I.N.A.

They sat for four hours before they received any word. A White male doctor came out and said she was fine and in the recovery unit. Kau told Yen to get the girls and leave because she had just seen two I.N.A. agents walking to the nursing station.

As soon as they left, one of the agents walked in, a tall slim White male with black hair, a faded coat and square black frame glasses.

He looked around the waiting room, it was full of people; men, women and children. He walked out to the hallway. She didn't know who he was looking for so she didn't get up.

Then it hit her, she called Len and told them not to say anything about Sonya's situation to no one, not even Kim. Len told the girls and they all agreed, then Yen told her to tell Kau she'll let her know where the dope is moved to. She smiled and hung up. She walked to the bathroom checked all the stalls, once she saw they were clear she called Rav.

She told him what the girls were doing and the Feds was there, He told her to destroy her phone and flush it and go buy another one. She took a piece of paper and wrote down all of her contacts and destroyed her phone.

She left walking down 147th Street trying to find a phone dealer or an electronics store. She noticed a Black guy and the same girl from the hospital wearing an all-black jumpsuit.

They were following her on the other side of the street, she didn't panic. She looked up into the early morning sky and prayed for Jesus to protect them through the day.

She looked at her silver Timex watch, it read 8:45 am. She stopped at the newspaper stand and asked if there was a Radio Shack anywhere nearby. A Black man told her to go three blocks and she would see it across the street.

She bought a paper to see if there was any info on Sonya's illness. There wasn't and all she got was business. The Wall Street Journal, August 17, 2004.

She stopped at a coffee shop a block away from the Radio Shack. She went to the bathroom to change the baby. She laid the paper on the floor, laid her on the paper and changed her. She smiled at her cause she was tough and no matter what she wouldn't cry. It was like she knew they were in danger and she was gonna play her role.

She changed her and cut the hand dryer on to warm her bottle. She knew she was hungry even though she never cried. She felt the bottle it was warm enough. She got the newspaper and diaper from the floor and threw it in the trash. She walked out and sat at a table by the window. She ordered a bagel and coffee and fed the baby.

The couple with the stroller came into the coffee shop, she got real nervous. She was thinking, *"What if they found her phone? What if they wanted to kill her?"*

She had no way to call for help, no gun, no nothing for protection. She came to go to school, trying to find him. Sonya sent her family a quarter million and had a hundred thousand in her account. She prayed cause if she could only make it through this situation she could go back home or go back to school. She'd only been out of school two months.

The moment of truth came when they approached her table. The man spoke to her in a soft tone.

"Kau, don't be afraid. We're with Rav. He sent us to watch over you. Here's your phone, now look at the black Navigator in front of the Radio Shack." It was Rav waving at her; she smiled and jumped up.

"Kau, where are you going?" the lady asked.

"I'm going to Rav!"

She put a $10 bill on the table for her food. Her order hadn't come yet and she didn't care, God answered her prayers.

For the first time Nodiya started crying. She knew they were safe and her daddy was only a few feet away. If she could talk she would be saying, "Daddy" instead of crying.

Kau ran out of the coffee shop to the end of the street, the light turned red and she crossed the street. Bill opened the door for her, she looked in. George was in the driver's seat and Mikky was in the passenger seat. She got in and sat beside him and closed the door. She took her hand and turned his face to hers and kissed him.

"I was so scared! Thank you, don't ever scare me like that again," she said.

Then she hit him on the shoulder and gave him the baby. He looked at her, she had on a blue "Baby Phat" pants and shirt outfit. She stopped crying as he held her up. Her little hands were touching him on the face then just like Nidiya she put her mouth on his nose.

He looked at Bill and said, "They did the same thing, just like sisters."

"They are tasting you," he said.

"What daddy baby been doing? Huh? You miss daddy?" she just smiled.

George pulled off taking him to the Hilton. The ride was silent and happy because he had seen his babies, he had both of them in his custody. Just when things couldn't get any better, she spoke, "Daddy."

"Y'all heard that? She just spoke! Please speak again baby!" She just laughed and played with his nose.

Then he thought about Nidiya and called Relena and said, "Relena, I got somebody who wants to speak with you!"

"Who?"

He put it on speaker phone and put it up to her mouth. She made all kinds of baby noise and Relena talked to her.

Nidiya then Nodiya said, "Daddy! Daddy! Daddy!"

"Rav, did you hear her speak?"

Before he could answer, Nodiya spoke again, "Daddy!"

"That's right baby you teach her how to talk."

He was so happy, they saw tears of joy in his eyes. He promised them both he would never leave them. Relena wanted her there with her and she wasn't taking no for an answer. She told him if he wanted her to stay still then give her, her babies. Everyone started laughing so he told her he would put Kau and her on a plane shortly. She thanked him and so did Kau.

They parked around the back and they walked through the kitchen. Mikky took the truck and parked it in the front so no one could ambush them. Afterward he walked the grounds and did a security check and George and Bill checked the house. Then they called Rav.

He walked in playing with the baby and said, "Kau, you look exhausted."

"I am I just want to shower and sleep."

Him, Kau, and the baby went into his room and closed the door. Kau undressed and showed off her body to him. She twirled around for him and gave him a good look at his property. He walked to her with the baby in his arms and gave her a kiss on both cheeks, rubbed her on both of her but cheeks. She turned and walked to the shower. Bill wore his usual black slacks, jacket and white shirt.

When he walked into the room he could feel the fatherly happiness and said, "I see you are enjoying your little princess, I can also see you don't know how to burp a baby."

"What do you mean?"

"Look at your $3,000 Outkast shirt, she just puked on it."

He looked down and said, "Dammit, I just asked if you were hungry."

"I guess she just answered your boss, she's not. So, what's up Boss?"

"I wanted to ask what to feed the baby, but it's too late for that, but you can go and get Sonya out of the hospital for me. I understand everybody wants her dead but she can't die. I can't explain to my girls that I killed their mom. So, tell everybody I want her protected."

"Rav, have you ever had a man to man talk before?"

"No, not really. What's up?"

"Why did you marry Relena?"

"To be the don!"

"Rav, there's more to life than this underworld. I have four girls, five boys, and 27 grandchildren. A wife who believes in you almost more than Jesus. That's what you need is a family. At the end of the day, I go home to Pereal and she kisses me all over. What I'm telling you Rav is to take advantage of love while you got it. You got four girls that love you to death and you don't even care. My take is that every move Gloria makes in life is for you. You'll see in the end."

He was interrupted by Kau entering the room naked. Her brown nipples spoke to Bill in a voice only a heated man could understand. He looked at her womanhood shaved smooth. He turned and looked at Rav and Kau; she smiled, grabbed the baby and handed her to Bill. He smiled and walked out.

Rav laid on the bed and she crawled up to him. She unbuttoned his shirt and raised it over his head. She kissed him from his lips to his navel, undid his pants and tugged them down and pulled him out and took him in her mouth. She licked him and took him all the way into her throat. She was jerking him off with her right hand and sucking his balls. She felt hot cum running over her fingers. She quickly put her mouth on it and sucked all of him into her mouth. She took him out of her mouth and told him to make love to her.

She stood with him and helped him out of his pants and boxers. She pulled herself across his lap and held his dick straight up and tried to put all of him inside herself. She put both of her hands on his chest and rocked back and forth until she cried out in pleasure.

Just as she begins to cum he flipped her over and put her in the buck, pounding hard and fast, she couldn't catch her breath. He was lost in the sound their bodies were making and he felt himself Cuming again. After he was through he laid with her head on his chest both of them panting trying to catch their breath. A knock came at the door.

"Who is it?"

"It's me, Mikky."

"Come in." He rolled off of her so she could cover herself. He told Mikky to throw him a towel.

He turned his head as Rav finished drying off and asked, "What's up Mikky?"

"We have the 86th Precinct Captain and the 129th Captain in the warehouse on Prospect. Do you want us to handle them or do you want to handle it yourself?"

He looked at Kau and said, "Sorry Baby girl, I've got to go. Lay me out an all-black Sean John suit and my black brim." He kissed her and got in the shower.

Kau had his clothes laid out for him when he finished.

"Where are you off to?" she asked.

"We're going to a movie and dinner; Georges grandson is taking us out. He just came back from Africa, we should have a lot to talk about."

"George, come in here please!"

"Your grandson, Kau, and my daughter?"

"They're going to our theater on 119th Street and after they are going to one of our soul food restaurants. They will be escorted by his three bodyguards."

"George, Nodiya is too young to go out on a date and your grandson is too old," he laughed at his joke, "anyway I want all of them to stay together until I get back, and you go back to school, okay?"

"Okay Rav," she said.

He finished dressing and sprayed Polo around his neck and walked out. He called Smokey to see have they made it to Chicago. They were in Hawthorne setting up shop. He smiled because Smokey and Leo were always on top of their game. They got on the elevator and rode down to the lobby. He remembered the last time he was in this situation he had to bail Relena out. He smiled because no one was paying them any attention. People spoke to Bill and Mikky; just as they were going out the door a young lady spoke to him. She wasn't any older than seven or eight and her hair was in braids; she was a pretty little dark-skinned girl. She smiled showing a missing tooth in the front. She grabbed his hand and tried to pull him towards the bar.

Her parents noticed what she was doing and came up to them about the time she was saying, "Come On Boy!"

"Alicia!" a short chubby Black woman called her.

The father walked up wearing black pants and a red T-shirt, grabbed the girl and picked her up and said, "Excuse me Sir. She's never done this before."

"She's a child with courage, Rav. She might have something to tell you," said George.

He reached for the little girl and the father gave her to him. He rested her on his hip and said, "High my name is Ravenion, what do you want to tell me?"

"My daddy needs work, we sleep outside, we came in here to eat."

He looked at the father and asked, "Is this true?"

"Yes! My name is Alonzo Edwards and this is my wife Tenisha. We go shelter to shelter, we went to St. Mary's but they were full so the manager let me bus tables for two hot meals and 10 dollars. I've had a record since I was fourteen and no one wants to hire a crook!"

"George, don't we have some apartments on 163rd?"

"Yes! Go to Old Fashioned Apartments, my niece Phillis is manager, tell her I sent you. She will hire you to drive the transit van, bringing the elderly to the park and bingo, stuff like that."

"Thank you so much!" Tenisha said.

"No don't thank us, thank your little girl cause she got tired of sleeping outside." Everyone laughed.

"Hell, that's the first thing she's said."

"Mr. Ravenion, now this is what I wanted to tell you. I seen a Chinese man put something under the black truck you came here in. That truck in front of the door right there."

Rav looked at her, "Are you for real, Baby?"

"Yes Sir! That's why you got to go out the other door. Cause the white policeman got in the blue van and told the other white van to go up the street."

"You seen all that young lady?"

"Yes Sir! I heard him when he was in here that he gonna pay to play," she said.

"Okay Baby girl, I love you!"

Mikky sent for another car. Rav told the man there would now be a quarter million waiting at that apartment for him. George called a tow truck to get the truck and they went out the kitchen door. They saw four unmarked cars as they walked up the street. They took a cab to Grand Central Station and waited for a car. They stood out front for 10 minutes. Mikky got on the phone to see what was up, before anyone picked up a black Limo pulled up.

Arod got out and opened the door; Rav got in first, then George, Bill, and Mikky. He sat with his back to the driver; facing them. Arod was beside him, cool and calm as usual.

"Why the death colors?" Rav asked, "you only wear those when you're on a mission. What's up Arod? Talk to me."

"Alex is in town and he's demanding to speak with you. Sonya called and she's at Gloria's. Alex knocked on the door and Sonya told Gloria to let him in. So, she paid the doctor in one of the examining rooms, he gave her a nursing uniform, and she left."

He told the driver to take them to Gloria's and to look for unmarked cars on the way. Then he called and checked on Kau. She said everything was fine but she had noticed some unmarked checking out the front of the hotel.

He told the guys, "They got away clean but there were some under covers at the hotel." George didn't feel comfortable about the situation so he called an old contact at the police station.

"Hello Melvin, this is Scooter. Is I.N.A. on us? Is it the FEDS or what?

"George no one knows Ravenion is in the country, they think he's in Cuba. They're trying to find Sandra Anderson though. She just walked out of the hospital so that's where their focus is right now. But they do know Rav's the don and they know someone was on his floor today. They seen his keeper Kau so they think Sandra is near her."

"Rav, how many jets do you have?"

"Three but I only fly in the 2-17. The black jet never leaves Cuba."

"The black jet has a tracker on it. Relenas too except its white. I doubt if any of them has left Cuba. I know hers is in New York. I sent mine back right after we arrived."

"My people tell me the forces aren't after you, they're after Sonya. Now they know you're the don, we need to find the leak."

"I believe I know who the leak is Rav," Arod said.

"Who?" they all asked.

"Raul, I never felt right about him, you were supposed to take the fall for him so he could come back. This is information. Alex wanted to tell you so you'll have to get it from Alex."

Rav called and got the black jet sent to Scotland, then he closed his eyes and meditated. He told himself several times he didn't want this life because no don in history had to go through what he had been through. Since he had no choice but to live it, he would live it harder than any gangster that ever walked the earth.

They pulled up in front of Gloria's apartment, Arod opened the door and stepped out. George, Mikky, and Bill stepped out, looked around and saw that everything looked normal. Rav stepped out and they rushed him into the apartment.

Alex jumped from his chair to greet them, he stepped to the side as they came through the door. He got on his knees at Rav's feet. Rav looked down at him and then reached down and picked him up. He stood looking him down.

"I see you are wearing the clothes I bought you, the jacket and everything. What's up with that?"

"Ain't nothin changed but your position, I'm still gonna honor you even if it's from afar. I never had any intention of killing you, I sat in this room and cried because the order came down from over your head. I only said I would take up the hit to see who was behind it and buy you some time. Raul put that hit on you and the Chinese are supposed to take you and Sonya out. Raul knows neither one of us can kill you so it had to be an outsider. Mr. Chin and Kim came here together but they had their differences. The way y'all met up was a set up to begin with. Now they are back together through Raul, none of their soldiers know. Raul has Chin hitting all of your spots so he can kill everyone who follows you and take over. He had all his people set up cause you were never supposed to make it to donhood."

"Alex, let me sit down and comfort Sonya, we'll get down to business later."

He sat to the right of the front door where he could see Gloria applying a cool cloth to Sonya's head. He placed her head in his lap; her eyes were barely open but she managed to smile at him.

"Rav, tell her to take this laxative, I keep telling her she has to flush her system out," said Gloria.

He looked at her and told her to take the stuff. She looked up at him and nodded. Alex got up and got her some coffee. He knew the coffee would rush everything through her system. She saw the doctor putting something in her IV. As soon as she got up enough strength she would leave but as she moved she got dizzy and Gloria got the trash can for her. When she was sure she was alright for a minute she helped her to the bathroom. Rav walked to the door, Gloria had dropped her head but he helped her raise it back up.

"Look at me! What's understood doesn't need to be explained." She wanted to test him by making him take her to bed but she knew if she was gonna be strong she had to resist.

"Worry about your girl! Don't make sure I understand nothin! Cause I don't!"

He hit the door again, so she flushed the toilet a couple of times. She came out and she was still feeling a little weak but she made it to the couch and laid down. He sat at her feet this time and rubbed her ankles. He twisted her left ankle and he told her she had 48 hours to get everything back or she would never see the twins again. All she could do was agree.

Bill got up and went to the kitchen and made some soup from the stuff that was there. Gloria fed Sonya while everyone else sat in the kitchen. Alex started the conversation about getting the dope back.

Rav told him she was in no shape to get the dope back. He really didn't care about the dope because they had plenty. He just didn't want the Chinese to enjoy the fact that they had jammed on him. He knew in the end everyone would die, including himself. If he could keep Sonya and the twins alive then he will have served his family well. He didn't want any of his children exposed to this life. He looked over at Gloria, she was eating her soup. Why would he let her love him? Did he think he was protecting her by not being around her?

Sonya grabbed her cellphone from the table and called Yennifer to send a Limo. She told her to have Tara drive the car behind her and to alert Kim to her arrival. She looked up at him and smiled.

"Juan, are you ready to get our shit back? I'm gonna get it back if it kills me!"

He looked at the green nursing suit and asked if she was gonna wear that. She told him the girls had extra clothes in the trunk in case something jumped off. His heart pumped fear for the first time because something wasn't right. He called Amali and asked what the business was? She told him they could hit at any given time and that Kim was in the building. He came up through the back, it's an opening in the fence. She told him to unsecure the connector to the sixth pole and roll the fence back and drive through it.

He sent them in and told her to capture everyone and not to act until he got there to make sure the sharp shooters are taken care of, he didn't want any death toll. She laughed and told him they would be straight by the time he got there. He hung up and 10 minutes later there was a knock at the door.

He heard a small voice through the door, "It's me Yenny."

Everybody jumped up and pointed there weapons at the door. Arod had a Glock 40, Alex had a Chrome 357. Rav went into the kitchen with his

Glock raised. George, Bill and Mikky went to the door with their 357's. Gloria stayed by Sonya's side pointing a 17 shot 9mm while Sonya lay down pointing a 41 at the door. Bill opened the door and Yennifer walked inside with Sonya close. Tara and Lin walked in backwards looking up and down the street. When they all came in Mikky closed the door. The girl didn't look surprised because wherever she was, she was well protected. Yen threw her a black fur, black blouse, black slacks, and shoes. The girl didn't say anything, they just sat on the arm of the chairs.

Sonya stood and stripped out of her nursing uniform; she had nothing but bra and panties underneath. Everyone besides Rav looked at her in lust as she undressed. Alex told Arod he could see why Rav protected her so closely. She was slim and flawless.

"Rav, let's go while the time is right, we're gonna need a place to do our business," said Sonya.

He walked out saying, "No, we'll go in silent and do all we got to do there; I'll get Chin to come in. I'm not trying to risk getting caught up, I already got five trucks waiting to take everything where there supposed to go. I already got spots here; I just got to talk to Fir Twon Woo in Chinatown; he's giving some of my people Hell! Now, he's going on a copter ride, you dig?"

As they headed out the door Tara's phone rang, she didn't know whether to answer or not. It would look like a set up; she looked at Sonya and shook her head no. She just let it ring. On the 10th ring Rav walked up behind her. She stopped with her head facing the ground; she went into her pocket and handed him the phone.

"Why don't you answer your own phone? You make yourself look guilty. If you ain't got nothin to hide answer your phone."

The skies were fading fast, by the time they hit it, would be night fall. Just as she was going to answer her phone it stopped ringing.

She looked down at the phone and said, "It's my brother Ben, he's part of Kim's circle. What do you want me to do?"

"Answer your phone," he replied.

"Ben what do you want? Why are you calling me like this?"

"Don't go to that warehouse with Sonya. It's a setup, they're gonna blow the place up! There's only about 50 men there; they're shipping everyone off to Chinatown to meet with Fir Twon Woo. The dope is here on Prospect but Chin is gonna move it at 5:30 p.m. Kim knows Sonya knows about the food poison and he knows she ran back to Rav. So, tell him me and Thai Wang have on yellow silk shirts; we'll be in the back with Kim and Chin. There's only 20 people here with us. There are six men in the front, two on each side of the door and windows, the rest are on both sides of the walls running up and down. No one should make it to the back door. Their weapons are mini 14's and Glocks. I'm in the back room; the wall is about 10 inches thick; Call before you come in."

She hung up and turned to Rav, "New plan, let's go back inside."

Rav turned around and walked back into the apartment. He sat in the middle, the same place he sat when Sonya gave him her hand. Sonya took the same position and laid in his lap.

Sonya got a glass of juice and took a drink and said, "Well, what's the new plan Tara?"

"Rav, you got a warehouse on Prospect, right?" He nodded.

"My brother said your dope is in that warehouse, the other warehouse got a bomb in it. Mr. Chin and Kim is there, they got 20 men with them. They're moving the dope to Fir Twon Woo at 5:30 am." Gloria grabbed her computer cutting her off.

"Rav this is how I knew about Alex and Nikko's plan; I followed them to that same warehouse, climbed the wall and placed the camera and sound mics in place so I can tell you whether she's lying or not."

She opened the computer and typed in view of everybody as they walked around her, it didn't show anything at first. They looked at Tara, she told them to move the camera at different angles. Gloria told her to chill that wasn't the warehouse yet, it was next door; they are on the same surveillance line as us, just give it a minute. Tara went to the computer and typed F-4 and a moment later the warehouse came into view.

It showed everything her brother said but it didn't show him. She started crying "Rav, my brother isn't in the place I can't see him!"

"Call your brother and keep the camera where he's supposed to be at," said Rav.

She called her brother and Ben walked out and locked the door. He picked up the phone out of his pants pocket.

"Yeah, Tara you know not to call this line unless it's an emergency."

"Ben, I panicked cause I didn't see you at the door!"

"Tara, what are you talking about?"

"Rav got that place wired up, I see you right now. I saw you come out of that room and lock the door. We see everything you see and everything you say. Rav, can they join us when this is over?"

Rav looked at Alex and he nodded; so, she told her brother yes and they hung up. Then Rav called Amali and told her to go to Prospect and wait till they got there; they should be there in two hours. They got into their cars; she rode with her people. Alex and Gloria rode with Rav.

He called to check up on Relena and no one answered after six rings so, he called Poco and she picked up on the first ring and said, "Rav what's up?"

"Ain't you with Relena?" he asked. Gloria, sitting across from him just looked at him; he wasn't paying her no attention.

"Yes! Kau and the baby are here, there all asleep."

"Wake her and get her on the phone."

"She's on medication Rav, I'm not sure waking her would be the best thing."

"What happened Poco?"

"Nothing, she just needed rest; she's here in the house, she's been in the garden. The nurse just gave her some stronger medicine cause for some strange reason she feels you are in trouble. She's been trying to warn you about a bomb, she kept calling but you never answered." He looked at his ringer and it was off.

"Yeah, my ringers been off, tell her you spoke with me and I'm with Gloria and Alex and I know about the bomb; so, I'm straight. How's my baby doin?"

"She's fine, her and Relena played and went to sleep."

He hung up, for the first time he didn't sense death, see death or feel death. He looked at Gloria and Alex and told them about Relena situation, neither one of them cared. Gloria wished she would've died, then Gloria broke her silence.

"Rav, your married right?"

"Yes, why?" he said with a curious look.

"I'm fixin to get married to my CEO Kelvin Kelley in a couple of weeks. Since you married I may as well do the same. I hoped to marry you but you don't want me, all you want is to be don. I'm fixin to move on. I shouldn't be here I should be next to my man."

He looked at her with a look of betrayal; he didn't say nothin because he needed her. But if she was gonna marry he was gonna kill her. He didn't want to spook her cause he was gonna kill her no matter what. He smiled and told her it wouldn't last long.

He was so mad he just stared at her; Alex looked at her and no one said a word. George broke the silence by telling Rav he had to let Gloria live her life. She was no longer part of the family, she had chosen her dream and to stop the car and let her out now.

Rav looked at him and for the first time he showed him disrespect. "Listen old man, as a matter of fact all of you listen up. Gloria is an important factor; if any of you treat her as an outsider I'll kill you. She ain't getting married, she's gonna sing until her voice goes out. She's gonna put in work like she's putting in now. Because of her we know what we are walking into. She can get into any state and kill anyone I need killed. Including one of you! I respect her choices but I love her life! Do you all understand me?"

"Yes Sir!" they all replied at once, that made her feel so important.

"When we get there Gloria, you, and Alex are going on top of the roof. You wait until everyone's focus is on the front door and then you come down killing everyone. Once that's cleared George, you, and Bill, Arod, and Mikky are to go to Ben, his job is to open that door. Me and Sonya and the others will be waiting. We're gonna find out where Raul is at."

They all agreed and rode in silence, he looked at Gloria and smiled. She told them to stop at Wendy's so she could use the bathroom, they pulled in. She got out and went inside, George wanted to say she was fixin to run but he kept his peace. He knew the pressure on her wanting to marry him and be free. It had to be Hell to be that deeply in love with someone and have to sit back and watch him be with someone else. To his surprise she came right out and got back in the car without saying a word.

Rav looked at his watch, it was 10:20 p.m. and they were a block off. When they pulled up they seen the five trucks at the side of the warehouse waiting to be loaded. He had forgotten about the dope that was already there or did they move it? It was supposed to be a meth warehouse. When they pulled down he saw Amali getting out of the white Limo crossing the street. Out of nowhere people appeared; his people and their people; they closed the whole street. Gloria set the computer up so they could see inside; her and Alex walked to the other side of the building and climbed on the roof.

Sonya jumped in the car with him while George followed behind the Limo with Tara. Once he seen them on the roof he kissed Sonya and told her he loved her. He called Kau and told her when Relena got better to take the girls to Tasha and stay until he contacted her.

Sonya looked at him and said, "All your kids will be together, I like that. That's all I wanted was for us to be a family."

He promised her in the end they would all be under the same roof. He meant it cause he still owned property across from his grandmother's property. Tony's house would be the house they would live and die in.

They got out and Tara gave them both AK's. He asked Sonya if all the guns had silencers on them, she told him he had been watching too much TV He smiled as they walked through the alley next to the warehouse.

As they walked they noticed there wasn't a bum in sight. All they saw was a rulable dumpster. It was another warehouse, she looked at it and went to the door. She sparked her lighter and saw the door was slightly opened. She walked back to him and looked at the camera. They were shooting but you couldn't hear it cause Nikko had sound proofed it.

Something about the door being open bothered her; she tapped him on the shoulder and told him to come to the dumpster. They rolled it and stayed behind it and the door exploded. There had been a trip wire. They knew what they were waiting for so they waited for them to come out. The explosion had knocked the feed off their computer. Sonya got up and told him to come on, they stood on the side of the building pointing their AK's. Kim, Chin and Thai Wong came out and Ben came out behind them. When they looked up and saw the AK's pointed at them they tried to run only to find six more in their faces.

Kim spoke in Chinese to Tara saying, "Y'all can't be Chinese, put the gun on them cause they got a billion-dollar price on their head."

Then Sonya spoke in Chinese, "You two are selfish Son of a Bitches, you care nothing about your people. You got your people in that warehouse with a bomb in it and they don't know it. Tara called that warehouse and told them to move out cause of the bomb."

She ordered them to walk to the truck and got in. He called Amali and told her it was over they've captured them. Alex and Arod got in the truck and Bill and the others got in the Benz with the girls. They drove to a warehouse in Manhattan by the Hudson River. You could actually throw something out the window in the river.

They rushed them to the dark warehouse; Bill cut the lights on, it was a furniture repair warehouse. Bill laid them on the floor and chained them up; he hooked them up to the pulley and hung them upside down.

George gave Rav a sledgehammer and he told Chin, "I'm only gonna ask you this once, where is Raul?"

"It's death before dishonor Ravenion."

"Get me two 55 gallon drums and fill them with water and put their heads in the water."

They did what they were told and their head was placed in the water and Rav hit Chin in the spine with the hammer. He made Amali take a knife and cut Chin from his stomach to his collar and made Tara and the girls cut him from one side to the other. George dropped them in the water while Sonya pumped AK rounds into them.

Bill and George were expecting to see what they saw. He made George pull them back up and he hit both of them in the mouth with the hammer breaking their jaws and knocking out several teeth. He had a statement to make and he made it.

He looked at Amali and told her to call both crews and bring them together and she was the leader. He said not to worry about Fir Twon Woo, he would deal with him. He looked at Sonya and told her to go back to work or get out of the country. He told Gloria to live her life and Alex was back in the family.

He told George, Mikky, and Bill to clean up the mess and go home to their families. He told Amali all the money would be in her account and if she tried anything her family would feel her mistake. With that, he walked out and got into the Limo, called Bill and told him to distribute the dope.

When he hung up he called to the singer Mario to be in Atlanta by the time he got there.

He boarded the jet and went to Atlanta, Mario was there waiting on him and they got into his Limo and drove to his house. He called and got her up. When they walked in she was coming out of the room with Nodiya.

Mario started singing, *"You Should Let Me Love You."*

ABOUT THE AUTHOR

I was born in Atlanta, Georgia on September 26, 1978. I grew up in what seems like every rough hood of Atlanta. I was a child that was abused until I was 6-years-old.

My mother went to prison in 1985, that's when the abuse stopped because she killed her husband. I was placed with my grandmother, who was also raising two of her grandchildren. It was a house full of adult "crackheads." Now, came three of my mom's children. So, she didn't have time to raise all five of us. Many times, Christmas missed us, but I went out and stole for my little sister Cara and little brother Neil. In addition, I started taking out trash for a dollar for candy for all five of us. I knocked on the dope man door and he took me in.

This is the time of my life that I was staying in the Scottsdale Oak Forest Apartments. I started out as a *"watch-out boy,"* moved to a *"delivery boy,"* and then a *"drug dealer."*

By the time my mother came home in 1989 from prison, I wasn't Torrey anymore, I was Charlie Cain. My mom tried to raise me, but the streets had my heart. Also, I didn't care for school; I went but wasn't mentally there.

I started my drug empire in the streets of East Atlanta from nickels and dime to ounces and half of kilos. I ran with a robbing crew, and that crew got me two consecutive life sentences at the age of 14. I've been in prison since 1993.

I educated myself and I went from a 14-year-old with an 8-year-old mental capacity; to getting my GED. In addition, going to Middle GA Tech for food preparation to writing books.

When I came up for parole, I was denied, and set off for three years due to the nature of my crime.

My mother has since passed away, my sister Tasha had a heart transplant, and my sister Cara survived cancer. I come up for parole in again 2016 and was set off two years due to the nature of my crime.

It's now 2018, I can only hope I make it this year. This year will be 25 years served in prison. I came to prison 9-9-93, 25-years-ago. When is enough a enough?

Every life has the Rubin Carter dream; someone would gain interest and help me out. I only hope that you'll pay attention to your children, brothers, or sisters and stop them from coming here to prison. Prison is an open door, just like an open grave that don't want to let you go.

Readers, if you want to, you can write to me and I'll write back to you. The address is below:

Torrey Flowers 814370

Jack & Rutledge State Prison

7175 Manor Road, Columbus, GA 31907

UNTIL THEN. . .PEACE!